Licensed to STEELE

The Most Expensive Thing In The World Is Trust

ALLISON —
THANKS SO MUCH FOR
BUYING MY FIRST BOOK!

Noland R. Mattocks

HOPE YOU ENJOY

Halo
PUBLISHING
INTERNATIONAL

ISBN: 9781612445779
Library of Congress Control Number: 2017911709

Printed in the United States of America

Halo Publishing International
1100 NW Loop 410
Suite 700 - 176
San Antonio, Texas 78213
Toll Free 1-877-705-9647
www.halopublishing.com
E-mail: contact@halopublishing.com

DEDICATION

This book would have never made it to print without help from several great people. I'd like to personally thank Holly Cuddington, Heidi Henrikson, Kim Kiger Barnard, Jill Baucom, Dave Bunting, Vince Willis, Scott Castleman, Julio Venegas, and Wayne Faber. Your support is greatly appreciated.

A special thank you to Robbie Helm, Stephen Smith, and Kim Johnson. Each of you went beyond simply helping to give this novel a chance. Your input and continued support was vital to completing this dream.

Many of my Kappa Sigma brothers also contributed their support for "Licensed to Steele." Blaine Brawley, Doug Drum, Robert Hooten, Dustin Shearon, Carl "Nukeydog" Cayton, Brian Clarke, Jeff "Knabbytoes" Knabb, and Jeff "Rojo" Denton. Brothers for life. AEKDB.

Throughout the book, you'll find a few of my friends. Vaughn Moore, your words of encouragement and generous support came at a perfect time. Jeff Knabb, you have always been there with a quick joke and a shoulder for support. Kevin Rickard, you've been "The Rock" for me for over thirty years. Your input was invaluable. Every time I started to lose faith, your voice kept me focused on the final product.

My first editor, Cherise Sherwin, plowed through the book in record time (without compensation). Your direction and input were instrumental in making Cameron Steele come to life. You also fed me several times. If you are in the Sarasota area, please stop by and visit with Cherise at Anna Maria Oyster Bar in Bradenton. Tell her I sent you.

A special thanks to Molly Nero. A great author of children's books, you pointed me to Lisa Umina with Halo Publishing International. A chance encounter changed the entire course of my novel.

The final push needed to complete "Licensed to Steele" came from Lisa Baldwin. Your constant words of encouragement were the lift I needed. When I was sitting at the computer at two in the morning, frustrated and ready to come to bed, you were the one who brought me sweet tea. Without you, I'm not sure this novel would have ever made it to print.

This book is dedicated to the memory of my mom and dad, N. Randy Mattocks, Jr. and Susan Mattocks. Since words cannot express my gratitude enough, I'll simply say thanks for not leaving me at a bus station.

Lastly, there is not a page written when I wasn't thinking of my daughter and son, Harris Gray and Nash. You may never know how much you mean to me and you are in my thoughts constantly. I love you both.

This book is a work of fiction. All the characters used are a figment of my imagination. A few names were used with permission. Any editorial mistakes are solely on my shoulders. If you feel the need to tell someone a mistake you found, please tell a friend to order the book online and point it out to them.

Throughout the book, you may find phrases or character banter that seem familiar. You are right. I purposely dropped a few lines from movies and other media outlets that stuck with me growing up. Look at it as a homage to Hollywood. I hope you enjoy.

Please visit www.NolandMattocks.com for updates about my next novel and book signing events.

PROLOGUE
PUNTA GORDA, FLORIDA

My name is Cameron Steele, but most people call me Cam. I rob banks for a living. Actually, that's a bit of an understatement. As of last count, I'm up to nine successful jobs and just a hair under $250,000. As far as I know, no one is on my trail and I seem to have found a system that works. I'm not some kind of computer whiz who has figured out a way to skim the books, nor do I steal by using identity fraud. I don't get dressed up as a dead president and go in guns ablazing with my "gang." I'm old-fashioned in my ways. I'm thirty years old and my friends think I'm a successful, independent financial advisor. Most of that statement is true. I am a stockbroker and I have found some success, but I want more.

Robbing banks is not a profession one seeks as a young boy. It's not like my high school guidance counselor suggested it as a second choice after auto maintenance. I actually went to college and graduated from East Carolina University in Greenville, North Carolina with a B.S. in criminal justice. You might think I got the idea while studying criminology, but you would be wrong. Some people might think the idea came from being a summer bank teller in 1997. They are wrong, as well. I became one out of despair. Let me take you back a few years.

CHAPTER I

It was the fall of 2002, four years after graduation and I was living and working in Winston-Salem, North Carolina, where I grew up. It was an entry level nine to five job for $12 an hour, installing local area networking for a communications firm and trying to make ends meet on $2k a month with a $3k budget. With a good used car, a one bedroom apartment, student loans, and credit cards, I always seemed to have more month than cash. By the way, I'm also in debt to my bookie for over seven grand.

I needed a new job. I was going backward and the creditors were starting to call. I had borrowed all I could from my family and even sold plasma. I often wonder if crime does pay. I didn't want to be a drug dealer or mug someone on the street. Stealing cars was no good. Who would I sell them to? Also, most of these crimes involved hurting someone, taking personal possessions, or involved other people or other criminals. That's a surefire way of getting caught.

My luck changed one afternoon when I bumped into my best friend Kevin and his sister, Valerie, at the mall. She was several years older than us and was working for KPTN, a coupon marketing firm in Winston-Salem. Kevin was in town from Greensboro, where he was a high school soccer coach. Kevin and his sister inherited a bit of money, not enough to drop out of the workforce, but enough, from a rich uncle whom Kevin had never met. His sister told me they were hiring and looking for account managers. The pay started at $32,000 a year and she assured me that I could move up to senior account manager, earning $43,000 a year in no time.

The next day, I stopped by KPTN and gave Valerie my resume. Before I got home that evening, there was a message in my voice mail from Ashley Van Der Hagen, Valerie's boss. She wanted to interview me the next day at noon. By two the next day, I was hired as a junior account manager on a team of four managers. I was designated to handle fourteen national accounts.

Luck was on my side. A week later, the senior account representative, Todd Willis, decided to go back to school to pursue a master's degree. Ashley approached me and offered me the position. In less than two weeks, I went from $12 per hour to $32,000 per year to a whopping $46,000 a year. Not bad for a twenty-six-year-old in 2002. After my first check, I paid my bookie half of what I owed him.

CHAPTER 2
WINSTON-SALEM NC

All was well for five months. Then April 1st, 2003 rolled around. Yes, April Fools' Day. However, at the end of the day, no one yelled April fools. Not one. It seems that KPTN was extremely over budget and drastic measures were taken to thin out the herd. They let go everyone that had been with the company for less than a year. I was one of ninety-four people fired that day.

The next day, I returned to KPTN for my exit interview and paperwork to continue my insurance. The company was nice enough to carry my medical insurance for six months. Not only that, but since I was a senior account rep., I received six months' severance! What a great deal. I work for a company for six months and they pay me for a year.

I'm out of here. I hop into my car, go straight to Foreign Cars Italia of Greensboro, and purchase a 1992 Alfa Romeo Spider Veloce. Why not? With extra cash in the bank, plus $23,000 coming to me next week, no problem. However, finding a new job wouldn't come easily. I paid my bookie the rest of what I owed him. Now, I have a clean line to start betting again.

CHAPTER 3

Three months later, still no job, my cash was starting to run thin. Again, for a second time, my luck would change while walking through the mall. I bumped into my dad's stockbroker from Legg Mason. I told him my situation and he offered to set up an interview with his manager.

Two days later, I'm sitting in a beautiful office off Knollwood Street, sipping coffee, and waiting for the manager to come in and interview me. This interview didn't go too well. Unbeknownst to me before the interview, the manager's name was Mark Jamback. This would have been of no consequence, if I hadn't dated his daughter, Michelle, in high school.

Here's the story. Michelle's parents were out of town and we decided to have a party. Nothing special, just a few of our closest friends and their dates. As all high school parties tend, the entire senior class showed up. Michelle lived in a beautiful colonial in New Sherwood Forest with a nice pool. At some point during the party, someone had a camera. Several photos were taken of Michelle and me, sitting at her dad's desk. Her hand was on my crotch and in my hand was a bottle of Southern Comfort. This was all very innocent until Michelle's dad developed the film.

Some dumb ass had taken Mr. Jamback's camera from his study and taken pictures. They placed the camera back in its case, without telling anyone. Two weeks later, Mr. Jamback forbade Michelle to talk to me again. To say the least, the interview was over before it began. He just came in the office and stared at me. He didn't look at my resume or glance at his watch. He just sat statue still and stared at me.

After three minutes of staring, I stood up and asked him if I had the job. Didn't think so.

I'm in the lobby of the same building a few minutes later looking at the directory. Dean Witter was on the fifth floor. What the hell. I'm here, dressed in a suit, and with resume in hand. I might as well try. I interviewed with Stuart McIntyre. This one went great. Unbeknownst to me, Mr. McIntyre hated Mr. Jamback. Somehow, the story of the party came out and through tears of laughter, he hired me on the spot. Only $24,000 per year, but plus commissions once I pass my exams.

On October 22, 2003, I passed my series seven, the securities license exam needed to become a stockbroker. After a few more minor exams, I was fully licensed and ready to sell.

Too bad I sucked at it. Try making two hundred cold calls a day, asking the person if they wanted to buy stock. Hell, I couldn't make one hundred calls per day. This was awful. Since I couldn't sell, I couldn't make commissions. Since I couldn't make commissions, I couldn't afford my car, my bills, and my new four grand debt to my bookie. Since I couldn't afford anything, a new plan was formed, out of despair.

I've always read about bank robberies. They fascinated me. It's almost always the same story, usually with two different outcomes. The robber either gets caught in the parking lot or within a few minutes of the crime or a week later. Always the same result. And always a small take. Generally, less than a thousand dollars. And it's almost always a drug addict trying to get a little money for a fix.

This got me thinking. If done the right way, knowing what I know from my short experience of being a teller, bank robbing should be easy. Very profitable, little risk.

You just have to plan. Two weeks later, plan in hand, I head off to Myrtle Beach, South Carolina for my first job.

CHAPTER 4
NORTH MYRTLE BEACH, SC

As I arrive in North Myrtle Beach on Highway 17, I pull off and head east toward the water. It takes me only a few seconds to find a little dive with a sign out front reading "Floyd's Eff. Apts." with the vacancy sign flashing. A few minutes later, after meeting Floyd, getting a room for $59 a night, and purchasing a few "Floyd's" T-shirts, I was sitting in my room staring at an old bulky television. I lie down on the bed and look up at the ceiling. Carved in the wood paneled ceiling is this: "We are the Fellas. I want some stew." Whatever the hell that meant. I closed my eyes and went over the plan for the hundredth time.

The next morning, I started the day off with a jog. Winding my way back to Highway 17, I turned south and pushed on for about two miles. I passed a Hertz Rent a Car on my run out and on the way back, I stopped in to ask for rates. I told the clerk that my car broke down and I needed a midsize rental for a few days. We made the arrangements and I told him I would return around noon with my ID and credit card.

Next door was a drugstore. I went in and bought the least expensive, least powerful pair of reading glasses and put them in my back pocket. I return to Floyd's, shower, change, and head on foot to Hertz.

Leaving the lot, I head south on 17. I turn left at a sign pointing to Arcadian Shores. A mile later, I'm staring at the Arcadian Shores Twin Towers, with the North Myrtle Beach Hilton to their right. Everything was beautiful. The tennis courts were busy, the parking lots were full, vacationers were carrying floats to the public beach, and a lawn maintenance crew was running several mowers and weed eaters. I parked in a Hilton guest slot and entered the tall building. I walked straight through to the back, where a huge swimming pool was busy keeping thirty or so guests cool from the one hundred degree heat. To the right of the pool, a steel band was playing reggae and behind it was an outdoor bar. Seconds later, I'm sipping a Corona sans lime, the way it was meant to be served.

The lime was started in Mexico. The locals plugged the opening of the bottle with a lime between sips to keep the flies away. Not until some Americans came back from vacation from Cancun did the lime actually make it into the drink.

I paid the bartender, Randy I believe, tipped a dollar, and headed for the beach. Upon hitting the sand, I turned left and made my way to the parking lot between the Hilton and the Twin Towers. I spotted the lawn maintenance truck by a dumpster. I could tell the crew was in the front from the sound the equipment made. I headed to my rental car, a very bland 1999 silver Ford Taurus. I pulled around to the dumpster, maintenance crew still out of sight, pulled the "Mr. Piggott's Lawn Care" magnetic sign off the driver side door, jumped in the rental car, and calmly drove back to Highway 17.

A few miles farther south, I repeated my actions. This time, I got a "Lawn Care by Jessup" sign. Satisfied, I turned around and head north. Passing a Bank of America, I hit the mileage counter and head back to Floyd's.

That night, sleep did not come easily. Visions of prison kept flashing in my mind. Although I had never spent time in a real prison, I have spent a night in jail. As a matter of fact, it was here in North Myrtle Beach during senior beach week. Ironically, it wasn't for underage drinking, but for streaking. It's not fun spending the night in jail with nothing but a towel to wrap around yourself. This was before the day everyone had a cell phone. I had to wait until the next morning, when my friends noticed that Ronnie Castleman and I weren't there. Usually, that's a sign that we got lucky the night before. But, we made a pact that we'd all report back to the rental house by noon the next day. If not, we would call the pokey.

I got caught when a policewoman chased me down a dead end beside a hotel. Ronnie got caught because he couldn't climb a wall. The next day, Ronnie took us to show us the four foot wall he couldn't get over.

But, that night was a walk in the park compared to what I imagine prison is like. Considering I'm only 5'10", 185 lbs, and own a sphincter that's exit only, I'm not sure I want to see the inside of a prison. This was even more reason to get out of bed and go over the plan again. Satisfied, I turned off the lights, said goodnight to the fellas, and went to sleep.

CHAPTER 5

Early the next morning, I drove to a store that sold Halloween costumes year-round. I purchased a fake mustache and beard, a package of temporary tattoos, and a fake witch's wart. I then pulled directly across the street to a Catholic church and walked in. It took a few minutes, but I found the room where they keep the Father's robes, grabbed one, tucked it under my shirt, and left through a side exit door. Minutes later, I was back at Floyd's.

With a fake tattoo of a spider on my left hand and one of a lightening bolt on my right, the wart was placed dead center between my eyes. Next was the mustache. It was a fat one, like Tom Selleck had in Magnum, P.I. or like the one Tom Selleck had for his entire career. Adding the reading glasses and putting on the robe, I looked very much the part of a Catholic priest.

With the "Piggott" sign on the driver side and the "Jessup" sign on the passenger side, I was off to Bank of America. I put a piece of electrical tape over the "Hertz" decal on the bumper. I pulled into the parking lot, making sure to avoid the ATM at the front of the building and its hidden camera inside. I take a deep breath, count to ten, and enter the lobby.

Although the parking lot was almost empty, there were six tellers, all female. To the right, in three waist-high cubicles, sat three customer service reps., one male and two female. In the corner behind them, a middle-aged lady with blonde hair and a "Branch Manager" plaque on her window helped a gentleman with his business. All the customer service reps. were helping customers. There were only two customers at teller windows. This means no time to think and also no time to get nervous. Or, more nervous anyway.

"May I help you?" nametag Christie asked.

"Yes, thank you. I would like to complete this transaction and I'll be on my way," I said and handed her the note. It read: "This is real. It's a robbery. No bait money. No dye packs. No silent alarm. LOOK AT MY EAR. Inside it is a radio receiver on the same frequency as the police. If I hear them respond, I will detonate the bomb I placed in the trash can. Please open your top drawer and put all your money into the bag. Then, open the second drawer and do the same. Lastly, open your bottom vault and give me all the hundreds, fifties, twenties, and tens. Do this and you will not get hurt. HURRY, AND DON'T LOOK AT ME."

Christie complied. They are trained to follow instructions and do as they're told. This was a piece of cake. She handed me the bag. "Hand me the note," I said.

"Here," she replied, looking straight down.

"Thank you." I turned and walked out. I got into my rental car and headed south on 17. Five miles later, I pulled into a Kroger grocery store. Having already removed the robe, the mustache, and the wart, I got out of the car and placed the items into a trash can at the edge of the parking lot. I pulled off the magnetic signs, wiped them clean of fingerprints, and put them in the trash can, as well. I opened the trunk and placed the bag of money into the compartment that holds the spare tire. With that complete, I leave the parking lot and head east to get as close to the ocean as possible. I then turned north and hugged the coast.

Once I was certain I was past Bank of America, I turned west to get back to 17, turned north, and headed for Floyd's. Once there, I retrieved the money bag and went to my room. I placed the bag in another bag that was watertight, sealed it, and put it in the back compartment of the toilet. I changed clothes, putting on a pair of running shorts, socks, running shoes, and my Floyd's Eff. Apts. T-shirt, which on the back had the slogan; "In Cancun there's no Floyd's." My personal bag was already packed and I took it out to the Alfa, placing it in the trunk. I got in the rental car and headed to Hertz. Once there, I turned in my keys to the clerk and headed out on foot.

It's been less than a half hour since I walked out of the bank. I ran south on 17 for about a mile, away from Floyd's but toward the bank, keeping an ear out for any nearby sirens. There were some, but they sounded several miles farther down. When the bank was barely visible, blue lights were flashing in the parking lot. I turned around and ran the mile and a half back to the turnoff for Floyd's. I jogged past the great apartments and didn't see anything out of the ordinary. I walked around the block and past the apartments again. I repeated the process two more times. Satisfied there was no danger, I entered my room, grabbed the money bag, left my room key on the nightstand, and left.

Starting the Alfa, I looked in the mirror and gave a little smile. I think I just pulled it off. I get back out of the car, opened the trunk, and placed the money bag in the spare tire compartment. Back behind the wheel, I head toward

CHAPTER 6
WINSTON-SALEM, NC

Back at home, I've got the weekend to relax and monitor the news to see if I hear of anything concerning the robbery. So far, all is quiet. I get up Saturday morning and go for a four mile run, anything to help release this adrenaline stored inside my body. Upon returning, I grab the Winston-Salem Journal for the local news. I enter my downtown apartment and jump straight into the shower. Minutes later, I'm dressed and out the door to the corner diner for breakfast, the newspaper tucked under my arm.

"Hey Vern, give me the Hungry Captain, scrambled with links, grits, wheat toast, and a coffee," I said directly over Gina, the waitress.

"No problem Cam. Gina, pour the man some coffee," replied Vern.

I spend the next few minutes flipping through every page, scanning the headlines. Nothing jumps off the page indicating any robbery in South Carolina. I turn to the sports page and read an article by Mason Crutchfield, local sports writer, covering a Mount Tabor baseball game.

My food comes, cooked perfectly. Life is good. That night, I stop by my bookie's house, pay him the six grand I owe him, and grab a USA TODAY to check out the latest NCAA tournament lines.

The rest of the weekend was not good for me. I ended up losing over four thousand to my bookie and now only have eight left to pay my bills, which were in excess of ten.

Monday morning, I book an online, first class flight to Las Vegas for the upcoming Friday. I work the rest of the week at Dean Witter, making about fifty calls per day. Every night, I rack my brain to think of another bank job. I also stop by Barnes & Noble and pick up a "How to Play Blackjack" handbook. I know I can't make the necessary daily phone calls to be a successful broker, so the plan gets kicked up a notch.

CHAPTER 7
LAS VEGAS

Friday is here and I catch my 6:00 p.m. flight out of Raleigh-Durham Airport to Vegas. I order a Bud Light the moment I grab my seat and pull out the blackjack book from my carry-on bag. I spend the next two hours rereading the system the book outlines and knock down three more beers in the process.

After a short nap, the flight attendant taps my shoulder and informs me to prepare for landing. I glance out the window and can already see the lights. It's beautiful. I've never been to Vegas. I've seen it plenty of times on TV, but nothing can compare to seeing it in person.

Outside the airport, I grab a taxi and head for the Bellagio. It's the first hotel to come to mind. Thirty minutes later, I'm in my hotel room recounting my cash for the third time. I left a grand at home, along with all my major credit cards, and a hundred in my car beneath the seat back at RDU. The only credit card I have is one with a measly thousand dollar limit and I used it for the room. I have exactly sixty-two hundred on me. I put half in my pocket, the other half in the room safe, and head downstairs to the tables.

I approach the low limit blackjack tables, ten dollar minimum and one hundred maximum. I give the dealer, a guy that looked my age, a thousand dollars and asked for green $25 dollar chips. With my chips stacked neatly in front of me, I play my first real hand of blackjack.

Playing one handed, two chips at a time, I double my chips in less than an hour. A few players join me at the table and I quickly lose about three hundred. I tip the dealer two chips and leave in search of a new table with higher limits.

Settling on a $25 minimum and $500 maximum, I take a seat in eighth position, so I can be last to play. The table is half full and the dealer is a blonde named Stacie. She's slim, about five-five, hair framing her face and shoulder length, with a fake rack, and cleavage tight enough to hold a Titleist. It was everything I could do to focus on my cards.

I placed my chips on the table and started playing. It was like I knew what cards were coming. I would double down with nine or ten showing against the dealer's upcard five or six. I split aces. I would double my bets after a hand following a slew of low cards. Face cards came when I needed them. Blackjack hit about every dozen hands. By one in the morning, two hours after sitting down with Stacie and about a six pack later, I was up nine grand and had the pit boss' attention. He approached me and offered an upgrade from my original room to a deluxe with a view of the fountains. I tip Stacie three one hundred dollar black chips and follow the pit boss to the lobby.

I retired to my new room an hour later and pulled out all my chips and the rest of my cash. The total tally, including my cash from my previous room vault, was over $15,000. I placed it all on my bed and just stared in disbelief. Then came a knock on my door.

CHAPTER 8

I grab the cash and chips, throw them in the vault, and activate the lock. Approaching the door, I look through the peephole and standing there was Stacie. I open the door and can't think of a thing to say.

"I don't think I thanked you for the tip. May I come in?"

"Of course," was all I could utter. I stepped back and let Stacie in. "Can I get you anything? Beer? Wine?"

"Any Merlot?"

"I think I can find some. If not, it's just a phone call away." I fumble around the wet bar and find a bottle of Fetzer Vineyards Merlot, not having any idea if it's a good wine or not. Trying to work the corkscrew as smoothly as possible, I open the bottle, along with a small chunk of my left thumb. "Damn." I stick my thumb in my mouth and grab a towel. I pour Stacie a glass, hand it to her, and fumble in my shaving kit for a band aid. "So, what's up?"

"Not a lot. I didn't get your name downstairs."

"Oh, uh, it's Cameron."

"Well now we know each other's names. It's nice to meet you Cameron. You had a good night."

"Thanks. Just lucky, I guess. How did you know what room I was in?"

"The front desk operator and I have been girlfriends for about a year. She told me."

"Easy enough. So Stacie, what should we do?" Then came another knock on the door.

CHAPTER 9

"That would be Darby, my girlfriend. Let her in. She's cool."

Sure enough, I look through the peephole and there stood the girl the pit boss introduced me to for the room upgrade. I open the door. If Stacie was a nine, Darby was a ten. Another blonde, this one with her hair in a ponytail. At five foot nine, we were nearly eye to eye. Apparently, she knew the same plastic surgeon as Stacie because her chest was just as impressive.

"Hey there Cameron, I'm Darby. Is Stacie here?" she asked.

"Uh, yes. Come on in. What can I get you to drink?"

"Whatever you're drinking," she replied. "But the real question is, what can we get you?" asked Darby.

"I'm not sure what you mean."

"Come on Cameron." I turn to the bed and look at Stacie. She already has her top off. "What can we get you?" she repeats.

I turn back to Darby and her top is off as well. She comes toward me and pushes me back toward the bed, pulling my shirt over my head in the process. As soon as my shirt is off, Darby kisses me, while Stacie grabs me around the waist from behind and drops my belt and slacks to the floor. She spins me around and takes me immediately in her hands, arousing me instantly. She takes me in her mouth, while Darby is rubbing her breasts on my back.

A few minutes later, Darby joins her. They finish the job together and start in on each other. I stare in disbelief and start to get hard again. We spend the next hour probing every inch of each other's body.

I'm totally spent when Darby reaches into her purse and pulls out a little baggie. She dumps the white powder on the coffee table and scrapes out several long lines. Stacie pulls a Franklin out of nowhere and rolls it up. She takes a line, then hands it to Darby. Two lines gone, fingers dipped, and rubbed on their gums, they hand me the rolled-up hundred.

"This will help us, well you anyway, for at least another hour or so."

I take a line and repeat the gumming process. Ready for round three, I crawl back onto the bed and lay on my back. Stacie crawls onto the bed and straddles my face, while Darby mounts me. Ten minutes later, they switch places until I'm completely empty. They toot a few more lines, then proceed to finish each other.

Seemingly done, they grab their clothes and both go into the bathroom. Minutes later, they exit the bathroom fully dressed and looking more beautiful than when they arrived. Darby nuzzled my neck and whispered, "That was great Cameron. I'd say that was good enough for a thousand. Wouldn't you?"

I get up and cross the room to the safe, punch in my code, and retrieve the money. Handing it to her I say, "That was so good, it will be worth twice that tomorrow night."

"Then, we will see you tomorrow Cameron," Darby said as she grabbed Stacie's hand and left the room.

I slept till noon the next day. I didn't have one sex dream. Hell, even in my dreams I couldn't get it up a fourth time.

CHAPTER IO

At 1:00 Saturday, I enter the fitness room and put in a fifty minute run on the treadmill. I mess with the dumbbells for awhile, then enter the men's room for a steam bath. By 2:30, I'm in my room taking a shower and planning my evening. I figure I'll take to the streets and see a little of Las Vegas.

In downtown "Old Vegas," I see and enter the famed Binion's Horseshoe. I find a blackjack table near the back and decide to try my luck. An hour later and a thousand dollars lighter, I head for the craps table.

I have no idea how to play craps, so I stand and watch. After several turns for the players, I give up on learning and walk to a row of roulette tables. There is a sign displaying the last ten numbers and colors the ball settled on. The last five numbers were red, so I decide to bet $200 on black. The wheel is spun and it comes up red. Pissed, I reach into my pocket and pull out $500 and bet on black again. This time, it hits. The attendant pays me $500, plus my bet and I walk away. Enough of this shit. Get me back to the Bellagio.

At exactly nine o'clock, after a great nap and a perfect room service filet mignon with garlic potatoes, I approach the same table that Stacie was working the previous night. She's not there. In her place is an even more attractive woman with long auburn hair, about five foot seven, slim, all original parts, named Summer.

I put down three grand and ask for the hundred dollar black chips. With my stack neatly arranged in front of me, I put a chip into the betting circle. The cards come up five of hearts and five of spades. The dealer shows four of spades. I double down and draw an ace, giving me twenty-one. The dealer's hole card is a nine and hits a face to bust, paying me two hundred. My luck continues for about an hour. I'm up over ten grand. I give Summer a four black chip tip, leave fifty chips, ask her to hold my spot, and head to my room.

Upstairs in my room, I pull everything out of my pockets. I also open the room safe and retrieve its contents. I'm staring at nearly $20,000 in chips and cash. Satisfied, I shovel everything into the safe, lock it, and return to the floor.

Back at the table, there is a new dealer named Steve, an older gentleman, probably about fifty, with piercing blue eyes. My chips are all there. I place a five hundred dollar bet. I'm dealt a face and a four. The dealer's upcard is a five. I stay. The dealer turns his hole card over. It is queen of diamonds. He hits his fifteen and draws the nine of clubs. Bust. Pay me.

A different pit boss approaches me and hands me a note. I glance at the folded napkin and open it. It read, "Thanks for the tip Cameron. Meet me at Ghostbar at midnight for cocktails if you're interested in having fun."

Holy shit. What's going on? I've ran my share in my time, but this is ridiculous. It's amazing what money attracts. In the next thirty minutes, I lose every chip I had on the table. Oh well. I look at my watch. It's 11:30. Time to head to the room, grab a few grand, and head to the bar to meet Summer.

CHAPTER II

I'm a few minutes early and there is no sign of Summer. I grab a stool at the bar and order a Corona sans lime. I believe that I'm going to have to start drinking finer beer to go with my new success. Glancing around the bar, there is still no Summer.

Minutes later, Darby rounds the corner and catches my eye. With a quick little wink, she mouths, "I'll be back."

Before I have time to smile and shake my head in disbelief, Summer slips onto the stool beside me. She's changed clothes. She's wearing a knee length black Nicole Miller dress with spaghetti straps, cut low in the front, but not too low, accented by peek-a-boo strapped high heels. She looks amazing. For a split second, I wonder how much this is going to cost me.

"You look incredible."

"Thanks Cameron. How'd you make out after I left?" she inquired.

"Well, after your note, I couldn't think. I crashed and burned."

"I'm sorry."

"I'm not. Can I get you a drink?"

"Absolutely. I've been working since noon. Last night, I worked till midnight. I need to let my hair down and have some fun. Can you order me a gin and tonic? I need to go to the ladies room and freshen up."

"It'll be here before you return." She touched my forearm, gave me the slightest kiss on the cheek, and left for the bathroom, leaving a trail of perfume in her wake. I watch her round the corner. I turn to order her drink and Darby is sitting in her chair.

"Cameron, Cameron, Cameron. What am I to do with you? I leave you alone for a couple of hours and you're having a drink with another."

"She's not like you and Stacie. At least, I don't think she is."

"We're all the same Cam. You'll see."

"I don't think so Darby. Anyway, what do you know about Summer?" I asked.

"Just that she's going through a rough divorce. She was a stripper at the Palomino and married one of the owners. He slept around, Summer found out, and the rest is history."

"So she's available?"

"Everyone is available for the right price Cameron."

"That's not what I meant. I mean, is she single?"

"Very. But aren't we all?" I ordered Darby a drink and waited for Summer to return. By the time Darby's cocktail arrived, Summer returned and took the bar stool on my left, leaving me in the middle. Darby said hello to Summer, then stood up to leave. She bent down to my ear and said, "You know where to find me. And Stacie. Bye Cameron."

Summer and I had a great evening that ended with her in my bed. The sex was incredible and didn't cost me a thing.

CHAPTER I2
WINSTON-SALEM, NC

Back in North Carolina, I received news of my great uncle Walter's passing from a massive heart attack. My uncle Walter married late in life and never had any children. When his wife died a decade ago, he retired and moved to Punta Gorda, Florida, a small town on the gulf located about an hour south of Sarasota.

Uncle Walter and I were always close and I sensed he wanted children, specifically a son. When I was little, he would take me fishing, hunting, and on long rides on his Harley. We had drifted a little over the years, more so since his move to Florida. But, I visited him on occasion and he would take me deep sea fishing. He had sold his boat a few years back when it got to be more than hecould handle.

He had a two-bedroom condominium with a spectacular view of Charlotte Harbor. On the times I would visit, we would sit on the back lanai, overlooking the harbor, and he would tell me stories about my parents. My mother died my sophomore year in high school and my dad, still living, is a workaholic lawyer in Mooresville, North Carolina.

Uncle Walter would tell stories my dad would never tell me. They included how my parents met and how Dad was the life of the party in his fraternity. He also told me about the time he had to bail my dad out of jail for a bar fight and how the case was dropped when my dad, while not in law school yet, had lined up nineteen witnesses, frustrating the judge and the DA till they dismissed the case.

We shared a lot of memories on that back lanai, so it wasn't a complete surprise he left the condo to me in his will. I took a week off from Dean Witter and flew to Florida to finalize his affairs.

In Punta Gorda, I met with Walter's stockbroker, Daniel Russo. Daniel is an independent adviser clearing through a regional brokerage firm. As we discussed Walter's assets, he told me how proud Walter was of me for becoming a broker. He thought I was a natural born salesman and possessed the gift of gab.

Walter died with a little over $200,000 in stocks and mutual funds. The will indicated his brokerage account was to be liquidated and the proceeds be given to the Peace River Wildlife Center in Punta Gorda. Daniel had contacted the center and informed them of the donation. A reception was to be held in Walter's honor the upcoming Thursday night at Ponce de Leon Park, complete with catered dinner and open bar and they wished for both me and Daniel to attend.

At the reception, I met many of Walter's friends. Since we shared the last name and everyone was wearing name tags, I shook a lot of hands and exchanged hugs with what appeared to me to be the entire retirement community. Even the mayor paid his condolences.

The president of the preserve, Vaughn Moore, presented me with a plaque in Walter's memory and for his generous contribution. At the end of the evening, Daniel approached me with an offer of employment. He informed me he couldn't continue servicing 30 percent of his book of business and he was looking for a young go-getter to lighten his workload. I would receive 50 percent commission on his clients and full commission on anything I generated on my own. On top of that, Vaughn Moore told me he was looking for an adviser for his organization. He had over two million in assets, $500,000 of which was in cash. He sweetened the pot with an intent to move their account to me if I joined Daniel. With nothing holding me down in North Carolina and a free place to live in Punta Gorda, the decision was pretty easy.

I joined Daniel at his firm, Sunset Advisers, two weeks later. Complete with a corner office, the suite only had two offices total, a newly hired but nearly retired secretary, and close to three hundred accounts given to me by Daniel. I picked up the phone and started to call my new clients.

CHAPTER 13
PUNTA GORDA

After a month, I've settled into a nice routine. After a morning run, I arrive at the office around 9:00, a half hour before the opening bell. I spend the morning monitoring the market and calling Daniel's clients assigned to me. I've also brought in a dozen new clients along with the Peace River Wildlife account. Vaughn Moore has been instrumental in introducing me to several new clients and we have a golf game today, where he is inviting two new prospects.

I lunch at Harpoon Harry's, a favorite spot of my late uncle Walter, and knock back a grouper stuffed with a crab mixture, lightly seasoned and broiled to perfection and served with apple cranberry orzo and steamed veggies. Kick in a Corona Light for good measure and I'm off to St. Andrews South Golf Club for 18.

Vaughn introduced me to our playing partners. Mark Ferrer, 44, was a real estate speculator who had netted a few million in the past few years. Our other playing partner was Jim Tulley, 66, a retired general contractor whose son now ran the business, net worth unknown.

After finishing our round, we headed to the River City Grill, where we enjoyed great steaks and a couple bottles of wine. By the time dinner was finished, both players had committed to opening accounts with me. Vaughn also pledged to open a personal brokerage account.

Later that night, sitting on the lanai and enjoying a beer, I realized how much my life had changed these past few months. Here I was, working my way up as the go-to broker in Punta Gorda, surrounded by wealth, multi-million dollar homes with million dollar yachts in their backyard canals, and it all seemed slightly out of my grasp. Even working hard and generating $300,000 in revenue, a third of which is mine, wasn't enough. I wanted more and I wanted it now. Something was missing. I needed a thrill. A challenge. A high only achieved with taking great risk. I needed to rob a bank.

CHAPTER 14

This particular bank job was easy to execute, but tough to plan. Once the concept was conceived and the target identified, I set out a time frame to achieve my goal. The target was a downtown BB&T bank in Winston-Salem, North Carolina, my home state. It is located on two streets and is twenty-one stories high. It's their headquarters.

I knew the branch, located in the lobby, very well. As a rule of thumb, you shouldn't rob a bank in your hometown. Although the grainy black and white video is generally too blurry to detail you, it will be seen by a million people, several of whom know you. This job, like many others in the future, will be accomplished only by a thorough disguise.

I fly out of Southwest Florida International Airport in Fort Myers to Atlanta and pick up a connector to Charlotte. In Charlotte, I grab a rental car and drive the seventy-two miles to Winston-Salem. For a moment, I consider stopping by my dad's house in Mooresville on Lake Norman, but ruled it out. I shouldn't let anyone know I'm in the state.

After stopping by the local Goodwill center and picking up a one-piece mechanic's uniform, I drive around Winston-Salem to make sure the city is how I left it months earlier. A lot of road construction closes roads and in some cases, turns one-ways into two-ways. I park the rental on 3rd Street and load the parking meter with three quarters that were carefully wiped to leave no fingerprints.

Wearing a suit, not the mechanic's uniform, and a fake goatee, I enter the parking garage of the high-rise on foot and walk past the parking attendant, who didn't even glance my way. Approaching the elevator that went up to the lobby, making sure that there are no cameras, I place an empty briefcase behind a FedEx drop-off box. The elevator door opens. I enter and ride to the lobby, where I pass a security guard reading a newspaper and I leave through the front doors. I've seen all I need to see.

Making my way back to the rental car, I realize that this job is going to be easy. This is not a busy branch, not a lot of foot traffic, and an unarmed security guard that is pushing seventy years of age. I decide to blow off some steam and head toward the row of bars that are off of 6th Street. Three hours later, I enter a Holiday Inn to get some sleep and make final preparations for tomorrow.

CHAPTER I5
WINSTON-SALEM NC

I wake at 7:00 a.m. and after applying a fake tattoo to the back of my left hand, a mustache, and a wig, I start wiping down the entire room for prints. Satisfied that it's clean, I get dressed and check out by leaving the card key on the dresser and exiting the back door. I drive to the exact same parking meter from the day before and repeat the quarters.

Walking to the parking garage, adjusting the mechanic's one-piece as I go, I reach into my right pocket to assure the note is there. In my left hand is a regular brown lunch bag with a pager and a cell phone taped together. Three identical but empty brown bags are in my left pocket. I pass the same parking attendant helping someone leave the garage and make my way to the elevators and up to the lobby.

Passing another bank of elevators that take employees to floors two through twenty-one, I enter the working lobby of the branch through a set of glass doors. The lobby is empty of customers and there are two tellers behind the line. An office to the left has a young lady, probably twenty-five or so, working on her computer with the phone pressed to her ear.

I go up to the table on the far wall to act as if I'm filling out a deposit slip. One teller is on the phone and the other looks to be reading a magazine. I approach her and hand her the note from my right pocket. It reads:

"Stay calm. This is a robbery. Please open your bottom vault and fill this bag with hundreds, fifties, and twenties.

Then, open your second and top drawer and do the same. Do not give me any bait money or dye packs. Do not trip the alarm. Across the room on the deposit table, LOOK AT IT NOW, is a bag with a bomb with a remote detonation device. The trigger is in my pocket. After you do your station, go to the other teller and hand her the note and do the same thing. BE CALM. I can detonate the bomb from a mile away. But, I won't if you follow directions. DO NOT TRIP THE SILENT ALARM. I WILL KNOW IF YOU DO AND TRIGGER THE BOMB."

The teller read the note, looked at the bag across the room, and started filling up the bag. After she finished, she went to the other teller who was now off the phone and showed her the note. I told teller one to take three steps back. She followed orders. Teller two read the note, looked at the bag, and followed suit. Once teller two gave me the money, I told her to take three steps back, as well.

"Hand me the note." Teller two complied. "Believe me," I said calmly, "I have a police scanner right here," showing them a walkie-talkie. "If I hear the police responding to an alarm, I will pull the trigger on that bomb," pointing to the bag. "Have a nice day."

I walk to the parking garage elevators, but took the stairs instead. Upon entering the stairway, I quickly remove the mechanic's one-piece and the fake mustache and wig, putting the mustache and wig in my pocket and tucking the uniform under my left arm. Now, I'm wearing a suit and tie. Opening the 1st sub basement door and walking to the FedEx drop off box, I reach behind it and grab the briefcase. I quickly open the case, shove the uniform and the money inside, and close it, latching the locks. I leave the parking garage, waving to the attendant as I do, turn left, and walk the block and a half to get my rental car.

I open the trunk, deposit the briefcase, and get behind the wheel. I drive until I come across a manual car wash I had scoped out yesterday and pulled in. I open the trunk, remove the mechanic's uniform, and place it in the trash can connected to the vacuum. I take out three quarters and deposit them in the vacuum, letting the suction take the wig and the mustache. Nothing like a lot of dust from a dirty vacuum to cover any DNA left behind.

Satisfied, I head to the Piedmont International Airport in Greensboro, about forty minutes away. I will catch my first of three flights, eventually arriving in Fort Myers, Florida. Upon dropping off the rental car at Enterprise, I grab my overnight bag and the briefcase and catch a bus to the terminal. Once alone on the bus, I open the briefcase to check on the money, not to count it, just to make me feel better knowing it's there. I'll count it later.

The next day, I arrive in Fort Myers at 1:30 p.m., $56,000 richer. I head to my car and I'm back in Punta Gorda by 2:45. I stop by Bank of America, go to my safety deposit box, and put all the money into the box. It's the largest one they rent. A few more jobs and I'll have to get another one.

One year later, six jobs complete.

CHAPTER 16
PUNTA GORDA

After a five mile jog over the Punta Gorda Isles bridge and back, I shit, shower, shave, and head out to get some breakfast and read the local paper. I want to see if my latest robbery was reported in the Nation section. Although you generally don't see articles written about bank robberies from 1,200 miles away, mine seem to get into the paper due to the cleverness of the job or from the amount of money reported taken. There is nothing there. I know I can check the internet, but the FBI are pretty bright about back checking. I'm afraid they could pinpoint everyone who clicks on the article and trace it back to me. Even if I use the computer at the local library under a fake library card, they could still trace it back to Punta Gorda.

This would be as good a time as any to let you know a few rules of the trade. Granted there are many, but here are the obvious ones. Never do a job in your hometown. I clearly broke that rule early in my career. Hey, it was my second job and I was learning. Since then, I haven't returned to North Carolina for any reason. I now have a strict one robbery per state rule.

You need to have several fake IDs, as well as several real credit cards, but with fake names. Having multiple P.O. boxes comes in handy, also. When getting a rental car, which you must do 90 percent of the time, use a fake credit card with a fake driver's license. It takes years to obtain these fake IDs and to learn how to make forged birth certificates and Social Security cards. You can use someone you trust, but this can be tricky. Remember, avoid getting others involved. If you find a competent forger, pay him well and never let him know your business.

The most overlooked battle of getting away with a bank robbery is the disguise. You know you are going to be on video. Most guys go in with a baseball cap and sunglasses. This is clearly not enough. You must learn real disguise techniques, including makeup, prosthetic noses, extra chins, padding to make you look heavier, even dressing as a woman. Tattoos are also a great diversion, as well as fake moles, changing your hair color, or giving yourself a unibrow. There are several great books to help you learn guidelines on applying makeup. I've done jobs as a priest, mechanic, tow truck driver, cross dresser, even a six-month pregnant woman.

Also, get a good optometrist to prescribe you several different shades of color contacts. Experiment with glasses, such as wire rim, round, square, all kinds of shapes. Work on an accent. Learn an English, French, southern, northern, and Hispanic accent.

Generally, when traveling, use large hotel chains. They see hundreds of people per day and the likelihood of them remembering you is slim. When dining out or going to a bar while on a job, don't tip too much or too little. You don't want anyone remembering you as a cheap bastard or a heavy tipper. Dress down, nothing flashy. You want to blend in, never stand out.

Since cell phones can be tracked, I only travel with a throw away smart phone that I buy from Walmart. I use this phone to make hotel, plane, and rental car reservations. You also never know when you'll need to use the maps app or look up a weather report. Weather is important and I try to do all jobs on a sunny day. Cops are busy writing tickets. If it's raining, you can be sure they are sitting in their patrol cars trying not to get wet, thus, more likely to be sitting nearby. After each job, the phone goes in the trash before I get on a plane to go home. I always leave my personal and work cell phones at home.

And lastly, anytime you plan to break the law, whether it's a bank robbery or a simple U-turn, do it between 3:00 and 4:00 in the afternoon. Statistics prove that's the best time to get away with any crime. Trust me on this one.

CHAPTER 17

I fly out of Fort Myers Airport on my first of three flights to Los Angeles, LAX. I arrive in the city of angels at 9:00 p.m. on a Sunday. I take a taxi to the Fairmont Hotel in Santa Monica, with a view of the Santa Monica Pier. After a late night dinner, I retire to my room and go over the plans for the following week. This is one of my most complicated heists and it's going to take a few dry runs to make it work. I could really use a partner on this one, but I still don't trust anybody.

Monday morning, I grab a taxi and tell the driver to take me to the nearest car rental agency. He deposits me at a Hertz lot and I enter and approach the counter.

"I need a compact. Something cheap and good on gas."

"No problem. Can I have your credit card and driver's license?" the attendant asked.

Minutes later, I pull out of the lot behind the wheel of a beautiful Ford Escort. I head east on I-10 until I see what I need. I pull into a Penske Truck Rental lot and inquire about rates for a sixteen-foot moving truck with a loading ramp. Satisfied, I reserve one to be picked up tomorrow and ask if I can leave my car on the lot while I move from my current apartment to my new one.

The truck taken care of, I head west on I-10 to find a place to grab some lunch. The next exit has signs for Taco Bell and McDonald's. I decide on the Taco Bell and grab the LA Times from a vending machine upon entering.

Halfway through enjoying my number four combo, I find what I need in the classifieds. I call the number on the listing, get directions, and am on my way. The house is a run down shack in East L.A. and I get a little bit nervous as I approach the door. Before I can knock, Juan Carlos opens the door and asks if I'm Nick.

"Yeah. Nick Wood. You got the bike?"

"Yes, it's right around back. Round here."

I follow Juan through a three-foot high chain link fence and see what I came for. It's a black 2002 Ninja 600, a crotch rocket.

"Can I start it?"

Juan puts the key into the ignition and motions me to go ahead. I crank it and it growls. It's a little loud, but a quick adjustment to the muffler will calm it down. I ask him if a helmet is included and if I could borrow it now for a quick test run. I give him the keys to the rental car to let him know I'd be back and steered the Ninja toward the street.

After a quick lap around the block, I was satisfied that the bike would do. Upon returning, Juan is drinking a 40 on the front porch, with my keys on a table next to him.

"How much you want?" I asked.

"Twenty-two hundred."

"Tell you what. I've got to take my car home. I'll catch a cab back and give you two thousand cash, an extra fifty for the helmet. What do you say?"

"Twenty-two and the bike and helmet are yours."

Not wanting to spend anymore time than necessary in East LA, I agree and tell him I'd return in an hour for the bike. I drive back to the hotel and tell the concierge to get me a cab.

Back in East LA, I tip the driver a finsky and ask him to wait until he sees me pull out on a motorcycle. He agrees and promptly squeals his wheels as soon as I close the door. Great.

Juan Carlos was true to his word. Twenty-two hundred dollars later and helmet on my head, no license plate on the back, I get out of East LA as quickly as possible.

Back in Santa Monica, I find a small strip mall with a hardware store. I purchase a Phillips and flat head screwdriver, a ratchet set, and a pair of pliers. An hour later, I have a new, but used, hot license plate on the Ninja. I park the bike a block from the Fairmont, tighten the muffler to reduce its noise, and walk to the hotel.

In my room, I raid the minibar.

CHAPTER 18
CHARLESTON, SC

FBI Senior Special Agent Martin Rickard is sitting at his desk in his downtown Charleston, South Carolina office. Due to the recent surge of bank robberies nationwide and in his home state, the FBI added more resources to help fight the crime.

Robbing banks might sound old-fashioned in today's high-tech, identity fraud, and cybercrime laden world, but the threat is still there. The FBI took the lead in investigating bank robberies in the 1930s, when John Dillinger and his gang grabbed the nation's attention with daring heists. In 1934, it became a federal crime to rob any bank that was a member of the Federal Reserve. Today, the FBI generally plays a supporting role in investigating the everyday common bank robbery and focuses most of their resources on those suspects who pose the greatest risk to the public. They also pay particular attention to suspected serial robbers who jump jurisdictional lines, moving state to state.

Rickard graduated from North Carolina at Chapel Hill in 1992 with a B.S. in psychology. He stepped out of a graduation robe and straight into fatigues, enlisting in the Army out of Fort Bragg. Six months later, he joined jump school with the 82nd Airborne. After a few years in Germany, he returned stateside and finished his time teaching counterintelligence.

Upon leaving the military, he joined the Charlotte Police Department and made detective in homicide in short order. It was a particular murder in 2001 that put him on the FBI's radar.

In July 2001, a Brink's truck was robbed at gunpoint by three armed men while making a delivery to a Charlotte-based Bank of America. They got away with over two million. Weeks later, when two of the suspects were found decapitated, they brought in Rickard.

Rickard followed the money. After a few days, he tracked down a storage unit rented by one of the deceased suspects in Wilmington, North Carolina. After getting a search warrant for the unit, he cut the lock and located the cash. Rickard was amazed at the sight. There were two small tables with the neatly stacked money in the form of pyramids. The Wilmington Police Department catalogued the find, with Rickard getting the credit. A year later, the South Carolina office of the FBI hired him to head up the entire state's bank robbery division.

FBI Senior Special Agent Rickard rekindled the flame of his high school sweetheart after the Army and married her quickly. Sally was a beautiful, petite brunette and only three months married, they were pregnant. They gave birth to a beautiful baby girl, Vanessa, and all was wonderful in their little world.

"Sally's on the line one sir," Agent Pete Knabb informed him.

"Thanks." Picking up the phone, "Hey dear. What's up?"

"Not a lot. Just wanted to see what time you'd be home for dinner."

"I'm not real sure. We've got some details to go over, but

I feel like I'll be out of here by six-thirty, seven at the latest. How's our little angel?"

"She's doing better. The doctor seems to think it's just a little bug, something going around. Anyway, she's napping right now and I'm trying to plan our meal. So, be home by seven-thirty or call. K?"

"No problem. Love you."

"Love you too."

"Everything good?" asked Knabb.

"Yeah, thanks. Vanessa was running a little temperature. We just wanted to make sure. Hey, let's go over the details of that BofA hit in Myrtle Beach in early 2004. You know the one, the eighteen grand the Father got away with."

"Why do you keep insisting that we continue to look at this case? There hasn't been a single robbery that even comes close to resembling that hit since. Come on Boss, let that one go."

"I can't Knabb. It just intrigues me. I mean, come on, was this guy cool or what? He doesn't go in and put a gun to anyone's head. No, not this guy. He puts on a Catholic priest's robe, puts a few tats on his hands, and what we believe is a fake wart placed directly between his eyes purposely to divert attention from other facial features. He slips the little honey a note and is out of there in less than eight minutes. He leaves in a white, four-door POS with some kind of lawn maintenance magnet on the side, never to be seen or heard of again. Now that just doesn't happen nowadays."

"Well, you're right, sir. I mean, this guy is no local. We'd've made him by now," added Knabb.

"So, who was this guy? Look, I know we've done this

before, but let's get out of the FBI database and check the internet for news stories. Maybe something slipped by the bureau. Google 'Catholic Priest Bad.' Shit, strike that. You'd be here for days. Try 'Catholic Priest Robbery.' You know what Knabb, try whatever you like. I'll do the same and let's look at it tomorrow morning. I need to finish up a little paperwork, then scoot home. Get out of here. Go do whatever it is you do when you're not here."

"Actually boss, I do that sometimes while I'm here, as well," Knabb replied with a grin.

"Yeah whatever. See you in the morning."

Senior Special Agent Rickard signed a few documents, got his files in order, locked all but one of them up, and headed home to his wife and daughter.

CHAPTER 19
SANTA MONICA, CA

I wake up in a slight fog and head for the bathroom. Minutes later, I've changed into my running shorts and T-shirt and head for the lobby of the Fairmont. With the Santa Monica Pier off to my left, I head south toward it. After passing several homeless people, I make my way down a flight of stairs and onto the pedestrian bridge that will empty me onto the sand. I hit the famed asphalt bike/jog path and kick it north till my legs burned. Instead of retracing my steps, I find another pedestrian bridge to get back to the main road. Unbeknownst to me, I have a three hundred plus step climb almost straight up to get to the main street. Damn! My calves ache, my thighs were melting, and I start to get dizzy. Ten minutes later, after resting twice, I make it to the top. Note to self, don't take the same route tomorrow. Even better, don't run at all.

Back in my room, I shower and shave and hit the in-house restaurant. After eating a western omelet, bowl of fruit, wheat toast, and a glass of orange juice, I'm out the door, giving the valet my ticket stub. There is nothing more embarrassing than having a valet bring around a rental. I slip him a few dollars and drive a block south to turn east on Wilshire Boulevard.

About ten miles later, I pull into the parking lot of the Wells Fargo branch on Wilshire Boulevard, steering clear of the ATM and its hidden camera. I'm wearing a long blonde wig under my UCLA ballcap and cutoff jean shorts with a wife-beater tank. I enter through the lobby doors and walk up to the deposit table in the center of the branch. After making a mental note of the branch layout, I pat my back pocket and make a show of not having my wallet. After glancing at the teller line and putting to memory a teller named Sharon, I leave through the front doors, get in my car, and pull out with my plan solidified in my head. Back to the Fairmont.

CHAPTER 20
CHARLESTON, SC

Martin Rickard pulled the covers up around Vanessa's shoulders and returned the Little Mermaid book to its proper place on the bookshelf. He kissed her soft cheek, said a prayer for her health, and left for his study.

He grabbed a Rolling Rock from the mini-fridge in his makeshift study, more of a large utility closet than an office. He booted up his laptop and checked his email. There was nothing worth noting, so he pulled up Google. He tried a dozen different searches and found several references to robberies around the country.

An armed bank robbery in San Francisco that netted thirty grand looked good until he read two people were involved. That's out. In Macon, Georgia, a suspect disguised as a satellite TV installer got away with $26k, but was caught a week later. The suspect was black. Another job took place in Little Rock, Arkansas. The robber, dressed as a security guard, lifted an undisclosed amount and brandished a gun. Not our guy.

CHAPTER 21
SANTA MONICA, CA

I hop on the Ninja and ride back to the Wells Fargo branch. I find an apartment complex a mile past the bank and find a vacant parking space without apartment numbers stenciled between the lines. Leaving the bike behind, I head out on foot and call for a cab, using the throw-away cell phone I purchased the day before.

The taxi drops me at the Penske rental store and after completing the needed paperwork, I leave with a sixteen footer. I head back to the same apartment building where I left the bike, park the truck in front of a different building, and walk to the bike. I fire up the Ninja and head back to the Fairmont, again parking several blocks away, and walking the last part.

At the Fairmont, I order room service and a movie. Ocean's 11 seems appropriate. I fall asleep as Don Cheadle grabs his nuts, waiting for the pinch to blow the lights in Las Vegas.

I skip my morning run and grab a light breakfast from a diner down the street. I hop on the Ninja and head for the apartment complex to get the Penske truck. I drive the truck to the back of the complex, out of sight from the front office, and lower the loading ramp. That secure, I walk to the bike and leave for the branch.

Upon arriving at the bank, I notice a cop getting into his cruiser and I watch from across the street as he pulls out and heads southwest on Wilshire. I pop the clutch, bringing the front tire slightly off the ground, and speed after him. There are three cars between us and I'm paying so much attention to him I nearly slam into the back of a Land Rover, having to lock it up and swerve slightly to the right to miss it. Several miles later, satisfied the policeman is not returning, I whip the bike around and head back to the bank. Parking the bike backward in a parking slot facing Wilshire Boulevard, I adjust my wig, check to make sure my blue-tinted contacts are in, and walk inside.

"Hello Sharon. I haven't seen you in a long time. How have you been?"

"Fine sir," she responds. "How can I help you today?"

I hand Sharon the note. It reads:

"I'm taking your money. STAY CALM. Open your safe and put all the hundreds, fifties, and twenties in this bag. Open your second and third drawer and do the same. Then, open your top drawer and give me all the cash. NO BAIT MONEY. NO DYE PACKS. I have a gun and will use it. Lastly, take your billfold out of your purse and put that in the bag. I want to know where you live. Don't trigger the alarms. I have a scanner and will know if you do. Have a nice day."

Sharon looks up at me and then back down to the note. She looks as if she's about to faint.

"Calm down Sharon. I'm not going to hurt you if you do as I say. Now, use this sack and follow the directions."

She puts the money in the sack and hands it to me. I ask for the note and she hands it over. I give her a huge smile, letting her get a good look at the black cap I've put over my left upper front tooth and walk away. Outside, I hear sirens.

CHAPTER 22
CHARLESTON, SC

Agents Rickard and Knabb are pouring over documents when the television in the corner interrupts with a Fox News alert. On the screen, a helicopter is following a motorcycle through the busy streets of L.A. A picture of the on-the-scene reporter is in the upper right hand corner of the screen, giving everyone a play-by-play.

"Bill, it seems a man robbed the Wells Fargo branch on Wilshire Boulevard just minutes ago. The armed man exited the branch and hopped on a motorcycle and headed northeast. The bike is faster than patrol cars and so they called us, WLAI, while we were doing a routine traffic report. We picked the guy up immediately. He looks like he's doing well over eighty miles per hour. I can't imagine that this will have a happy ending."

"Look at that idiot Knabb. When are these people going to realize that it can't be done?"

CHAPTER 23
LOS ANGELES

I tear out of the parking lot and head northeast on Wilshire. Several police cars pass me heading south, but they can't cross over, due to a two foot high median. I check my mirrors and don't see any blue lights. I can't hear sirens anymore. I'm not sure if it's because of the helmet or if the police are going the wrong way. I take an exit three miles past the apartment complex exit and head east. Immediately, I pull into a shopping center with a Target as its anchor. And that's when I notice the helicopter.

"Shit shit shit! Think Cam. What now!" Then, I see it. Two motorcycles are leaving the shopping center. I pull up beside them, reach into the bag for the purse, and hand it to one of them.

"This is my girlfriend's purse. I just found her fucking my best friend. Take it."

The guy takes the purse. I smile at him. They turn left and I turn right.

From the helicopter:

"It seems two or three of them are working together. We just saw the main guy hand off something to his partners. It looks like two of them are getting back onto Wilshire and the other is going in the opposite direction."

"Which one should we follow?" asks the pilot.

"Follow the money, man. Follow the money."

CHAPTER 24
LOS ANGELES

I gun the bike for about a mile and turn right. Heading toward the back entrance of the apartment complex, I look and see the helicopter fly in the direction of the two bikers. I pull in the back lot and around the back building where I parked the truck. Looking around, I see no one. I ride the bike up the ramp and quickly bungee it to the wall of the truck, jump out, close the roll-door, and put a padlock on for good measure. I climb into the driver side, start the engine, and slowly drive out of the complex.

I drive north on 15 toward Las Vegas. Within two hours, I'm on the east side of the Mojave National Preserve. I pull off on a gravel road and drive about three miles in until I'm satisfied. I unlock the roll-up, lower the ramp, and coast the Ninja off the truck. Certain that no one is within earshot, I crank the bike and ride it off the gravel road into the woods. A few hundred yards in, I lay the bike in some thick growth and after wiping the entire thing down to remove any prints, I try my best to cover it up. I remove the license tag and head back to the truck.

Back on highway 15, I seriously consider going to Vegas, but head back to L.A. By the time I hit the city limit, it's after six p.m. I return the truck to the Penske lot and place the keys in the night dropbox. Back in the Ford Escort, I drive to the Fairmont and I'm in my room by eight. As I empty the contents of the sack onto the bed, I turn the television on to Fox News.

"We have exclusive footage of the capture of two bank robbers apprehended earlier today. Our traffic helicopter tracked the two alleged robbers and directed the police on the ground of their exact location. Unbelievably, they stopped at a Burger King just blocks from the bank they robbed and were captured while eating. A third alleged robber has not been captured. Back to you in the studio Steve."

"Thanks Jim." Looking to his right and speaking to his co-anchor, "Where do these people come from? Well, it just goes to show you, crime doesn't pay. Now, let's check sports with Andrew."

I laugh so hard I piss my pants.

CHAPTER 25
PUNTA GORDA

Back in Punta Gorda, I do some serious thinking about a quick trip to Vegas. I haven't fed my gambling fix in over a year. Squashing my desire to research flights for McCarran International Airport, I head to the office needing to get some serious work done and make a few calls. The market is doing well and it's time I make some legitimate money.

I call Mark Ferrer, one of my better clients. He's unloaded more of his real estate investments and needs to park some cash with me. His net worth has improved by a million and he's finally listening to me and starting to sell his land holdings. He spends his days at the beach and his evenings playing guitar at local open mic nights. After meeting him at the reception at the Peace River Wildlife Preserve held in honor of Uncle Walter, he became a client and a good friend. I advised Mark to sell short three thousand shares of a tech stock that had risen from $32 a share to about $150 in the past year. Order confirmed, I surf the net till lunch.

At lunch, I head for the public library to do a more complete search on the internet. I picked up an article on Foxnews.com detailing the robbery in L.A. It seems the two arrested for the crime know nothing about it and tell the cops that a stranger rode up to them in a parking lot and handed them a purse. They haven't a clue who the stranger was and the only description they can give is "a white guy."

The helicopter pilot and traffic reporter confirm the report. As far as Sharon can remember, it was a white guy, five foot ten to six foot two, between 175 and 210 pounds, and around thirty-five years old. The only solid description was he was missing an upper tooth, had piercing blue eyes, and wore a long blonde wig.

Exiting Foxnews.com, I google Chase Bank in Maryland. I'm not sure why. I've never been to Maryland. I don't need the money. I just pulled the L.A. job last week and I'm already looking for another. It's like a drug. I need the rush.

I come across a branch in southern Maryland in Saint Mary's County. From the Chase website, I enter the hyperlink for directions. After a few minutes zooming in on the map, I realize it's perfect. I check the flights to Baltimore and D.C. from Dallas. Then, I check Tampa to Dallas. Although Fort Myers is closer, Tampa is a much larger airport, thus less of a chance of me being remembered. With my flights booked one-way two weeks away, I log off and return to the office.

CHAPTER 26
CHARLESTON, SC

Rickard scans the National Crime Database for bank robberies, looking for some connection to his robbery in South Carolina. The only description he has from the Myrtle Beach robbery three years ago is a white guy, mid-thirties, five foot ten, and a wart between his green eyes. He also has a tattoo of a lightning bolt on his left hand. He weighs approximately 175 pounds and is apparently wearing a long blonde wig.

Checking the records for the L.A. heist, he reads the description by head teller Sharon. He searches the database for bank robberies in the past three years using this white guy's description. The search produces 935 hits. He narrows his search to include only those that are unsolved. That narrows the field to 376. He reduces his search once more by adding the word "wig" and hits enter. Now, the list has only twenty-six names.

CHAPTER 27
PUNTA GORDA, FLORIDA

That night, I head to the Punta Gorda tennis club where Mark and I previously planned to meet to play a doubles match with a couple of girls he knows. He guaranteed me that I would like my partner and he is seldom wrong. When I arrived, Mark was already warming up with both the girls. I'm not sure which is my partner, but either will do. I watch from a distance as I sit on a bench and change into my tennis shoes. Mark catches sight of me and yells out my name.

"Cam, how are you?"

"Better than I deserve, Mark. We already look good on our short today, closed down over a point. You owe me dinner.»

"Not to worry. We'll go get drinks after our match. Cam, meet Gina and Michelle. Gina is a real estate agent for RE/MAX and Michelle is a branch manager for Colonial Bank."

"Nice to meet you both," I offered.

"Mark has been singing your praise for the past thirty minutes. Do you play tennis as good as you give stock advice?" asked Michelle.

"Unfortunately, no. I just picked up the game a year ago. Mark got me interested and invited me out a few times. When I realized I couldn't keep up with him, I took a few lessons."

"Well, I've played since I was a little girl. Let's you and I partner up and let Mark take Gina. That sound OK to you guys?"

"Not a problem. Gina and I are going to rip you a new one!"

And indeed they did. Mark was on his game and Gina held her own. They finished us 6-3 and 6-4. Michelle had a great serve and a wicked backhand, but we couldn't catch a break. Afterwards, we went to our respective locker rooms, showered, and met on the veranda for drinks. Realizing we were all starved, Mark made the announcement to head over to the Slip-Knot, an outdoor restaurant a few blocks north, and finish the evening over salmon and a bottle of Merlot.

Comfortably seated at the Slip-Knot, Michelle turned to me and asked about Colonial Bank's stock.

"It's not bad. A decent P/E, good management, and market penetration. Right now, it's trading near its fifty-two-week low because of its overexposure to the Florida real estate market. But more than that, how do you like working for them? That's usually one of the best signs to me about a company's performance."

"Oh, it's great. Like you said, good management means a lot. I'm also in a great area at the right time. With a flood of northerners with lots of cash coming to Punta Gorda almost daily, it's like shooting fish in a barrel. That's how I met Gina. I was attending a trade show at the convention center and she introduced herself to me. We've literally been partners since. Do you live in Punta Gorda?"

"Just down the street. I live on West Marion Avenue, a few blocks past Fisherman's Village. And you?"

"I'm on the Isles, like you, but a few blocks in. It's canal access."

Dinner was served, drinks were consumed, and as the saying goes, a good time was had by all. I, however, was a thousand miles away. Although Michelle was strikingly beautiful, I was busy planning my next operation in Maryland. Just before 11:00, Mark invited the girls and myself back to his place, a gorgeous Spanish-themed villa overlooking the harbour and his fifty-five-foot Sea Ray. I declined, giving the excuse of a long day, and thanked everyone for a wonderful match and dinner. As I was standing up, Michelle gave me her business card and asked for me to call her tomorrow concerning some stock. I left the restaurant and drove home.

With a Corona Light in hand, computer booted up, I searched the internet for hotels in Saint Mary's County, Maryland. A few hours later, a plan was in place.

CHAPTER 28
PUNTA GORDA, FLORIDA

The next morning, back in my office, I have a few appointments with existing clients to discuss their holdings. Shortly after noon, I'm staring at the computer as little abbreviations and numbers light up green or red, depending on if they are up or down. Unfortunately for most of my clients, the screen is littered in red. Good for Mark.

I decide to call Michelle, get her voicemail, and leave a message. I leave the office by one and head home. After a quick change of clothes, I pack my cooler and head for Gasparilla Island, also known as Boca Grande, a well kept secret thirty miles north. I like it, due to the fact it costs four bucks to get on the island. That keeps the riffraff away. Plus, the local police totals two patrol cars and that's one more than they really need. I get my iPod, grab the cooler and my beach chair, and plant myself in the sand overlooking a beautiful turquoise blue gulf. This is what I want to do for the rest of my life. All I need is a girl by my side and about 800,000 more dollars.

Shortly past five, awakened by a couple of gulls, I jump in the water to cool off. After a quick beachside shower, I jump in the Alfa, crack open a cold one, and drive around the island, looking at and dreaming of living in one of the beachfront properties. This is paradise. Forty-five minutes later, I'm at my condo in Punta Gorda, going over last-minute details of the Maryland job ahead.

CHAPTER 29
WASHINGTON, D.C.

Arriving at Reagan International Airport in D.C., I realize it's colder than I previously planned. After getting a rental car at the airport Hertz, I make the hour or so drive it takes to get to St. Mary's County. I find a Holiday Inn several miles south of the Chase Bank that I've targeted. After checking in, I put on a small disguise and head out to pick up some supplies and do a little reconnaissance at the bank.

A Walmart I passed earlier is my goal. I pick up a set of obnoxious bubba teeth, a blue and black striped short sleeve button-down made of heavy cotton, and a set of iron-on name patches. The rest of my simple disguise, wig and makeup, I brought with me.

At the bank, I enter and approach the teller line. I ask for information about opening a savings account and take a business card of the teller who handed me a brochure. I make a mental note of the layout and also pinpoint my pigeon, the cute teller at the end of the line.

That night, in the hotel, I get in full costume, complete with a unibrow and forehead scar. Satisfied with my results, I settle down and walk through the steps while lying in bed. Sleep comes easily.

I start the next day with a short workout in the hotel's fitness room. After working the treadmill for forty minutes, I try the universal weights. I give up after a short bench press rep. These damn things are too heavy.

The continental breakfast did little to curb my appetite. I read the USA TODAY and check out the latest NCAA and NFL lines. I return to my room and try to take a nap. With only six hours before showtime, I'm somewhat restless and give up, deciding to turn to Fox News and waste the morning. Shortly after noon, I start to prepare and get in full criminal mode.

CHAPTER 30
CHASE BANK, LEXINGTON PARK, MARYLAND

As I enter the branch lobby, my bubba teeth almost fall out. I approach the counter with the large bouquet of flowers in hand and toward a young twenty something teller on the end.

"I have a delivery for," looking down on my clipboard, "uh, Allison Crumpler."

"That's me"! All the tellers, except for the one on the opposite end, approach Allison and the flowers, anxiously awaiting the note and the sender's name.

I look down at the teller that stayed put and and asked her if I could cash a check while I was here.

"Sure sir. How are you today?" asked Chloe.

"Better than I deserve," I responded. However, because of the bubba teeth, it came out sounding like "vetter dan I deserve." I hand her the note. She looks up at me and makes a motion to her left, blindly trying to reach something. "Please don't do that Chloe. I won't hurt you. Just stash the cash in the bag." Looking at Chloe, I realize her beautiful green eyes, much like my own. She is five foot six, maybe thirty years old, with very long sandy blonde hair with highlights and a cute little nose. She's quite striking. She stared back at me, into my pale blue contacts. She looked down at my mouth, obviously noticing the brown crooked teeth, and back up to my eyes, focusing just above my fake unibrow to the scar on my forehead I had stenciled on earlier that morning. I tuck my long black hair behind my left ear and adjust my flower delivery hat a little.

Chloe looks to her left for the other tellers, but they are all focusing on Allison's flowers. She reaches into the drawer and starts following the directions. She is very innocent looking. Scared. Hands shaking just a bit. Like a child in the principal's office caught cheating on a test. A tear falls down her cheek as she finishes and hands me the bag. I put it in my oversized pocket and turn toward the door.

I walk out calmly and get into the rental car. Pulling out of the parking lot, I turn right and head in the general direction of the hotel. There are no cops, no sirens, nothing. After ditching the disguises, I go back to the Holiday Inn and take the money bag with me to my room. This was too easy. Turning on the TV and looking for a local station, I grab a beer from the cooler and plop down on the bed. On the bed, I open my laptop and fire up the WiFi. Checking the local TV news website, I don't see anything about the robbery.

What's going on? Did Chloe do anything? Seconds later, there it was. A full report about the robbery, but very little details of the suspect.

That night, all I can think of is Chloe. I awake in the morning, drive back to Reagan International, and catch my first of three flights that will eventually touch down in Tampa.

CHAPTER 31
PUNTA GORDA

At home, I go through my morning routine and leave for the office. I have a light day ahead, with no scheduled appointments. My hope is to leave the office after lunch and make a safety deposit box run to park the cash. I also need to drop by the public library and search the internet for any news on the Maryland job. After several phone calls and poking around the office, I return home for lunch and my deposit.

At the library, after my bank run, I sit down and open a browser at one of the many open computers. A few local reports of the robbery came up quickly, nothing national. Clicking the top search, I'm hyperlinked to the BayNet news and a four-paragraph story. Few details are released and I don't see any real reason to get concerned. In the last paragraph, I learn the last name of the teller, Chloe Wilson.

I enter her name in a new google search and get too many results. I narrow down the search by adding Lexington Park to the queue and get four other articles highlighting her name. The first three articles are more or less the same from the BayNet source. The last was about a Georgetown Hoyas basketball game where they beat the Butler Bulldogs. There was a picture of Chloe and three other girls cheering in the stands, with their names in the caption.

I decided to search her using Georgetown as a parameter and found a few more hits. Within a few clicks, I learned she was an education major, member of the pep club and Young Republicans Club, and played in the marching band at least her freshman year. A picture of her in her band uniform was listed in the yearbook.

"What a geek! I love it."

By then, I had made up my mind. It was probably one of the biggest mistakes I could make, but I wanted to see her again. I found her Facebook page and that gave me all the information I needed. Per her pictures, she frequented the Tiki Bar in Solomons. Her relationship status had her as single and interested in men. I then found her on a popular dating site and found her likes and dislikes.

I had to tackle this just like a bank job. I needed to form a plan to bump into her.

That night, I booked a flight from Tampa to Reagan National in D.C. for the following Friday. I reserved a suite at the Holiday Inn in Solomons, Maryland, a few miles from the Tiki Bar, for the weekend and spent the rest of the evening researching the area and her Facebook profile.

The rest of the week was perfectly uneventful. I called my T. Rowe Price mutual fund wholesaler and scheduled lunch with him in Baltimore the day I arrive. Since I'm doing a little business, I can write off my expenses.

CHAPTER 32
WASHINGTON, D.C.

A rriving at Reagan National Airport at 10:00 a.m., I've got about a half hour before I'm received by Marc Landon, my T. Rowe Price wholesaler, and driven to The Capital Grille for lunch and a soft sales presentation.

Marc and I have a good working relationship. I've dropped over two million of my client's money into his funds in the past few months and he received a commission of twenty basis points, or roughly four thousand dollars. A nice lunch was in order. Afterwards, he drove me to my hotel and told me a driver would return at nine this evening to chauffeur me for the weekend.

My plan was to grab a nap and then a shower, have a small dinner, and be at the Tiki Bar by ten this evening. My driver for the weekend, Alberto, was at the front entrance promptly at nine in a black, 2003 Lexus LS 430. He opened the passenger door and after I was seated, delivered me to Zahniser's Dry Dock Restaurant. I enjoyed a casual dinner on the back patio overlooking the docked yachts and sailboats moored in the harbor. After a perfectly cooked, eight ounce, butterfly filet mignon oscar with a fully loaded, iceberg wedge salad and Corona Light, I tipped my waitress a nice bonus and summoned Alberto. Minutes later, I'm entering the Tiki Bar with a full belly and looking for Chloe.

It only took an hour and two beers before a small group of girls came stumbling in the bar. Chloe was instantly recognizable in what looked like a white ASOS cotton mini sundress and brown cowboy boots. She was accompanied by three other girls of similar dress and age. They saddled up to the outdoor bar and ordered a round of drinks. I had previously spoken with the bartender and asked if she knew Chloe Wilson. She did and expected her and a crew shortly.

Their drinks served, I waited for a few minutes and made my approach. Since they were still seated at the bar, I walked up empty-handed and waited for the bartender's attention, making eye contact with Chloe. I ordered a Bud Light and turned my back to the bar and looked over the crowd. After a minute, I made my approach.

Looking her dead in the eye, I extended my hand and introduced myself.

"Hi Cam. I'm Chloe," she responded.

"It's nice to meet you Chloe. You guys having fun tonight?"

"Well, it's early. But we'll see. How about you?" she asked.

"Not bad, so far. I'm not from here. Is this the place to be?"

"It's a good local hangout. Usually, a laid back crowd. You here for pleasure or business?"

"Business, but that was completed earlier. Figured I'd stay the weekend and fly back Sunday."

"Where do you have to fly to Sunday? Where's home?"

"I'm originally from North Carolina, but I live in Florida," I answer.

"My parents retired to Florida, in Sarasota. Where in Florida are you?"

"About an hour south of there in a little town called Punta Gorda. Do you ever visit?"

"I have twice. They just moved there last year. It's always so warm. What do you do?"

"I'm a financial adviser for a small firm," I answered. "How about you?"

"Right now I'm a bank teller for Chase Bank. According to my degree, I should be teaching middle school, but I just can't see myself pandering to tweens."

Our conversation lasted for an hour. Both of us let down our dating guard a little, telling the other only the positive aspects of our lives. Not wanting to break up her girls' night out, I asked her to dinner for the following night. She said "yes" and we exchanged numbers. I told her it had been a long day and I was ready to turn in for the night. We decided to talk tomorrow and I let her know that I'd call her after noon. I would take care of the travel, she would pick the destination.

Saturday Noon, Solomons, Maryland

"Hi, is this Chloe?"

"Yes. Good morning Cam. How was the rest of your evening?"

"Very relaxing. A little lonely, but I needed a good night's rest. So, since I'm not from here, I'm relying on you to show me around. What do you suggest we do?"

"Don't you stress. You're in my backyard. I'll take care of everything. Why don't you pick me up around two. I can show you a few sites and we can get dinner afterwards. Dress casual. If it's ok, I might bring a change of clothes for dinner. It's going to be warm all day, but when the sun sets in Maryland, the temperature drops quickly. Where are you staying?"

"I'm at the Holiday Inn Solomons."

"Cool. Go check out the marina there. Nice boats."

"Will do. Where do you want to meet?"

"You can pick me up at my apartment. I'm just over the bridge in California. I'll text you the address."

"Sounds great Chloe. See you at two."

I called my driver, Alberto, and gave him my plans.

At exactly 1:30, I'm out front of the hotel when Alberto pulled up in a black 2003 Lexus LS 430. He jumps out of the car and greets me with a firm handshake.

"Where to today, Mr. Steele?"

"Please Alberto, call me Cam. And truthfully, I have no idea about the first stop. An apartment in California." I gave him the address and he entered it into his GPS.

"No problem. About a fifteen-minute drive. Relax and leave everything up to me. Who's our guest?"

"A girl I met last night. How long can I keep you today?"

"Today, I'm all yours. Mr. Landon told me to take you wherever you like."

"Great. In that case, we'll both be in for a surprise. The girl, Chloe, is making all the plans. I'll do my best to have you home by midnight. Is that too late?"

"Not at all Mr. Steele. Sorry, Cam. Midnight is just fine."

Pulling up to the apartment complex, Chloe is waiting outside wearing a cute little white sundress, with her hair pulled back in a ponytail. According to Alberto's barely audible whistle, he approved. So did I.

Alberto is quickly out of the car and introducing himself.

"You must be Ms. Chloe."

"That's me."

"Good afternoon Ms. Chloe. I'm Alberto."

"Nice to meet you Alberto."

"And you as well. Please," he opened the driver side rear door and Chloe looked in.

"Well, look who's back here. Hi Cameron."

"Wow. Chloe, you look stunning."

"Why thank you sir. My momma told me to never get in a stranger's car."

"But, I've got puppies and ice cream," I respond.

"What flavor ice cream?"

"Cookies and cream."

"Well heck yeah. Scoot over."

Chloe climbs into her seat and looks around at the car. "Do you always have a driver?"

"No. Not at all. I advise certain clients to purchase different investment products. The driver and car are compliments of a mutual fund representative whose product I sell. Beats having to get a rental car."

"It is nice. So, do I just tell him where to go?" Chloe asked.

"Yes. I'm in your hands."

"You might regret saying that. Alberto?"

"Yes, Ms. Chloe."

"Are you familiar with the Calvert Marine Museum?"

"Absolutely. Should I start there?"

"Yes, please."

Chloe and I talked the entire drive to the museum. There were no awkward pauses. She told me that after the museum, we were scheduled for a one-hour leisure cruise of Solomons Harbor and the Patuxent River. During the museum and the cruise, it's like we couldn't stop telling stories about ourselves. We talked about our parents, how we are both an only child, high school and college, careers, and even life ambitions. She wanted to visit her parents in Sarasota soon and I felt that was a wonderful idea.

After the cruise, I recommended we go to my room at the Holiday Inn so we can both freshen up for dinner. To my surprise, Chloe jumped at the idea. Alberto dropped us off and I asked him if he could return at seven. I slipped him fifty dollars and he happily replied that he'd be back.

My room was nothing special. It was a standard room with a king-sized bed and a nice view looking out over the marina and the harbor. Chloe has brought a change of clothes and I offer her the bathroom to do as she wishes. I head to the minibar and fridge and offer her something to drink. I got a Diet Dr. Pepper for her and a Land Shark for me.

I pull back the drapes and open the balcony sliding glass door. Being on the fourth floor offers a pretty good view of the water. As I sip my beer, I realize how comfortable I already am with Chloe. It's not quite sunset and a soft breeze kisses my face. From behind, Chloe puts her arms around my waist and places her chin on my shoulder.

"This date is going pretty well, wouldn't you agree?" she asked.

"Yes. And it's not over yet," I respond.

I turn around and remain in her arms. With my hands cupping her face, I pull her in gently for a soft kiss. She kisses back.

"You look perfect," I said. "Do you mind if I change shirts and clean up a little?"

"You look plenty clean to me, but I've been wondering what you look like without a shirt. Be my guest."

I retrieve a fresh, solid green, Tommy Bahama dress shirt from the closet and remove the Izod golf shirt I was wearing. I face Chloe and put my arms through the short sleeves, taking my time buttoning it up and keeping constant eye contact.

"Do you approve?"

"Very much. You better take me to dinner before…"

I move forward and kiss her again, this time with a little more passion, a little more force. She reciprocates, grabbing my biceps. We pull back simultaneously.

"You're right," I said smiling. "I better get you to dinner."

"Yeah," she exhaled. "Nice dinner would be."

"Come on, Yoda," I replied laughing. "Alberto is probably waiting for us."

We dined at the Lighthouse Inn overlooking the harbor. The food and service were perfect. We even ordered for Alberto and had it sent to the car. After dinner and a couple of cocktails, Chloe recommended we head back to the Tiki Bar to enjoy some live music.

We could have walked, but Alberto happily drove us the short distance. Upon entering, Chloe bumped into several friends and was greeted by name by a waitress. Chloe introduced me to a few friends and they invited us to join them. The party consisted of three girls and two guys, all about Chloe's age. We drank, played darts, laughed, and swapped stories to close to 10:30.

I reached toward Chloe and whispered, "I promised Alberto that he'd be home by midnight."

"That's fine. Let's get another drink, then you can get me home."

A little past eleven, we walked to her door holding hands. "I had a great time tonight, Chloe."

"Me too, Cam. That was a near perfect first date. Can I see you tomorrow?"

"My flight leaves at four. How about lunch?"

"Perfect."

"Since my check out time is eleven, and I won't have Alberto, would you like to meet me somewhere or pick me up?"

"I'll be in the lobby at eleven sharp."

"Sleep tight Chloe." I kissed her briefly and turned and headed down the walkway.

"Good night, Cam!"

I looked over my shoulder and she had her hand on her chest looking upward. Ive still got it when I bring my A game. In the car, I ask Alberto to take me to my hotel.

Sunday 7:00 a.m. Holiday Inn

I'm up and pounding the pavement, my mind running in circles, while my legs are running for distance. Yesterday was a perfect day and Chloe's touch was unforgettable. There are a few moments in life when everything falls into place. Most of the time, you only recognize that moment days, months, sometimes years later. You think about it nostalgically. When you replay it in your mind, you make it better than it was. I'm replaying yesterday and it was wonderful.

You meet a lot of people during a lifetime. Everyone has the potential to change your life. You generally realize this after the fact. I realize it now and will not let this one get away. Chloe is perfect.

Back in my room and having skipped breakfast, I shower, shave, and pack my only bag and backpack. I double check my airline ticket and head for the hotel lobby. As the elevator doors open to the atrium, Chloe is standing dressed in a man's black suit complete with chauffeur's hat and a sign reading "Mr. Steele."

"Mr. Steele, I presume," she smiled.

"Yes. I'm Mr. Steele."

"Please follow me. Your car awaits."

I follow Chloe outside and to a red BMW. She popped the trunk and deposited my bag, then moved to the passenger side and opened the door for me. After closing my door, she bounced around and got behind the wheel. She leaned over and gave me a little kiss on the cheek.

"Good morning, Cam."

"Good morning, Chloe."

"I figured you needed a new driver. Will I do?"

"Absolutely. Where to?"

"Let's have brunch at Cape Bistro. You'll love it."

Chloe drives and points out local areas of interest. She works the five speed performance car with ease, downshifting into curves and throttling out after the bends. I double check my seat belt, not that she's dangerous, but to keep me in my seat. She notices this and smiles.

"I got you," she reassures me.

"I hope so."

Brunch at Cape Bistro was busy. Either the church crowd let out early or we dined with a lot of sinners. As like yesterday and Friday, our conversation had its own pace. Nothing was forced. We sat on the back deck, my back to the sun and Chloe facing it. She pulled down her sunglasses that were perched atop her head. She reached across the table and took my hand.

Chloe looked at me for a second, then removed the sunglasses.

"There is something unique about you Cam."

"Unique is good, right?"

"Yes. But it's more than that. In this light, you remind me of someone, but I can't seem to place it."

"Well, I'm sure he was handsome," I replied with a smile.

"Yes, but it's not that. It's like I've met you before. Are you sure this is your first visit to Maryland?"

"As far as I know," I responded cautiously.

"You just remind me of someone. Oh well. I'm sure I'll think of it later."

The waiter showed up and we ordered. We remained silent for a few minutes. I was looking around and Chloe seemed to be pondering where she might have met me in the past. Besides that awkward moment, our brunch was just an extension of our date yesterday. I told her I'd like to visit her again. I didn't want to push the issue too much and decided to tell a little lie.

"I've got a due diligence trip scheduled with T. Rowe Price in two weeks. I'll be arriving on Thursday and if you're interested, I can stay through the weekend."

"Really Cam? That would be nice. I'd love to see you again."

"Of course, I can get a hotel for my visit. I don't want to rush you."

"Tell you what, book the hotel and we'll see how it pans out. Deal?"

"That's a deal, Chloe."

After brunch, she drove me to Reagan National Airport.

It's about a two-hour drive, depending on traffic, and we arrived at 2:30. There was plenty of time for me to make my four o'clock flight. Chloe found a spot in short-term parking and walked with me inside.

"Well, Mr. Cameron Steele, I've thoroughly enjoyed your company."

"Thank you, Ms. Chloe Wilson. So have I."

We kissed lightly and she said the most romantic words to me.

"Call me when you land safely."

"I will."

The next six weeks, I visit Chloe every other weekend. We talk and text several times a day. Our weekends were spent jumping all over Maryland, Georgetown, and D.C., checking out every tourist attraction. Chloe was a perfect host. After the first weekend in a hotel, the other two visits we shared a bed at her apartment. I haven't closed the deal yet and I think the anticipation is mounting for both of us.

CHAPTER 33
PUNTA GORDA

Back in Punta Gorda, I couldn't get Chloe off my mind. She told me her parents lived in Sarasota and a quick check on the internet found Rylie and Grace Wilson at 320 Mimosa Place in south Sarasota. Mapquest put them about an hour's drive north from my place.

Another check on the internet and I found that the annual Punta Gorda Arts Festival is three weeks away, on May 23-26th. The town blocks off the streets downtown Friday through Sunday and throws a big party with cardboard boat racing, a 5K run, face painting, and wine and beer tasting. It is a good family-friendly affair, with a local artist selling their goods.

I decide to call Chloe and invite her down for the week. It is a Thursday to Thursday affair. She can stay with her parents or me, hopefully me, Thursday through Sunday and then with her folks till the following Thursday. It would be a good way to get her in Florida for a week. I check airlines online and find her an affordable ticket for the exact days I want, leaving Baltimore and landing in Punta Gorda. Making a decision to call Chloe later, I switch into shorts and a Nike golf shirt and head to Punta Gorda Isles Golf Club to meet a client.

After carding a decent seventy-nine and my client a seventy-seven, we head to the nineteenth green for a cocktail. Of course I paid, since I lost. After two Coronas each and discussing the market and my client's account, it's close to 6:00. I head back home, grab a quick shower and another beer, call my office line to check messages, then head up to the Slip-Knot for dinner alone.

Same time that day
Charleston SC

"Hey Knabb, did you happen to see CNN's coverage of a bank robbery in Maryland that happened about two months ago?" asked Senior Special Agent Rickard.

"Maybe. The guy who didn't get caught?" Knabb said. "Eyewitnesses put him as white, five foot ten. That one?"

"That's the one. Could it be our guy?"

"I guess anything's possible, but I highly doubt it. Sir, you've found over forty bank robberies across the U.S. that you think could be our guy. Just because he's white, between five foot nine and six feet, 165 to 185 pounds, and wears some type of disguise ..."

"It's more than that. It's also the description of the note, the amount taken, and the time of day that the crime happens, always around 3:30, give or take an hour. Look," said Rickard, "I want details of all unsolved bank robberies with a white perp, five foot eight to six feet, 160 to 180 pounds, aged twenty-five to forty-five, committed between 2:30 and 4:30 p.m., in the US. Can you get that by noon tomorrow?"

"Shouldn't be a problem sir." Knabb answered.

"Cool. See you tomorrow."

"Night sir."

CHAPTER 34
PUNTA GORDA

I get up, gulp down a tall glass of water, throw on running shorts and shoes, and head out for my morning run. Four miles and about forty-five minutes later, I return to the condo. Chloe was on my mind all last night and throughout my run. My plan is to call her on her cell around noon. I've got to get to the office to make some legitimate money and some phone calls. The market, mainly the Nasdaq, has been on a good run lately, so calling some of my tech-heavy clients ought to be easy conversations. It is a good time to pick up more commissions.

Chloe answered on the second ring. "Guess where I am!" I said.

"Let's see Cam? Hmm, Hooters?"

"Nope and bad guess. Food's no good! I'm at Harpoon Harry's. It's where I'm going to take you on our first date when you visit me in Florida."

"Oh really? And do you have a date in mind for this first date in Florida?"

"Absolutely! It's Friday, May 23rd, three weeks from now."

"And how do you suppose I get there Cam?"

Oh I love the way she says Cam. Just the way the "M sound" lingers a little, so it comes out "Camm."

"There is a flight leaving Baltimore, Thursday, May 22nd, landing at Punta Gorda at 5:30 in the afternoon and returns the following Thursday evening. I figure you could stay with me till Monday, then I'll drive you to your parents, so you can visit with them till it's time for you to leave. What do you think?"

"How expensive is the ticket?" she asked with a whimper.

"Nothing! You say the word and I'll purchase it online."

"Oh Cam. Really?"

"And that's not all! That weekend is the Punta Gorda Arts Festival. There will be things for us to do Friday through Sunday. I'll show you a great time, my little town, and of course hit the beach, as well. So?"

"So?"

"So, say yes, Chloe!"

There was a pause and then "Yes!"

"That's awesome Chloe. Look, call your parents and let them know and I'll call you around 3:30. Hey, I also need to give you my new cell number. I picked up a new phone this morning to keep my personal and business lines separate." I gave her a number that only she has. It's a new smart phone from Walmart, but I might need to keep it with me when doing a job. I rang off and could not wipe the smirk from my face. I pay my tab and head for the short, half mile drive home.

Fifteen minutes later in Maryland

"Hey Mom. It's me!"

"My Chloe, what a surprise! To what do I owe the pleasure of a middle of the day call?"

"It's good news. I'm coming to see you guys in a few weeks and I want you to meet someone."

Chloe spends the next few minutes giving her most of the details, promises to call her parents back that evening with all the details, and rings off.

During that same fifteen minutes in Punta Gorda

"Bow-ty Florist, can I help you?"

"I hope so," replied Cam. "I need flowers quickly! Delivered today!"

"How much are you looking to spend?" the lady asked.

"About $100 round trip. Mainly gerbera daisies and throw in some baby's breath. Main color theme is red, purple, and gold."

"No problem. And what should the card read?" she asked.

"Is it May 22nd yet?"

"And the card signed by?"

"Just leave that part blank. There is an extra $10 tip if the driver calls me on my cell five minutes before the delivery."

I give the lady my credit card info and Chloe's branch address, and I change for the beach.

Twenty minutes later in Punta Gorda

Cooler with a six-pack of Corona Light, check!
Sliced lime, check!
Beer hugger, check!
Towels, check!
Beach chair, check!
Cell phone, check!
Top down on the Alfa Romeo, check!
I'm off to Gasparilla Island.

Thirty minutes later Gasparilla Island

Paying the toll and crossing the small drawbridge just a few minutes past three, I smile just thinking of my week with Chloe. It's a short drive from the toll to the beach, maybe five miles. But, the speed limit is thirty-five, so with stop signs, it takes about three-fourths of a beer. Now I'm not endorsing drinking and driving, but with only two cops on the island, it's almost impossible to not enjoy a cold beverage. It's beautiful, eighty-eight degrees, low humidity, and not a cloud in sight.

Parking beside the old lighthouse, paying for the $3 visitor pass, I grab my beach goods and head for the sand.

Relaxing in the beach chair, I open two Corona Lights and put a lime in each neck. I put one in the beach chair's left cup holder and one in the right cup holder. I lean back, grab my cell phone and take a picture, put one beer back in the cooler, and go jump in the water. A minute later, and much cooler, I'm loving life!

Twenty minutes later

My cell phone rings....

"This is Cameron, can I help you?"

"Yes sir, this is Bow-ty Florist. I've got orders to call you five minutes before a delivery to Chloe Wilson. I wanted to let you know that I'm about ten minutes out. Is that good enough?"

"Perfect. Thanks!" and I rang off.

I open my cell phone to the saved pic, select send pic message, enter Chloe as the recipient, add the text "Someone is missing from this pic!," and hit send! Ten minutes later, I receive a text from Chloe with a picture of the flowers and the message "I wish it was the 22nd also :-)."

I lean back, drain the last swallow of my third Corona, adjust my sunglasses, and dream about the future.

Three hours later, Punta Gorda

Back home, I grab a quick shower, then boot up my laptop. First things first, get Chloe's ticket. Booking Chloe, I realize I don't have all her personal information. With a quick call to her to get her address and driver's license data, her ticket is now bought. I get her a one-way ticket to Punta Gorda. Maybe I can get her to stay.

Now to business. I pull out a college English literature type notebook, you know the one, black and white spotted, and check my coded ledger. It's riddled with codes and numbers that, hopefully, only I know the key for. It's an old jeweler's trick I learned years ago from a client and it's really quite simple.

Take any nine- or ten-letter phrase or word where no letter is repeated, such as "cashmoney." Now, assign each letter the corresponding number of one to ten. For example, C=one, A=two, S=three, and so on. The number ten, or zero, is X. So, $150,400 would be CMXHXX.

The phrase I use is "JackHoldem," a combination of blackjack and Texas hold 'em.

In my ledger, I have the name of the banks I use coded one through six, with one being the closest to my house and six being the farthest. All of these branches are located on Highway 41, better known as Tamiami Trail, so named because it runs from Tampa to Miami. Pronounced as a rhyme, Tammy-Ammy, it runs through all the small west coast beach towns before crossing the bottom of the state to Miami.

I start at the bridge that links Punta Gorda with Port Charlotte and work my way north on Tamiami. There are easily one hundred banks or branches in a seventy-mile stretch. I don't have to go more than four miles to hit my six. In my ledger, I use only the first numbers and corresponding letters, dropping the last three. For example, $210,000 is just 210 or AJM. $405 is KMH.

My ledger reads as such:
1 = LH
2 = DM
3 = JKM
4 = JJH
5 = JED
6 = JKK

The total is LHA. That's $752,000 cash! I'm about $250K shy of my quitting goal and a year ahead of schedule.

10 p.m. same day Maryland

"Yeah Chloe. What's up?"
"I just thought you were going to call me back after you booked my flight."
"I'm sorry babe. I should have, but I got tied up doing work. Not to worry. It's done."
"Oh Cam, thanks so much! I told my parents and they can't wait either! They really are interested in meeting you!"

"Me? What did you tell them about me?" Cam asked.

"Not much, just that you were a triple threat."

"Triple threat?"

"Yeah. Cute, funny, and smart!" Chloe added.

"Why thank you Chloe. I'll have to try and be all those things when I meet them."

"But, the thing they liked about you the most is that you live in Punta Gorda. They've already asked me to move home to Sarasota and live with them. Oh, how I just love the beach!" exclaimed Chloe.

Trying not to sound too eager, I replied, "You should really think about it!"

"I think I'm going to look on Craigslist for one-bedroom apartments between Punta Gorda and Sarasota, and jobs, as well," Chloe said, trying to hold back her excitement.

"Well, we could always look around the week you are here," I said.

"OK. I'll text you later. I'm going to get online."

10:30 p.m. Punta Gorda

Well, after six years and having done about five to six jobs per year, and averaging about $25,000 per job, I've successfully stolen right about $800,000. I've spent $160,000 and have made about $112,000 gambling.

Let's plan a job for the week before Chloe gets here. I can take her to play casino boat blackjack in Fort Myers one night and launder a few thousand bucks. Then, after she flies back, I can plan a weekend trip for me and her to Las Vegas and wash the rest.

I get up from my couch and go into the spare bedroom/ office. I have a map of the U.S. on the back wall. I grab a dart from my dartboard and aiming for the general area of the center, toss the dart. It lands on Manhattan, Kansas. To be more specific, Fort Riley, Manhattan, Kansas. It is research time!

Back to the couch and using my laptop, I google Manhattan, Kansas, population 56,000. I then google banks in Manhattan, Kansas. I get a ton of results. Scrolling down, I see numerous national and regional banks I've hit. Then, I come across a name I've never seen, KS StateBank. I find it on Anderson Avenue, a few blocks west of Kansas State University. Using google earth, I switch to satellite feed and get a street view. It's beside a McDonald's and a grocery store and a few hundred yards from a decent thoroughfare. It looks perfect. Now, what disguise?

CHAPTER 35
FRIDAY, MAY I6TH PUNTA GORDA, 6:30 P.M.

"Hey Chloe. How was work?"

"It was a little stressful, Cam," Chloe said, sounding out of breath.

"What's up? Everything OK?" I asked.

"Not really. This guy came into the bank today, and at first glance, it looked a little bit like you. For a split second.....I thought it was you. That you somehow flew up to surprise me. The guy had his back to the line, filling out a deposit slip. He had the same build as you and about the same height. He turned around and I realized it wasn't you at all. He looked like the guy who robbed us, robbed me. It was bizarre!"

"Chloe, Duchess. Slow down. You're talking too fast. I can't understand you at all! You said he had on a brassiere?"

"What? A brassiere? I didn't say a bra. I said it was bizarre! Now shut up and let me finish!" shouted Chloe.

"Okay, okay! Take it easy....Go on!"

"It was so weird....First I think it's you, then the guy turns around and I think it's the bank robber. I nearly faint when he hands me his deposit slip. It looks just like the robber's note. Then I realize that it's just a deposit slip and a check. He smiles and has all his teeth. Not only that, he owns the tire shop two blocks over and comes in here every Friday to make his week's deposit. Like I said, I almost fainted!"

I almost faint, as well. "What did you do?"

"Well, I told the guy I felt nauseous from something I ate for lunch. I asked if Christy could wait on him. The customer said 'no problem'. I went to the back, splashed some cold water on my face, and grabbed a Diet Cherry Dr Pepper from the drink machine."

"Did you tell anyone? Did you mention it to the branch manager? What's her name....Megan? Megan Bennett?

"I was going to, but didn't. I might say something to her on Monday morning" Chloe said.

"I wouldn't say anything Chloe. You don't want them to think you're losing it. First you think it's me, then you think it's the bank robber. Believe me, Princess, you want to keep this to yourself."

"You think so Cam?"

"Absolutely!" I replied.

"Look, I'm just getting home. Let me get off here, change out of my work clothes, grab a good imported beer from the fridge, and I'll call you back in an hour."

"Okay babe. No problem."

"Thanks Cam. I don't know what I'd do without you in my life right now."

CHAPTER 36
CHARLESTON, SC

"Here's the data you wanted sir," Knabb said. "It's a little more than I thought. Going back about five years, we've got about seven hundred cases that fit that description."

"No shit!" Richard shouted. "Seven hundred? I can't get a pattern with seven hundred! This guy, even if he was working his ass off couldn't have done more than forty or so, maybe fifty! What's that......ten a year for five years?"

"I can do a little better," said Knabb. "If I go on what our robbery and forensics experts found on height and weight, I could get it down to two hundred. Now we know he's white. If we condense the weight range down to 165 and 190 pounds, move the height range from five foot nine to five foot eleven, tighten up the time frame from to 3:00 to 4:00, now we've got one hundred fifty cases. Put in a range of money taken from $25,000 to $60,000 and we now have seventy. Now, just ask the computer to expand the locations since we don't think our guy does two jobs in a one hundred-mile radius, we get a result of just forty-three!"

"Fuckin' A, Knabb, now you're earning your paycheck!"

"Thank you, sir!"

CHAPTER 37
SATURDAY, MAY 17TH, MANHATTAN, KAN-SAS

I was wheels down at 1:45 at Manhattan Regional Airport via Tampa Airport via Dallas/Fort Worth. My return trip Tuesday will take the same route. I pick up a rental car at the Enterprise agency at the airport, then check into a Holiday Inn Express. I do all this under fake credit cards and IDs under Richard Sutton of Sarasota, Florida. That address is forwarded to a PO box in Punta Gorda. This is where the credit card statements were sent and promptly paid by a Visa debit card that carries a healthy balance of close to $20,000 that is linked to a checking account opened online with Colonial Bank.

Leaving the Holiday Inn and driving to KS StateBank took less than eight minutes. After stopping at Walmart and Target, buying all needed supplies, I head back to the hotel. By 5:00, I'm enjoying a beer and burger at Applebee's located across the street when I get a call from Chloe.

"Hey Chloe," I answer.

"Hey Cam. Sorry I never called you last night. After three glasses of wine, a hot bath, and curling up on the couch, I fell asleep and didn't wake till noon. What are you up to?"

"I just sat down at Harpoon Harry's," I lied. "I played in a captain's choice golf tournament with three clients. We finished up about an hour ago and I headed straight here. You?"

"Just running some errands. I just wanted to call and, um, I guess I just wanted to apologize for yesterday."

"No need to Chloe. I'm sure it did freak you out a bit. Don't worry hun. You were fine."

"But I'm not fine Cam," Chloe whimpered. "I think about that day all the time. Every time the lobby door opens, I look up to see if it's him. When I'm at the grocery store, when I turn down any aisle, I look to see if he's there."

"Didn't you tell me the bank offers free counseling for those who want it?"

"Yeah, but I don't want the bank to know."

"I'm pretty sure it would be completely confidential, Chloe."

"You're probably right, but I don't want to take any chances. I'm going to call my doctor and see who she recommends I see."

"Sounds like a good idea to me," I replied.

"Hey, I've got to go Cam. I'm meeting a sorority sister for dinner. I'll call you later, and oh, I can't wait till Thursday!"

"Me too," I countered. "Me too," and it hit me just then how much I meant those words.

CHAPTER 38
MONDAY, MAY 19TH, CHARLESTON SC 10:00 A.M.

"This is good stuff, Knabb. Give me your gut feeling."

"Well, it's still early," Knabb started, "but let's go. There are a total of thirty-two states that didn't get a hit. Of course, Alaska and Hawaii didn't. All other states that weren't hit are northern states. From Oregon and Washington on the west coast to Maine, Connecticut, Vermont, etc. on the east coast and all those in between. However, you can draw a line from Maryland to California and every state under that line has been hit. All except Florida."

"Except Florida?" asked Rickard. "Why not Florida?"

"Not sure," replied Knabb. But follow me sir." Knabb walked into an empty office, where he had a four by five foot map of the United States taped to the back wall.

"Now I've put green sticky notes on all the states that got a hit from our search. Do you see any kind of pattern?"

"Well, like you said," replied Rickard, "draw a line from Maryland to Cali and everything below it has a green sticky note, but not Florida. Maybe he has outstanding warrants in Florida and he doesn't want to risk it."

"I thought about that also. But look at the other states he's skipped over. All cold weather states. What does he like? Warm weather states. So why hasn't he hit Florida?" Knabb let that linger for a few seconds. Finally, Rickard answered.

"Fuckin A, because the son of a bitch lives there!"

Manhattan, Kansas later that day

The magnetic letters and numbers purchased from Walmart look good on the white rental van I picked up this morning. My overalls fit well and my name patch and matching laminated ID on my chest look authentic. My black wig with a three-inch ponytail hanging out my worker's cap look real and I've got a real goatee that I haven't shaved for a week. I've got a clip-on silver hoop earring in my right ear and finally, I have ice blue contacts on my eyes.

The metal garden-style sprayer I bought from Walmart has about a half gallon of ammonia in it. I can smell it now, even as I munch down a combo from McDonalds with all the windows down and the canister all the way in the back of the van, covered by a large beach towel. I'm camped out in the McDonald's parking lot across the street from the bank, with about an hour to kill.

Same time, Maryland

"Hey Mom."

"Chloe! I'm so excited you're coming this week. You said your flight gets to Punta Gorda at 6:00, so you guys should get here in time for a late dinner. What's Cam like to eat?" Mom asked.

"Oh, about that Mom, I'm staying with Cam till Sunday. Then he's going to drive me up there. I'll spend Sunday through Wednesday with you guys."

"Well, that's fine honey. But you know how much your dad and I want to spend time with you, and Cam is welcome to stay in the extra bedroom in the poolhouse. What time does your flight back to Maryland leave on Thursday?"

"I don't know Mom. Cam only emailed me my boarding pass for getting down there. I'll forward my departing info to you now and the rest to you once I get it from Cam. Anyway Mom, I've got to go. I'll see you soon and I love you. Send my love to Dad, as well."

"We love you too Chloe! Be safe."

3:15 Manhattan, Kansas

I've backed the van into a parking spot in front of the bank and quickly raise the back door, which holds the license plate which I replaced with a stolen one, so I guess it really doesn't matter. On both sides of the van, the magnetic letters read: "Jackson's Rid-A-Bug...Because I've Had Bugs Too. 785-555-1212." My name tag reads Edward. I walk into the branch. The assistant branch manager tells me the branch manager is out sick today.

"Well, I'm supposed to spray today. I usually do it at night when no one is here, but this is some kind of emergency. Here, look." I show her some paperwork. "It's signed by a Joanne Paulson. I think she's your regional or something."

"Yeah, she's over maintenance for the area. How long will this take?"

"About fifteen minutes," I replied.

I start in the assistant manager's office and pump spray a few squirts of ammonia. I go to the branch manager's office and repeat the process. I walk behind the teller line and ask the three tellers to take a step back. The assistant manager is with us and there is a break room behind the line. The assistant manager follows me into the break room and in one quick motion, I grab the phone and rip it off the wall.

Looking at her I say, "Sit down now!" I open the door and tell the tellers to step into the room. "Everyone, please have a seat." I walk around them and the small kitchen table and spray the solution on the floor.

"Everyone, empty all your pockets onto the table." They comply and a cell phone is placed on the table. "Where are the rest of your phones?"

"In my purse," one answers. The others just nod and I grabbed the cell phone off the table.

"Don't try anything stupid. I'll be right back."

I return within seconds with their purses in hand. "OK, I've got all your phones and can contact and track down your ICE contacts and loved ones. I also have your licenses, so I know where you live. Don't leave this break room for ten minutes. If you do not follow my instructions, I will know and I will find you. Have a nice day."

I go back to the teller line and empty all three tellers' top and second drawers, avoiding the bait money and dye packs. Two of the tellers' vault doors are closed, but not locked. I open them up and BINGO! Straps of bills. I'm out of the branch by 3:37. Within seconds, I'm on the highway heading toward the hotel. In an apartment complex, I remove all the magnetic letters and toss them in a dumpster. I check all the cell phones and make sure they are turned off. I get rid of the stolen license plate and put on the real one. I strip off the overalls and put them in the van. I'm now wearing a T-shirt and shorts. I drive to the next dumpster and toss the overalls, as well as the hat, but keep the wig. Ten minutes later, I'm in my room. I remove the wig from the money bag, go to the bathroom, and with my bare hands, rip it up and toss it into the toilet, flushing a quarter of it at a time. I dump the three money bags and the purses on the bed. A quick count of the money puts it around $60K. Shoving the cash under the mattress, I grab the purses, put a "Do Not Disturb" sign on the door handle, and leave the hotel.

Same time, Charleston SC

"The son of a bitch lives in Florida!" exclaimed Rickard.

"That's what I think," replied Knabb. "Makes sense. He likes warm weather. All descriptions of him usually says he has an "olive complexion" or he had a "great tan." He doesn't do any jobs up north. He won't mess with Florida. Maybe he's afraid one of those grainy black and white videos might be viewed by someone close to home who might recognize him."

"All right, what do we do now?"

"I don't know sir. I really don't know."

Twenty minutes later, Manhattan, Kansas

I drive thirty minutes west to Junction City and find a Walmart. Walking in, I locate the DVD section and turn on one of the teller's cell phones. I let it boot up, then quickly turn off the ringer volume. I then hide the phone in the DVD section behind a box set.

Back on the road, I drive to the Manhattan Regional Airport and turn on both stolen cell phones. One has full battery, the other less than half. I turn them both off, pocketing the one that was full. I park in short-term parking and approach the ticket counter.

"Where is the nearest bathroom," I ask.

"All the way to the right, sir."

"Thank you."

I head to the bathroom and immediately find exactly what I'm looking for. An old man is trying to wheel his check-in luggage into his stall. I take out the phone and power it up, turning the ringer off. I slide it into the side pocket while making a show of trying to help the old man with his bags.

He thanks me and while avoiding eye contact, I said "you're welcome."

135 minutes after robbery, Manhattan, Kansas

"Sir, we just got a GPS location on one of the stolen cell phones."

"Where son? Where?" Captain Lew of the Manhattan Police Department yelled.

"In Junction City. I should have an exact location any minute. Okay, got it. It's at 521 East Chestnut Street."

"Is that a residence or what? Lew barked.

"No sir. It's uh, a Walmart sir."

"Shit!" Lew responded. "Get the Junction City Police Department on the line and patch them through to me."

Same time, Manhattan, Kansas

Last phone to ditch. I head toward downtown Manhattan, just on the outskirts, and find what I'm looking for, a corner liquor store. I enter, turn on the phone, mute the ringer, and place it behind two bottles of Seagram's dry gin. On my way out, I grab a six pack of Bud Light, pay, and promptly exit. I drive three blocks down and go behind what looks like an abandoned apartment complex, making sure no one was watching me. I then put all three purses, including wallets, beside a trash can and then get the hell out of Dodge.

My phone rings.

"Hey babe, what's up?"

"Not much. How's your day going?" asks Chloe.

"Pretty uneventful. You know, same old stuff. You?"

"I just got off the phone with Mom and she said it's gorgeous there today. Did you go to the beach?"

"Not today babe. I've got a bug problem and some cell phone trouble. Look, can I call you back later? I'm kind of in the middle of something."

"Sure dear. Call me at 8:00."

"Okay. I'll talk to you then."

My adrenaline is pumping and I need beer.

Twenty minutes later, Manhattan Police Headquarters

"Captain Lew, we got a GPS location on the second phone taken from the robbery."

"Bring it," said Lew.

"It's at the Manhattan Regional Airport."

"Can we get any more specific? I mean, it's a pretty big fucking airport."

"Not yet sir. I've informed airport security and given them a description of the perp. They're searching everything now. Do you want me to send some of our uni's out, sir?"

"Does a one-legged duck swim in a circle, dip-shit?" replied Lew.

"Sir?"

"Yes, yes, yes. Send at least four units. I feel like Buford T. Justice from Smokey and the Bandit," Lew said to no one in particular.

Seventeen minutes later, Holiday Inn Express. Manhattan, Kansas

Holy fuck nuts, that's a lot of money. I still haven't counted it. I'm just staring at it scattered on the bed. Sitting down on the other queen bed, I finish my beer and take a deep breath. I go to the bathroom and take a leak, while looking into the mirror with big eyes and a huge smile.

"Holy shit, that's a lot of cash," I say out loud to my reflection.

Twelve minutes later, Manhattan Police Department

"Captain Lew."

"What?"

"Just got a hit on the third phone."

"Don't tell me, it was spotted at the movies."

"Uh, no sir. Downtown."

"Oh, picking up a prostitute?"

"No sir. We've got units in the area and they should be on it in minutes," he reported.

"Get back to me when we have the phone."

One minute later, Holiday Inn Express

$77,420. My biggest take yet. If I could do two, maybe three more jobs like this, I could give it all up and retire. I take $12,420 and put it aside. I bundle the $65,000 left into four equal stacks. Calling the front desk, I ask for the closest FedEx location. Tomorrow morning, before I leave, I'll overnight the $65,000 to my home address in Punta Gorda and will be there to sign for it on Wednesday.

I'll take it to bank number two, which has $80,000, and add the $65,000, making it $145,000 total. I keep the $12,420 liquid on me for my big week with Chloe.

Fourteen minutes later, Manhattan Police Department

"Talk to me guy," Lew demanded.

"Okay. The phone at Walmart in Junction City has been surrounded. All male employees and customers are being checked one at a time and released if they don't have the phone. The local police department will get back to me shortly. The phone missing downtown was picked up by Officer Charles and he has detained a very drunk homeless guy who claims he has no idea how it got into his pocket."

"Holy shit," cried Lew. "Are you fucking kidding me? What happened to the one at the airport?"

"It just boarded a flight to San Francisco via Southwest Airlines flight number BA 2268 nonstop to San Fran."

"Fucking great. I got one phone drunk with a homeless man, the second on a fucking shopping spree at Walmart, and the other suddenly comes out of the closet and heads to San Fran. It'll probably join the mile high club before I do. Contact the SFPD and ask them to search the plane and passengers upon landing," Lew said.

"Sir, they found the phone at Walmart. It was hidden in the DVD section behind the box set of Airplane!"

"Well spank my ass and call me Shirley," said Lew. "Looks like I picked the wrong day to stop sniffing glue."

8:00 p.m. Holiday Inn, Manhattan, Kansas

Chloe answers on the second ring. "Hey Cam, did your day get any better?"

"Not really. Sorry about earlier. It seemed like I had a dozen things going on all at once. How about your day?" I ask.

"Well, it's better now. I was about to think you were not going to call me back. It's after 10:00."

"What? No, it's just after 9:00."

"What time zone are you in babe?"

Holy shit, she's right. I'm an hour behind. "You're right dear. Damn. Where has the day gone? I'm sorry. It's just been one of those days."

"Don't worry about it. Anyway, are you going to give me any hints about our plans this weekend?"

"Not a single one. You've got nothing to worry about. I'll handle it all. And it wouldn't do you any good for me to tell you anyhow. You don't know these places."

"I know more than you think, Cam."

"What's that mean?" I ask a little nervous.

"Google is a powerful tool."

"Yes, and?"

"The menu at Harpoon Harry's looks good and affordable. And I bet you go to a bar called Mooseheads every Wednesday night, right?"

"Uh, yeah. And how do you know that?" I ask.

"Mooseheads' website says it has Texas hold 'em night every Wednesday, that's how."

"Oh, right. Their website." Holy shit Cam. Keep it together.

"Do you know what I really want to do for a day, but I can't really afford it?"

"What's that Chloe?"

"Go shopping at the Ellenton Outlets near Sarasota. But money is a little tight for me right now."

"Honey, please don't worry about money. The week you're here, you'll be my guest." I look over at the cash bundle. "I've had a good month at work."

"Oh, did you get a big deal," she asked.

"Yeah, you could say that."

"That's great babe. Do you have a busy day tomorrow?"

"Yes, but I'll call you before my flight." Shit!

"Your flight? What flight?"

"What? Oh, my golf flight. I'm playing in a tournament and I'm in the second flight. Golf lingo, Chloe."

"Oh, okay. Well, good luck and call me in the morning. Sweet dreams."

"And to you, as well dear." I rang off and grabbed my last beer from the mini fridge and turned on the television. The local news anchor was interviewing a pink-faced Captain Lew of the Manhattan Police Department, who was obviously pissed off about something. By the time I could turn up the volume, it changed to sports.

CHAPTER 39
TUESDAY, MAY 20TH CHARLESTON SC 8:00 A.M.

"Okay Knabb," said Rickard. "We've got another bank job to add to our research. Yesterday, at precisely 3:30 local time, KS StateBank of Manhattan Kansas was robbed by a Caucasian male. He is thirty to thirty-five years old, five foot nine to five foot ten, approximately 175 pounds, dark hair, a ponytail, blue eyes, goatee, silver hoop earring in right ear. He was disguised as an exterminator making his quarterly rounds. He got away with approximately $75,000. That's a pretty damn big haul. Now get this. He takes everyone's cell phone, plants two of them in the area, puts the third one on a plane to San Francisco, and had the local police chasing their tails for hours. As of 7:00 a.m., the Manhattan Police Department has no suspects."

"That's a lot of money sir," responded Knabb. He knew not to interrupt Rickard till he put in a long pause. "I see a couple of things we can do."

"Such as?" asked Rickard.

"Well, if he is from Florida, we know he didn't drive. We can check all flights from Manhattan Regional Airport to all destinations in Florida and cross reference with all white male passengers who fit our description. Maybe even interview the flight attendants. Couldn't be too many flights from Manhattan to Florida locations," Knabb responded.

"Knabb, I don't think this guy is that careless. My bet is

he has at least one flight between Florida and his destination, this time being Kansas."

"What about rental vehicles?" asked Knabb.

"Not sure. But I would think he would use fake IDs and probably fake, but real, prepaid credit cards."

"But if the IDs and credit cards were fake, but good, the perp would have the statements sent to a Florida address."

"And" Rickard interrupted, "I bet the drivers' licenses were fake names, but a legitimate address for our perp. I also bet the licenses are Florida issued. Get on it, Knabb! I've got a meeting to go to and explain to the Director the expenses we will need approved to continue to explore a bank robbery cold case that took place nearly five years ago. Let's meet at Halls Chophouse at 1:00 for lunch and a drink."

"Yes sir. See you at 1:00."

Manhattan, Kansas, 9:00 a.m. local time

My cash shipment to my Punta Gorda address should arrive between 9:00 a.m. and noon tomorrow. I should be home by midnight tonight. Then, I run the cash to bank number two. I need a haircut, to shave the goatee, and to pick up Chloe at the airport by 6:00. Oh shit! My place is a mess. There is nothing in the fridge. There is no wine, but dirty clothes, dirty sheets, and dirty towels. I call Carmina, who does a complete clean for me twice a month. Please be home. I explain to Carmina what I need done, today if possible. I told her to grab $400 from the petty cash box in my office, keep $200.00 for cleaning, take the other $200.00, and purchase groceries. I want her to make the place smell good. Cool. Done.

I've got three hours before my flight to Charlotte, North Carolina, then Charlotte to Tampa. I'll get to Tampa by 8:00, out of Tampa by 8:45, and with luck in Punta Gorda by 11:30. It's a long four days. But, even if you count it as twenty-four hours per day x four days as ninety-six hours, that is about $800.00 per hour. That'll work!

From the rental car, I text Chloe. "Less than thirty-three hours until you're in sunny Florida!" She responded within minutes with "I can hug my man in thirty-three hours!"

Although I wore latex gloves the entire time during the job, I hop in the back to start wiping down the van. Oh shit, the ammonia-filled garden sprayer! Minutes later, with the ammonia sprayer wiped clean and disposed of, I pull into the rental return lane. I take an additional few minutes to wipe down the instruments within reach of the driver's seat, grab my carry-on luggage, leave the van, and walk to the ticket counter. Twenty minutes later, I'm enjoying a coffee and bagel with a half hour to spare.

1:00 p.m. Charleston, SC Halls Chophouse

"Knabb, what are you drinking?" asked Rickard, who was working on his second Amstel Light.

"I'll take a Bushmills straight," Knabb replied. "How did the meeting go? Did we get a little funding, a little discretionary spending?"

"Very little. He wants results."

"But we get tons of results! We've got dozens of arrests and prosecutions in the past year. I think it's close to fourteen, to be exact. Let's just take the Florida Bandit off his radar. Tell him we gave up on it." Knabb was getting braver just knowing his drink was on the way.

"The Florida Bandit?" asked Rickard. "That's original."

"Well, what do we want to call him?"

"No, that'll do for now. For us."

"I've been thinking sir. If we can find any ID used at any airport rental agency rented on Friday, Saturday, or Sunday, returning it on Monday, Tuesday, or Wednesday, run all those names, match names that fit the age range, we may get lucky. I've already checked. There are only six rental agencies at Manhattan Regional Airport. Probably twenty returns per day. So six agencies times twenty rentals per day times six days equals 720 contracts. Shouldn't take us too long to narrow the search."

"Okay Knabb. I'll give you three days starting tomorrow. See what you can dig up." Their steaks were served and another round of drinks were ordered. They didn't speak of the Florida Bandit until the next morning.

11:00 p.m. Sarasota

Returning to Tampa Airport, I realize my phone has been off since 3:00. I've only got three bars.

"Hey Chloe."

"Cam, where have you been? I've been trying to call you all day!"

"You know how the other day I was telling you I was having phone trouble? Well, the battery died today and I didn't even notice it. I charged it for thirty minutes so I could call you. I'm actually driving around with it plugged in just to talk to you. I'm sorry if I made you worry!"

"Oh, it's okay, now that I can hear your voice."

"Are you packed and ready to come down?"

"Hell yeah. I'm just so ready to do what you say for a few days!"

"That sounds good to me.....like anything I say?"

"Stop it Cam. You know what I mean."

"Look, I've got about twenty minutes of driving to do. Why don't you keep me company and talk to me till I get home."

"If I was beside you, I could think of a few ways to keep you company for fifteen minutes!"

"Stop it Chloe. Save that until you're here, or are you all talk?"

"You'll just have to find out!"

We continued to talk for the last fifteen miles of my trip. When I hit the Punta Gorda exit, we hung up. Minutes later, I carry my laptop and enter my immaculately clean condo, complete with fully stocked fridge. Thanks Carmina!

CHAPTER 40
MAY 22ND THURSDAY, PUNTA GORDA

I wake at 6:30. I'm out the door for a four mile run and return to the condo by 7:30 drenched. I love Florida, but sometimes it's eighty-five degrees by sunrise. I shit, shower, shave, and dress like a native Floridian, with tan Armani slacks, a yellow Tommy Bahama silk shirt, and leather sandals. I turn on Fox News for Fox & Friends, boot up my laptop, and wait for FedEx to deliver. This is the most money I've ever mailed before and I'd be lying if I said I wasn't a little nervous. They train dogs to find drugs, but some are trained to find money. I google Manhattan, Kansas news and find out that the robbery made website headline news on WMKS.

Just then, Steve Doocy from Fox & Friends starts talking about the Manhattan robbery, telling the viewing audience how the cell phone sendoff was brilliant and the "Edward the Exterminator" disguise was pure genius. Then, they showed a Jay Leno clip.

Jay: "Monday, a bank robber disguised as an exterminator robbed a Manhattan, Kansas bank in broad daylight. Eyewitnesses say the van he was driving advertised 'Jackson's Rid-a-bug' because I've had bugs too."

Back to Steve … "Authorities, including the FBI, are linking this robbery with several others, some estimates as high as thirty bank robberies across the U.S."

They show typical bad quality black and white video. You can't tell who I am.

"Authorities estimate that this is a white male, thirty to thirty-five years old, five foot ten, and 170 to 175 pounds."

"Shit, shit, shit!" That's me on national television and they just described me perfectly. I'm thirty-three, five foot ten, and 171 pounds. My phone rings. "Shit, shit, shit!" It's Chloe.

"Hello."

"Hey babe. I'll be there in nine more hours. You excited?"

Oh, thank God, she knows nothing. Stay calm Cam.

"Excited is not the word. I mean wow or amazing, maybe even unbelievable!"

"Are you okay there Cam? You don't sound yourself and you're not making a lot of sense. Cameron?"

"Yeah, I'm here I'm okay. Just got some stuff to take care of before you get here. Business stuff."

"Okay Cam, big breaths, take it easy. Whatever you're stressing over, I'm sure is no big deal."

"You're right." It's just my fucking life. "It's no big deal." Just life in prison. "I shouldn't stress." I should fucking flee to Antigua or Jamaica or wherever the fuck they don't extradite to the U.S. "I'm okay Chloe. Just have a lot to do. I want our time this week to be perfect." Perfectly free of cops. Perfect, because it could be my last as a free man.

"Okay, I got you. You need to go and get stuff done. I'll leave you be. I'll text you when I'm boarding the plane. Bye Cam."

"Fly safe Chloe."

I check CNN. It takes them about ten minutes before they talk about the robbery. I turn to MSNBC. It takes three minutes before it's mentioned by the crawling banner at the bottom of the screen.

My doorbell rings.

I go to my kitchen window and look to see if I can identify who's there. The bell rings again. In the parking lot I see a FedEx truck. I open the door.

"Delivery for a Cameron Steele," said the driver.

"That's me. Thanks." I sign the digital pad and hand it back to him.

I close and lock the door and stand in the middle of the kitchen, looking at the package in my hands. I place the package on the counter and open the kitchen window. Then, I go to the guest bedroom and open its window and make my way to the den and mute the television. It's perfectly quiet. All I hear is a faint Florida breeze coming off Charlotte Harbor that rattles the blinds on my lanai. I fully open the four sliding glass-door panels that recess into the walls and stand perfectly still for ten minutes. No sirens. No car doors opening or shutting. Nothing. It's so peaceful.

Same day, Charleston SC 10:00 a.m.

"Dammit Knabb, I think we got him," exclaimed Rickard.

"You think it's him? It's got to be! Of course, we don't really have him and don't really know who he is, but with this kind of national attention and nationwide TV news coverage, we are sure to get some kind of break," Knabb responds.

"But, it will also do something else. It will shut him down, at least for a while," said Rickard.

"I don't think so sir. It's probably just the attention he is looking for. Some lonely little mama's boy geek who never got the girl. Always last picked to play kickball. Probably, some kind of independent IT contractor that pays him $35K per year, but he wants more. And being an independent contractor would allow him to pick and choose his jobs. This gives him the opportunity to travel and set his own schedule."

"I respect your opinion Knabb, but I think you're wrong. This guy doesn't want attention. He's clever. He wants to be completely under the radar. I don't think he's a loner and I bet he was popular in school. All the descriptions of him or jobs we think he has done are: handsome, charming, a gentleman, tanned, and pretty eyes, despite the fact that he caps out a tooth or two, used a fake wart or a huge nose, even a unibrow. This perp doesn't want to be famous for robbing banks. He doesn't want to be famous at all. And right now, I bet he is scared shitless."

Fifteen minutes later, Punta Gorda

I'm so scared I can't even shit. I'm not kidding. I'm sitting on the toilet and can't shit. Screw it. I got things to do."

In the kitchen, I grab the FedEx package, pull the ripcord, and empty its contents on the kitchen table. $65,000 large. I go to the bedroom to my master closet and open an extremely old iron safe that was my uncle's. Inside the safe, I keep my fake IDs and fake credit cards. It's also home to my ledger and my safe deposit box keys.

After scooping up the IDs, credit cards, and keys, along with the $65,000, I'm out the door. Firing up the Alfa Romeo, I can't help but put the top down. See, that's the thing about living here. It's hard to have a completely bad day. The sun is always shining. You've got water all around you, beautiful girls wearing skimpy outfits, and just an overall Jimmy Buffett laid-back attitude and lifestyle.

I go to bank number one. It's my biggest safe deposit box. I sign the card and the assistant manager escorts me into the vault. She takes my key, along with her master key, opens the door, and steps back.

Taking the box to the semiprivate stall, I open the lid. I place the IDs, credit cards, ledger, and deposit box keys for banks three through six inside. Giving the assistant manager the box back, she places it in its slot, closes the door, and removes both keys. Handing my key to me, along with a folded sheet of paper, she smiles at me and wishes me a great day.

Outside, I hop in the Alfa and look at the note. It reads "Catherine Jones 941-555-1212. Let's get dinner sometime." Wow, didn't see that coming. Throwing the note in the glove box, I leave bank one. Turning north on Tamiami, in less than half a mile, I turn into bank number two.

I repeat the process from my previous stop, but only leave the $65,000 in bank number two's deposit box, along with the key to bank number one's box. So to recap, the only thing I'm keeping in my possession is bank number two's safe deposit key, which I will tape to the underside of my safe at home. The safe weighs over four hundred pounds and I'm hoping no one will think to look under it. Okay, let's go to the office. There are sure to be clients to call.

I work till I get the text from Chloe that she's boarding the plane in Maryland. I reply "two more hours!" I'm off to Harpoon Harry's for a cocktail. After three Corona

Lights and a basket of fries, I'm off to the very small Punta Gorda Airport.

Punta Gorda Airport 6:00 p.m.

I'm holding up a cardboard sign that reads, "My Chloe". As she deplanes on the tarmac (Punta Gorda Airport does not have an airport connected walkway), the wind whips her sundress, which she holds down with one hand. The other hand is pulling her luggage. Once she enters the airport and walks past security, she sees me and the sign and immediately smiles broadly. She runs and jumps into my arms and we kiss briefly.

"Oh, I've missed you so," she said.

"Me too, Chloe. Me too. Is this all your stuff?"

"Yep. I travel lightly."

"Cool. Let's go."

"Where to first," Chloe asks, while we walk to my car.

"I figured we'd go to my place, get your stuff inside, and give you a chance to freshen up, if you'd like. Then..."

"Is this your car?"

"It is. Is the top down okaywith you?"

"Sure. But what is it?"

"It's a 1991 Alfa Romeo Spider Veloce I picked up in '95. I've always had a second car, so it's only got, let's see, 65,000 miles." Wow, that number keeps popping up. "But right now, she's all I got. Anyway, after you freshen up and maybe a glass of wine, I figure I'd drive you around Punta Gorda. I can show you everything in less than an hour. Sound good to you?"

"Your voice is what sounds good to me."

"Aren't you sweet," I say.

An hour and a half later and after showing Chloe the quaint downtown area, Punta Gorda Isles, and the yacht club, she turns to me and says, "Take me to Harpoon Harry's."

"I thought you'd never ask."

Minutes later, we pull into a parking lot set against Charlotte Harbor.

"This is Fisherman's Village. Over there are tennis courts." Pointing toward the back, I say "and over there are about fifty or so commercial and private boat slips, mainly for gulf fishing. Then, over here are the village shops."

"It's all so clean and bright and cheery. I can see why you come here a lot."

Chloe grabbed my hand and we strolled through the shops, making our way to the back of the property, the last structure being Harpoon Harry's. Taking her to the back deck near the bar, we grab a booth on the deck.

"The view is perfect."

"This is usually where I sit. So in the future, if we talk by phone while I'm here, this is probably where I'm sitting."

"Now it's our table," she said as she reached across the table and took my hand in hers.

"Now," I said, "look over there. Do you see the five-story building with the green roof?"

"Yeah."

"The white building to the left is my building and the condo on the second floor far left is mine."

"So, does this place become a bar at night?" she asks.

"Around ten on Friday and Saturday nights it's a club, live bands. It's usually more of a college crowd those nights.

I like it during the week around sunset, like now."

"I can see why. I can also see why you love living here. It's perfect."

I squeeze Chloe's hand and reply, "Almost perfect."

We order our meals and have perfect service, food, and conversation afterwards. We walk around the village to see the other half of the shops and retire home.

At the condo, I offer her something to drink.

"I'm fine. But what I'd really like to do is take a shower. Do you mind?"

"Not at all," I say. "Let me get you a towel and anything else you might need."

"I won't be but a minute. I promise."

Chloe shut the door to my bedroom and a few minutes later, I heard the shower running. I grab a Corona Light and turn the TV on to SportsCenter. Chloe kept her promise and the shower was off before I finished my beer. She opened my bedroom door wearing only my robe, which wasn't sashed.

"I think it's time we took our relationship up a notch."

I jump off the couch, taking off my shirt at the same time.

"Slow down, babe. We've got all night," she said as she backed onto my bed. "Come here."

I walked to her and she opened my belt and unfastened my shorts. I stepped out of them and my boxers, already standing at attention.

"Oh my," she said, looking at my manhood. "That looks tasty."

She pulls my waist toward her and takes me into her mouth. The warmth of her mouth makes me feel like I've already exploded. She works me gently with long, slow, deep motions and uses her right hand to cup the boys. It's finally her turn and I pick her up and place her further on the bed, losing the robe in the process.

I start by kissing her neck, move down to taste each hard nipple, and finally make my way to her hairless treasure. She's wet with anticipation and eagerly spreads her legs, giving me room to work. With my fingers, I open her folds and tease her a little with my tongue. It's pure joy for me and according to her gasps, for her too.

She grabs my hair and pulls my face deeper. I grab both her arms and pull each one down by her sides, holding each hand firmly under her ass, so she can't move them. Shortly, her hands are shaking, twitching with each flick of my tongue. This drives her crazy and after several minutes, she pulls her hands away and pulls my hair and face up to her mouth.

"I want you inside me now, Cam."

I'm so hard, I feel like I'm back in high school. I enter her missionary style and she grabs my buttocks, matching my rhythm. We kiss deeply and explore every inch of each other with our hands. I'm moments away from climaxing and Chloe slows me down. She rolls over and guides me in her from the back.

With my right hand, I grab a handful of her hair and pull it back, arching her head upwards. My left hand is on her shoulder, pulling her deeply into me. The pace picks up and I'm doing my best not to cum, wanting to enjoy this moment, this visual, the intense euphoria shooting through every nerve of my body. I don't want it to end. I move both hands to her hips, thrusting harder and harder and inviting her body to mine, working toward a simultaneous end.

Just as I'm no longer capable of holding out, I release and feel the warm sensation of both our fluids combining like a perfect summer rain.

She slows down and asks me not to pull out just yet. "Just stay right there."

"Baby, don't worry. I can't move," is all I can utter.

"Flex for me."

"Flex?" I ask.

"Yes. Stay in me and flex what's left of that hard-on."

I comply and do my best to swell what's left of my erection.

"Again, baby."

I cowboy up and try to push as much blood flow to my shaft as I can.

"That's it. That's perfect. I love you Cam."

"I love you too Chlo. God, that was like, I don't know how to describe it. Like, sunshine."

"Well, this sunshine is all yours."

Chloe is on her side and I'm spooning her from behind. In a matter of minutes, I hear the deep rhythmic breathing indicating sleep. It's soon my breathing is in sync with hers.

CHAPTER 41
MAY 23, FRIDAY CHARLESTON, SC, 8:00 A.M.

"Sir, with all the publicity the Manhattan, Kansas bank robbery is getting, will the Director increase our budget?" asked Knabb

"Just the opposite," Rickard snapped. "He feels there is enough heat on this guy that we should let the other states pursue it and we can just ride their coattails once someone IDs this guy."

"That's bullshit sir."

"Well," retorts Rickard. "Yes and no. I see where you're coming from, but I also see his point of view. We waste our funding figuring out the perp. Let someone else pay for it. The Director asked us to sit it out for three months or so and see what develops. I'll tell you this much. I'll lay four to one that we don't see a hit that matches him for a year."

Punta Gorda, FL 8:30 a.m.

"You keep sleeping honey. I'm going to grab a run. I'll be back in an hour." I kiss Chloe on the cheek and lace up.

Fifty minutes later, I return and grab a bottled water from the fridge. Tiptoeing into the bedroom, I kiss Chloe on the cheek and slip into the bathroom. Stripping down, I hop into the shower, leaving the water cool for a few minutes. A hand touches my back and Chloe joins me.

"Whoa. Throw some heat into that water!"

"Sorry. Trying to cool down after my run. How'd you sleep?"

"Mmmm, perfect. You?"

"Pretty good." With the exception of a recurring prison shower scene nightmare. "Pretty good."

As if on cue, Chloe says, "Oops. I dropped the soap."

She bends over, putting her butt in my crotch, moving it and me from side to side. She pops back up and starts to lather me up. "We've got to get you clean." She soaps my chest and works my arms and pits. She squats down and lifts my left foot and places it on her right thigh and soaps my leg. She repeats with the other leg. By now, I'm flying half staff and she's still squatting and I'm poking her on her forehead. She gently cleans my staff and the boys, grabs my waist, spins me around, and says, "Now rinse."

I comply and she spins me back toward her. Still squatting, she says, "I'll take it from here. You finish up by washing your hair." She takes me in her mouth and gives me the warmest, most sensual, oral sex I've ever experienced, completing the act in five minutes.

"Thank you," she says.

"What? Thank you," I reply.

"Now get out and make me breakfast, while I turn up the heat and take a real shower."

"Can I stay and watch?" I ask.

"Just go and make me breakfast."

I make a simple breakfast of scrambled eggs and bacon. Carmina had purchased some diced fruit, cantaloupe, honeydew, and mandarin oranges and I prepared two bowls. Chloe came out wearing my robe and we ate together, looking out at the beautiful sunrise on Charlotte Harbor.

"Today, I thought we'd pack a lunch, hit the beach for a few hours, come back here, and shower and possibly grab a nap and then head to the Slip-Knot for dinner. Sound like a plan?"

"That sounds perfect. I'll be ready to walk out the door in twenty minutes."

I cleaned up the dishes, then slipped into the room. Chloe had just put a T-shirt on over her bikini top. I change into my J.Crew swim trunks and we head to the kitchen.

"I'm going to pack a cooler. Is Corona Light okay?"

"For you maybe. Let's stop and get some Red Stripe or Killian's."

"No problem, dear."

Packing the cooler with the rest of the fruit, two deli-sliced roast beef and Pepper Jack cheese sandwiches, eight Corona Lights, and plenty of ice, we are off to Venice Island.

An hour later, top down on the Alfa Romeo. Venice Island

"Right over there is a private airport whose claim to fame is training one of the 9-11 terrorists how to take off."

"Really?" Chloe asked. "Right here in Venice."

"Yep. The little stretch of beach we're going to is nicknamed Shark Tooth Beach and on our way there, we'll pass a good restaurant, bar, and pier called Sharky's. They catch a lot of sharks off the pier, but don't worry. The water is so clear, if there was a shark nearby you'd see it."

"That doesn't really make me feel much better," she says. "Doesn't the saying go that most shark attacks happen in three feet of water or less?"

"That's true, because that's where the people are," I say, laughing.

"Cam, that's awful," she replied, playfully pushing my shoulder.

"And by the way, we are around thirty minutes away from your parents in Sarasota. If you want to, call them and see if they want to meet us at Sharky's around 1:00 or 2:00 for cocktails."

"That's a great idea. I'll call Mom now."

Chloe calls her mom and they decide to meet us at 1:00 for cocktails and a late lunch. That gives us a little more than two hours sun time. We pass Sharky's and I point it out to her. About a minute later, we're parking, grabbing our beach gear, and walking the short distance to the sand.

Chloe and I had a blast. It's as if we've known each other for years. We hunt for shark's teeth, find half a dozen or so, and played in the water. Even just soaking up the sun, there were no awkward pauses. Our conversation just drifted along with no pressure, like the simple low-key waves of the gulf, lapping their tides against the soft sand of Venice Island.

"Didn't I tell you life here was great?"

Slightly past noon, we both jump in the crystal clear warm water of the gulf and just stare out to the horizon. Holding hands, we get out and towel off. Collecting our gear, we head to the outdoor showers. After thoroughly rinsing ourselves, the cooler, the flip-flops, and the beach chairs, we cross the street and load up the Alfa to head to Sharky's.

Walking into the restaurant, we are greeted by Chloe's parents, who had snagged a great table on the patio, overlooking the beach.

"Mom, Dad!"

"Chole!" said her mom.

"Angel", from dad.

"It is so great to see you both Mom and Dad. This is Cameron. Cam, meet my mom, Grace and this is my dad, Rylie."

"Nice to meet you both," I say.

"Good to meet you Cameron," said Dad. "Let's get a drink. Girls, you catch up with each other. I've got Cam here." Grabbing my shoulder and steering me toward the bar, he asks, "What's your poison, Cam?"

Looking at the cute bartender, I reply, "I'll have a Blue Moon with an orange slice."

"Is that good? Sounds good. Bartender, make that two."

Chloe and her mom talk like best friends, giggling together like friends do about an inside joke. Her dad and I got along well. Rylie is a big classic car buff and by the end of our -ong talk, I felt I was an expert on the subject, as well.

A pleasant afternoon was had by all. Chloe informed them we had dinner reservations at 7:00 in Punta Gorda, so we had to leave by three to make sure we had enough time to drive back to Punta Gorda and shower. We said our goodbyes. Chloe promised to call them Sunday afternoon before we came up to Sarasota. I promised to stay Sunday night in the poolhouse. Rylie promised to take me out on his thirty-eight foot Sea Ray on Monday. We all made promises.

I PROMISE TO TRY AND KEEP MY BUTT OUT OF JAIL.

Friday night was awesome. Dinner at the Slip-Knot was perfect. Sex from 11:00 to 1:00 just about killed me. Here comes tomorrow.

CHAPTER 42
SATURDAY, MAY 24 PUNTA GORDA

After waking, eating breakfast, a shower, and more breakfast, it was time to head to the Punta Gorda Arts Festival. It was a perfect southwest Florida day. The temperature was in the low eighties and with a soft gulf breeze, we didn't even break a sweat.

By the end of the day, we had made several purchases, including a watercolor on canvas of Fisherman's Village by a local artist, a silver ring, a couple of T-shirts, hats, and mugs, all to remember the day. I'm also talked into buying a Wyland shark drawing titled "Trio."

After dinner, we were exhausted. At the condo, I moved the couch ninety degrees, so it faced the harbor. Chloe fell asleep on my chest as we watched a beautiful fireworks display light up over the water. It was a perfect ending to a perfect day.

The rest of the week went off without a hitch. I was constantly worried about the latest developments on the news concerning Kansas, but all seemed to die down, media wise, as quickly as it started.

As Thursday was quickly approaching, I found myself missing Chloe already. I didn't want her to leave. There had to be something I could do to get her to stay or at least consider moving here. And then it struck me. Michelle, the girl I played tennis with, works for Colonial Bank. I pulled out my cell phone, found her in my contacts, and called her, setting an appointment for Thursday at 11:00.

CHAPTER 43
THURSDAY, MAY 29 SARASOTA

I picked up Chloe at her parents' house. I told her parents that I had special plans for her today and that we needed to get back to Punta Gorda ASAP. We left their house by 9:45 and pulled into the parking lot of Colonial Bank in Punta Gorda at exactly 10:50.

"What are we doing here?" she asked.

"Now just stay with me for a moment. We need to go inside and I want to introduce you to a client of mine. I only want you to keep an open mind, okay? Can you do that for me?"

"Sure. I guess so. What's going on, Cam?"

"Nope. No questions yet. Come on."

We go inside the bank and I let the teller know that I have an 11:00 appointment with Michelle Jones. We were seated in the lobby and asked to wait a few minutes. Michelle was finishing with her 10:00 and would be with us shortly.

"Is this where you bank?" Chloe asked.

"No questions Chloe." I smiled and she returned it.

"Cameron, so good to see you again," Michelle says as she gives me a small hug. Turning to Chloe, "and this must be Chloe."

"Thanks Michelle. Yes, this is Chloe," I say proudly.

"So nice to meet you. First time in Punta Gorda?"

"Yes. And it's nice to meet you, as well," Chloe responded extending her hand.

"Well, come on back guys. I hope you weren't waiting long?" She took her seat behind a well-appointed, but conservative, desk in a decent-sized corner office.

Looking at Chloe, she says, "Cameron tells me you're in the banking business."

"Yes. I guess I am. I mean, right now I'm a teller for Chase Bank in Maryland, but I'm in line to get the assistant manager's position," Chloe responded.

"Cam also tells me you graduated from Georgetown with a degree in education. Probably not doing you much good in banking, huh?"

"True. I only got into banking because I wasn't ready to teach, I guess."

"Cam also tells me you have family in Sarasota."

"That's right. My parents live downtown, near Marina Jack."

"Are you interested in pursuing a career in banking?"

"Sure."

"Well, I just happen to have a branch manager position open in Port Charlotte, about eight miles north of here. It's a branch manager one position, kind of a starter branch manager position. The pay starts at $45,000 a year. Is this something you might be interested in?"

"Goodness. I haven't given a lot of thought to moving. I mean, it would be great to be near my folks and I absolutely love the weather here. Wow! When would you need an answer?" Chloe asked.

"Well, the current manager is transferring to Miami in six weeks. The position is not advertised and I'd like to keep it that way. No one knows she is transferring. I'd need the person to start in four weeks, so they can have a couple of weeks to shadow the current manager. So, I'd need an answer in three weeks max. Are you interested?"

"Wow. Umm, sure. I mean, it sounds great. Would you be my direct manager? Would I report to you?" Chloe asked.

"Yes to both questions. You'll find me easy to work for. And being new, you wouldn't have high goals for a year. Plus, it's a great market. I'll also throw in a $7,500 relocation allowance. Sounding better?"

"Very. Can I have two weeks to think about it?" asked Chloe.

"Sure. But the earlier the better. Here, take my card. My cell number is on the bottom and if you have any questions, just call. Oh, and although Cam has told me all about you and I have the final say so on who gets hired, forward me your resume so I can send it through the proper channels."

"No problem. Send it to this email on your card?"

"Yes. I really look forward to hearing from you. Soon, I hope."

"I'll forward my resume tomorrow and I'll call you as soon as I make a decision," Chloe responded.

"Okay, let's go get some lunch," I said. "I think we should celebrate at Harpoon Harry's!"

"I'm going to gain twenty pounds in the first month if I move here," Chloe chided.

"We'll have to figure out ways to work it off!" I said.

"Cam!"

Harpoon Harry's, fifteen minutes later

"Holy cow, Cam. Did you set this up? I mean, how did you know they were looking for someone?"

"I didn't. I called her earlier because she's one of my clients. We were discussing her portfolio and I asked her about work. She said she was losing one of her best managers and next thing I know, she wanted to meet you."

"Thank you so much Cam. What do you think? I mean, the job is definitely better than what I have in Maryland. That's not the question ... but moving here, that would be, uh, well, a big step in our relationship. So, what do you think?"

I reached across the table and took her hand in mine, looked in her eyes, and said, "The fact that I took you to meet her, knowing that there was a job opportunity in Port Charlotte, should be answer enough of what I think." Chloe squeezed my hand and smiled in response. "Now, let's order lunch and discuss our future together."

An hour later, we leave for the airport. Although the goodbye was tearful, it also had the feel of a new beginning, the start of something that could have long-term implications. Chloe and I just matched. We matched in music, restaurant styles, leisure time, eye color, family dynamics, and of course, in bed. I also had the feeling that some earth-shattering news was yet to come. Things were too good. Something had to derail this perfect lifestyle. I felt a dark cloud was on my horizon, but for some reason I didn't feel it was for the obvious reason.

CHAPTER 44
PUNTA GORDA, FL

The next week was a blur. There were constant calls and texts back and forth with Chloe about the job offer. She was so excited and so was I. She looked on craigslist for an apartment to rent. She didn't want to stay with her parents, but after a little discussion, we decided that her parents' house was her best bet. Staying the weekends with me, we could look for her an apartment together. Or maybe I can find us a bigger place to live together. Maybe.

I spend a lot of my spare time monitoring the news. The story has lost most of its national television appeal, but it was still easy to find online. However, most of the online content was not new, and if it was new, they were just rewrites of the original story. No new details.

There were a few opinion columns on who this state-hopping bank robber was, or rather, what type of person he is. Most profiles read the same:

A smart person. Tests very well, but didn't do particularly well in school. Has some college, maybe a B.S./B.A., but not a postgraduate degree. He's got a decent job that earns him a decent living, but is not considered by others as successful or highly skilled. More than likely, he lives alone. He doesn't spend a lot of the money, with a few exceptions. He spends it on electronics (i.e. the latest cell phone, flat screen, home entertainment, and computers), vehicles, and most likely frequents gentleman clubs, where his money makes him feel like a CEO, like someone important, rich, and well respected. He buys respect. No, better yet, he rents their respect. The respect has to be repurchased each time he visits. He greatly wants a full-time relationship, but he can't get the supermodel, unless she works the pole at the Bada Bing. When he ventures outside of strip clubs, he most likely employs escort services. Eventually, he will get caught and when he does, he will want to take the credit for all his accomplishments, especially the bank robberies.

That's a lot of information, but completely wrong. Not me at all. This gives me more confidence. The only real fear I have is a profiler figuring out that I live in southwest Florida. I believe there is a strong possibility that information could be deduced from the robbery statistics and patterns. I'm actually thinking of doing a job in Florida, just to change up my modus operandi. Maybe the Panhandle, but still far enough away that I shouldn't be too worried about local coverage of the grainy black and white video.

CHAPTER 45
FRIDAY JUNE 6 PUNTA GORDA

I convince myself that a Florida job is needed to keep the profilers honest. However, is it too little, too late? Will the experts identify it as a diversive technique? I've spent the last thirty-six hours trying to decide the best location. Of course, I'm staying away from the southwest. Nothing below Tampa all the way down to Naples. The east coast from Orlando down to Miami is out. There is way too much police activity. To me, the obvious location would be the Panhandle. However, would the profilers think the same and put me in the south? And if they do assume south Florida, wouldn't most think the east coast? If the same profilers think I'm hanging around strip clubs, wouldn't they think of the east coast? Gulf Coast south Florida is way too laid-back for the "profiler's" suspect.

I also have to make this look like one of my original jobs. I need a heavy disguise and it needs to be detected as a "disguise." I need to be recognized without being recognized, and during all this, I still need to get away. The money range needs to remain the same. The time of day needs to be around 3:30. The delivery and message of the note has to be similar. All in all, it needs to be a Cam job.

The location research has to be thorough. Nothing will be left to chance. I also need to execute it in about six to eight weeks, about the average time I've used between jobs in the past.

CHAPTER 46
SATURDAY JUNE 7 PUNTA GORDA

"Good morning, Cam."

"And to you too Chloe. Did you sleep well?" I asked.

"Better if I was there. Have you got big plans for the day?" she asked.

"Not really. I'm going to Gasparilla Island to relax for a few hours. Then a client of mine, husband and wife, asked me to stop by their house on Manasota Key around 3:00 and look over their portfolio. They have a few questions about an investment they are considering. I should be home around 8:00.

"Are you going to be in North Port some time today?" she asked.

"Actually, yes. I go through North Port on my way to Gasparilla. What's up?"

"I need you to stop by an apartment complex and check it out for me. Do you think you can?"

"I wonder if the apartment complex office will still be open around 7:00 tonight. Might not on a Saturday," I said.

"If it's not open, still ride through the parking lot and get a feel for it and its location. Okay?"

"Not a problem. I don't know the area real well, but I can say that North Port doesn't really have a bad section by definition. All of these medium to small Florida towns have very low crime rates."

"That's kind of what I saw online. It looks like a decent little town, rent seems reasonable, and it's about a ten-minute drive to the bank. It's about dead center between your place and Mom and Dad's."

"Sounds like a good choice. What's the name?" She gives me the name and address and I write it down. "Okay. I'll check it out."

"Great. Thanks Cam. Look, I need to call Mom and run a few errands. Call me later and have fun at the beach."

"Will do Chloe," I rang off.

Yet another awesome day at Gasparilla. Although I have become accustomed to going by myself, I'm really looking forward to having someone I can share the wonderful, laid-back lifestyle and beautiful beaches of southwest Florida with. Life is good.

Leaving the island, Corona Light in hand, I head north toward my client's house. They have a nice four-bedroom, three-bath, second row house on Manasota Key about five hundred yards from the ocean. It's about a twenty-minute ride and I should be there around 2:50. The top is down on the Alfa. It's eighty-five degrees, slightly overcast and a soft breeze coming off the gulf. I've got Jimmy Buffett's "Pencil Thin Mustache" pumping through the speakers and all is good in my life.

At exactly 2:55, I pull into Jim and Sara Nagle's driveway. It's a traditional southwest Florida beach house, a Spanish-inspired ranch bungalow. Sara is outside working in the yard. Jim is in the garage messing with the Sea-Doo.

"Hey Cam. Jim is in the garage. Go save our Sea-Doo. Beer is in the mini fridge."

"Thanks Sara. You doing okay today?" I asked.

"With this house, the work never ends. I keep bugging Jim to hire a landscape company, but he insists on doing it all himself. Thus, I'm doing it. But it's worth it. Actually Cam, there is a little two-bedroom that was recently put back on the market last week. Only a block down. You should check it out. Very cute."

I met Jim in the garage and after a few minutes of small talk, we got down to his and Sara's investments. They were doing well, with a little over 2.2 million with me, mostly in mutual funds, except the $400K that Jim has in a variable annuity from his 401(k) from IBM. Jim was in sales and had worked his last twelve years with IBM before retiring at the young age of fifty-six. Sara was a school teacher for twenty-five years and retired last year at fifty-four. They have no debt. Both of their kids have finished college and the house is paid off. Relaxing in the gulf on their thirty-eight foot Wellcraft is currently their main occupation.

After reviewing everything and recommending a slight rebalancing from their overweight position in small cap funds to large cap value, I remarked, "Sara tells me a house went back on the market next block down. What's the price range?"

"Not sure Cam. That's Sara's wheelhouse. Now, don't let her pressure you into anything. She'd love to have you as a neighbor. Why do you ask? Punta Gorda too far from the beach?"

"It's great living on the harbor, but I hate having to drive thirty minutes to get to a good beach. What you have here is more what I want. And don't you have a private boat dock on the sound side?"

"Yeah. It increased recently to $9,000 per year, but it's still the best deal going. You looking to get a boat?"

"If I lived where I could have year-round access, I would."

"Well, I'm thinking of upgrading. Maybe a fifty footer or more. I'd give you a great deal on mine."

"Ballpark me."

"I don't know. $55K to $60K. Hey, let's get a beer, hop in the golf cart, and head over to your new home."

"Easy Jim. Not sure I can afford it."

"It's actually been on and off the market for the past two years. It's been reduced from $699K to $450K. I bet you could get it for $399K. Hell, if you don't buy it, we might as an investment."

We pull up to the house, same Floridian style as Jim and Sara's, circular crushed shell driveway, half a dozen palms dotting the front yard. "Can we get in?" I asked.

"Sara has a key. Stay here. I'll go back and get her."

He spun shells as he left the property, leaving me to walk around the house. It wasn't very big. It didn't even look to be two thousand square feet. My condo has 1,600. No garage. Big wraparound deck in the back. Outdoor shower for when you get off the beach. It was very quaint. From the outside, I really liked it. I was making my way back to the front at the same time Jim and Sara returned, Sara with a huge grin on her face.

"Do you like it?" Sara asked.

"From the outside, yes. You have a key?"

"Right here," she responded, smiling. "Let's go in."

Sara unlocked the front door, explaining that the owner (it being a sell by owner) left her a key and had already moved to Naples to start a new job. The owner, Linda Stutts, lived alone. Nice lady, kind of homely, and is only ten years from being called the crazy old cat lady. However, Sara explained, she was a neat freak. Upon entering the house, you could not smell a hint of any pets.

The master bedroom was a good size. The second bedroom was a little closer to an office and could maybe hold a queen-sized bedroom suit. The kitchen was updated with new stainless steel appliances. Overall, the entire house needed some upgrades. It had an eighties feel about it. It shouldn't take much to bring it up to speed, possibly $30K or so.

"Sara, what is she asking?"

"I think she's down to $425K, but I'm willing to bet she'd take $399K."

"She also has a boat slip paid for till the end of the year. That's worth $4,500 right there," Jim added.

"I thought you said she was homely. What did she do with a boat?" I asked.

"She had a homely boyfriend with a POS boat."

"Stop it Jim!" Sara punched him in the arm.

"Well, it was. The boat was. And he was homely," Jim laughed. "And the cats always looked sickly too. They didn't say 'meow.' It was closer to 'meow-tha-pa'," Jim smirked.

"Jim!"

"Meow-tha-pa?" I asked laughing. "What kind of cats? Never mind. I can't believe I just asked that question. I don't care, as long as they are gone cats."

Sara locked up the house and we took the golf cart down to the marina. There were about thirty boat slips, most for thirty-five to fifty footers. On the back side, closest inlet, were about a half dozen that could house sixty footers. By quick glance, I'd say about eight slips were vacant. There was a pumpout and restroom for the owners. Each slip had a water faucet, several electrical outlets, and a full-size 5x7 foot locker for storage.

"Your slip would be number twelve," said Jim. "Sara and I are in seven. Would you like to see the Wellcraft?"

"That would be great," I replied.

The Wellcraft Excalibur is considered a weekender, built for cruising with enough room to sleep four adults comfortably and an inviting galley. This particular Wellcraft was a 2000, thirty-eight footer, with a smooth riding deep-V hull. The master stateroom has a privacy door rather than a curtain and the twin MerCruiser 385 horsepower sterndrives would propel you nicely at thirty knots, without breaking a sweat.

"I like it Jim. If I get the house, give me a reasonable cash price on the boat. Throw in a year warranty on the motor and I think we can work something out. Sara, call Ms. Stutts for me. Let her know I'm interested and that I'd like to make her an offer. Give her my number and ask her to call. Meanwhile, I need to shuffle a few things around and line up some financing."

"You'd do cash?" Jim asked, eyebrows up.

"For the boat, yes. I think I can swing it."

"Cameron, you look excited. There's also something different about you. You've got a certain spark about you," said Sara.

"If I tell you I met someone, don't ask me a lot of questions. I will say, however, that I'd be buying the house for me. She is looking for an apartment in North Port.

"North Port? That's too far away! Jim, tell Cam that North Port is too far away."

"Well, is she awesome in the bedroom?" Jim asked.

"Jim!" yelled Sara.

"Well, yeah Jim. She is."

"Well then, North Port is too far away," he said and winked at Cam.

"Slow down guys. Let's just say the house would be big enough for the both of us in the future. I just think it's time to sell the condo or maybe rent it out as an investment and get some real property. I really love it here on the island."

"Well, we do too," said Sara, "and you'll feel like a Manasota Key native in no time."

We rode the golf cart back to their house. Jim and I made plans to talk at the end of the week. Sara said she would call Linda Stutts. Then, she added that whether I buy the house or not, my new friend and I were invited for cocktails and dinner as soon as it's convenient for all.

I took off in the Alfa, top down, more excited about the future than ever. Within a few miles, I passed a roadside policeman with his radar pointed directly at me. I wasn't speeding, but I suddenly realized, maybe for the first time in my life, I had a lot to lose.

The funny thing about total and complete happiness is you realize how much you have to live for. The entire time touring the house, I envisioned Chloe and me sharing it. Grilling out, entertaining guests, working in the yard, boating the gulf, and long walks on the beach at sunset. It's like, all of a sudden, I have someone else to live for ... and I only knew the half of it.

On my way back to Punta Gorda, I stop in North Port, following the directions Chloe texted me. Cruising through the apartment complex, I snap a few pictures with my phone and send them to Chloe. Leaving the complex, I turn south on Tamiami and relax in the open wind for my twenty-minute ride home.

Back home, I take a quick shower, then make my way to Mooseheads. I need a good cigar, a tall Blue Moon, and some good jazz to finish my night. After a dozen or more texts with Chloe and two Blue Moons later, I carefully make the less than a mile drive home.

Exhausted, I hit the couch shortly after midnight and didn't wake till 8:00 in the morning.

CHAPTER 47
JUNE 10, CHARLESTON SC

"Knabb, I'm meeting with the Director this afternoon. He's going to tell us to continue to take a back seat on the Florida bandit. Is there anything you can think of that can add to the argument for us to stay involved?" Rickard asked.

"I don't know sir. What time are you meeting him?"

"Two this afternoon. So you've got less than five hours to come up with something. Meet me here at 1:00 and please have something I can use."

"I'll see what I can do." Knabb went to his desk and got out his file. He also went back to some websites that he bookmarked. Clicking on a link, he's directed to four different profiles by criminal justice professors from four different universities. All have undertaken the task to predict the who, what, when, and where of the perp's next moves.

The first, a sixty-year-old professor from UCLA, says the following: Single white male. Age thirty to thirty-five. Lives alone. Not overly intelligent and most likely gets his ideas for his crimes by watching movies and fantasizing. Loves Oceans 11, The Italian Job, etc. Attended some college, but quit before finishing, complaining to his professors that school was "keeping him down." Has a decent job, probably in sales, which allows him to travel. His business itinerary is probably three months in advance, allowing him time to research possible targets. He lives in a flashy place. He wants to be a star. He wants to get caught. I put him living in L.A., San Diego, Dallas, New Orleans, or Miami, most likely L.A. or Miami. Likes the outdoors. One or both parents likely deceased.

The next profiler was a professor from UNC Chapel Hill: Single white male, early thirties. Classic narcissist. Did well in high school. Did well in college, but most likely dropped out. Pissed at society, thinks he deserves the best. Probably had a good job, paid well, and had respect. Fired from position and now makes his living illegally. My money is on he's a former bank employee. I'd also guess that he took drama in high school, maybe even had the lead (back to narcissism). Has minor experience in makeup/costumes. Dates multiple women, but unable to keep long-term relationships afloat. Lives alone. Owns/rents a house. Does not live in an apartment/condo. Probably well known in his community and active in community service. Wants the accolades of being a giver. Wants praise from others, awards. Most will think he comes from family money. He makes others think that he's made a few good "business deals" or "investments." Center of attention. People really like him at first, thinks he's obnoxious after some time. Flashy. Drives a sports car or a big SUV that screams "look at me." Can become dangerous/violent if he doesn't get his way. Lives in a small town, where he can be a big fish in a small pond. I'd place him west coast (California) or east coast (South Carolina down to Florida).

A professor from Florida State: White male, twenty-eight to thirty-six, of medium intelligence. Has common sense, will excel in sales, but fail in most any other profession.

Does pay attention to detail, might have majored or at least studied accounting, engineering, or political science. Divorced or single, no kids. One or both parents deceased. Only child or youngest if not. Wants extravagant lifestyle, but can't afford it. What he does buy he shows off. Flashy car, flashy women (most likely escorts). Wants all the attention. Wears jewelry. Has low profile by day, loud profile at night. Has simple sales job, possibly retail clothing or car sales or the like. Has decent income, but wants more. Most likely home is in the south, North or South Carolina, Georgia, or Florida. Although he loves the spotlight, I expect him to lay low for a year, due to recent publicity.

Knabb was most impressed with the fourth profile. It kind of fits what he was thinking and it made the most sense. It was from a tenured professor from UNLV:

White male, thirty to thirty-eight. Single, never married. College graduate, quite possibly a criminal justice major or pre-law. Self-assured, but not cocky. Very careful, deliberate, and a detailed planner. Successful in his profession, probably sales. High-dollar sales; high-end cars, stocks, yachts to aircraft. He knows his product. Has a taste of the good life, but it's just beyond his reach. Very popular and liked by many. Very good first impression. Probably an only child. Wants to be married, wants a long-term relationship. Wants/desires normal life with extras. Smart, will likely strike again within three months, thinking that another job so quickly will help prove it's not him. Lives in Florida. Will likely strike in Florida, again to prove to profilers and law enforcement that he doesn't live in Florida. Has a dollar goal and will retire once obtained (or caught). Will not take extra risks. Has likely "not" done numerous jobs due to certain risk factors. I'm willing to bet that he tried to write a fiction novel about the lead character robbing banks, but it failed, so he's making it his reality. I doubt he will get caught. If so, it will be extremely bad luck on his part or dumb luck on the investigators.

Later that same day. Manasota Key, Florida

I just had to drive by. I stop by the marina to check out Jim's boat again. It's locked up, but I wanted to take some pics with my phone. I've changed out of my suit and I'm wearing cargo shorts and a T-shirt. Behind the front seat of the Alfa and under the boot is a small cooler holding a six pack of Bud Light. I grab one and walk down to the boat.

I absolutely love it. And I want it. And the house too. I wander around the docks, checking out the other boats and admiring their sleekness. Back in the Alfa and up to the private beach, I pop out and take the short walk to the crystal white sand. This is it. Walking and thinking about the future, I realize I have to quit. I have to hang it up and go legit. I have to figure out a way to have the lifestyle I want without any more bank jobs. But I don't want to work. How can I do that?

Back in the car doing the speed limit on the back roads from Manasota Key to Gasparilla Island, I enjoy the sun on my face and the wind whipping around me, Bob Marley's greatest hits pumping, and a cold beer in the cup holder. I need to check something out before I make a decision about the house on Manasota Key. "Don't worry about a thing, 'Cause every little thing gonna be alright," I sing along with Bob.

1:15 p.m., same day Charleston, SC

"Sir, I think I might have something. Some intel you can use. I spent all morning looking at several different profiles of our Florida Bandit," Knabb said confidently. "One of the profiles is from a UNLV criminal justice professor. He painted the picture of our perp in a light that warrants a little more work on our part. Even though the profile predicts the next hit to happen in Florida, I think we can make the argument we have a decent lead on this guy."

Knabb recapped the profile that, unbeknownst to him, described Cam very accurately. Knabb had typed out a report with bullet points, pointing out several key factors placing Cam on the east coast.

Rickard liked what he heard and agreed with Knabb, although not as heartily. Rickard actually believed the accuracy of the profile, but didn't think the Director would buy into it.

"I still think the Director is going to tell us to go pound sand. Let the other states blow their budget closing the case. As the Director said earlier on the phone, 99 percent of the residents of South Carolina are not even aware of, nor do they remember, the Myrtle Beach bank robbery from four years ago. But we'll give it a shot Knabb." Senior Special Agent Rickard dismissed Knabb, checked his reflection in the window, straightened his tie, and left his office for the short walk to see his boss.

2:00 Gasparilla Island

As I pay the tollkeeper four dollars to get on the island, I reflect how I love the privateness of Gasparilla Island, also known as Boca Grande. The toll keeps out a lot of the riffraff. It's a small price to pay to not have to worry about police and crowded beaches.

As I cross over the first bridge, I'm amazed at the clear blue water. Boats are scattered about, some occupying fishermen. Others are out enjoying the sun, a few beers, and the warm swimming water. I absolutely love Manasota Key, but Gasparilla Island is a close second.

I drive through the little town square. There is a small grocery store, a bar, restaurant, dive shop, real estate agency, and several other boutique stores selling clothing and beach goods. I enter the real estate office, ringing a little bell triggered by the door, and am greeted by a stunning blonde, about five foot six, late twenties, blue eyes that one could get lost in for days, and dressed in a casual sundress accentuating her perfect little frame.

"Hi there. I'm Amanda Taylor. How can I help you today?"

"Hi Amanda. I'm Cameron Steele and very pleased to meet you. I want to inquire about some property on the island. Is there a master list of available properties?"

"Sure, Mr. Steele. My mom is showing a house on the other side of the island. I'm just answering the phones for her till I pass the real estate exam. We've got a golf cart out back. I'd love to show you around the island," she said smiling, with her left hand playing innocently with her shoulder-length hair.

"Please, call me Cam. I'm pretty familiar with the area. Thank you though for the offer. Does the master list include the prices?"

"Yes." She went and picked up a stapled portfolio off an end table and walked it over to me, pressing her body against my right side as she pointed to a few highlighted properties.

"Let me write my cell number on the top so if you have any questions, you can call me. Or if you need me for anything else," she said coyly, looking sheepishly at her feet.

"Thanks Amanda. I'll keep that in mind."

"Let me have your number and if something else comes up, I can call you."

"Okay." Sounds innocent enough. I give her my number and actually hope she doesn't call. She looks mighty tasty and she's dropping hints like egrets on a newly washed car.

"What's your price range?"

"I'd say $400 to $600. Maybe seven if it's a good deal."

"Not too many first or second row houses in that range. There are a few golf course houses under six. There are also some condos below three."

"No condos. That's what I have now in Punta Gorda. Thanks for your help Amanda."

"It was my pleasure Cameron Steele. I hope you enjoy our island and everything it has to offer."

I pause briefly at the door with my back to her, sport a little smile, and then continue out to my car. The island is a little over a mile wide, one and a half at its thickest, and about eight miles long. I drive south and pass the lighthouse and public beach access that I generally use when beaching. About a mile later, you come to the end of the island and the little state park. I crack open my second Bud Light and weave my way back toward the center of town, going down every side street and consulting the list Amanda provided. As she said, not much under a million.

Past the square and a little east are two houses listed, both above seven hundred. Heading back toward the toll, on the inlet side of the island, I find the golf course. There, I find a few villas priced anywhere from $450 to $600. I also come across the marina.

I love the feel of Gasparilla. It's about fifteen minutes off the beaten path, which is nice. But it also seems ... too quiet. Not enough action. Manasota Key feels more like home. More like ... the beach. Mentally, I make up my mind. If I'm going to buy, it's Manasota Key. And Amanda is way too tempting.

Same time Charleston, SC

"Why do you have such a bug up your ass about this case Rickard?" the Director asked.

"It's just crazy sir. From all records and research, when we put in our crime details nationwide, it looks as if the Bank of America job in Myrtle Beach is ground zero for this guy. He never comes back to South Carolina. He goes on a spree that so far has lasted almost four years and netted, we think, close to a million dollars," replied Rickard.

"But, what makes you think we have any chance of catching him? We don't know who he is, where he is. Hell, we're not even sure what he is."

"The report you have in your hands is one of many profiles the experts are pursuing. My staff and I feel that one is very accurate. Matter of fact, my staff and I came up with almost the same profile as the UNLV professor," Rickard commented confidently.

"Who the hell is this staff you keep mentioning? And you better not say Knabb!"

"Um, Knabb and a few others."

"The others being you, right?"

"Right sir, but it makes sense. Let me make a deal with you. I believe in the profile you're holding. The profile states a lot of stats, but the one that jumps off the page is the prediction that he'll hit Florida next. We, Knabb and I, believe he lives in Florida and that's why he hasn't done a job in his home state ... yet. I also think he's smart enough, resourceful enough, that he knows others will think he lives in Florida, unless he pulls a job there.

Here's my proposition. I think he will strike in Florida within three months, quite possibly sooner. I believe he thinks that will put the investigators' and profilers' focus off his trail in Florida. And it will, for most of the pundits. But not me. He knows that he needs to hit the state, but far from his hometown. I believe he lives in south Florida, possibly Miami. My prediction is he'll hit somewhere in the Panhandle. If this happens, I want you to allow us to stay on the case. If I'm wrong, we'll lay low and let others do the work, as you've said," Rickard stated.

"You're that confident, huh?"

"Yes sir."

The Director leaned back in his leather chair and looked toward the ceiling. After a few seconds, he looked at Rickard and said, "Well, I'm confident that YOU believe that's what will happen, but I'M confident it won't. Look Rickard, you're a smart man and a damn good agent. But, I think it's too much of a long shot. However, since the odds are in my favor, you've got a deal."

"Thank you sir."

"Don't thank me yet Rickard. Be careful what you wish for."

"Thank you nonetheless. You can keep the report. I'll be in touch if there are any updates."

5:00 p.m. Harpoon Harry's, Punta Gorda

"Hey Cam."

"Chloe! How are you?"

"Nothing new here, except I just gave my two weeks' notice! Oh Cam, I'm so excited and scared at the same time. I can't believe I'm really doing this. Florida, I'm on my way!" she exclaimed.

"Wow, you just made my day. When are you going to tell Colonial that you'll accept their offer?"

"I thought I'd call her tomorrow afternoon around 2:00."

"Awesome. Have you given any thought to hiring a moving company?" I ask.

"I called Penske and U-Haul. I think I'll save some of the relocation allowance and do it myself. How am I going to get my car there?"

"I've been thinking about that. Why don't I fly up there on Thursday, we get the truck Friday morning, load it up, and I'll drive the truck and you follow in your car Saturday morning. Sound like a plan?"

"Oh Cam, that's what I wanted, but didn't want to ask. That would be great. I'll stay with Mom and Dad the first few weeks till I find a place of my own. Dad said I can put my furniture in the extra garage."

"And of course, you can stay the weekends with me!" I said. "On the beach."

Later that evening, I relaxed with a few good friends, a perfect Cuban Cohiba, a Blue Moon, and a friendly game of Texas hold 'em at Mooseheads. I'm debating all the while my next move.

CHAPTER 48
JUNE II, PUNTA GORDA

The more I look at it, the more I think Tallahassee might be a good location for my next job. It's Florida, 350 miles from Punta Gorda, and in the Panhandle. It also has easy routes to and from. This will be a job I drive to. No flights.

Time is my problem. I'm flying to Maryland on June 26th, only two weeks from today. I've got a lot of work to do at the office and possibly buying a new house and a boat soon.

Online, I find Bank of Tallahassee off Third Street. It's a decent location, with a busy shopping center right behind it, with Target as an anchor. A large mall is located just a few miles south and the police department is north of town, eight miles away. It's about a six-hour drive to Tallahassee from Punta Gorda.

Later that day, Maryland

"Hey Mom!"

"Chloe! Hi baby. Getting excited yet?"

"You have no idea Mom. I can't wait to get there and start my new job and being closer to you and Dad."

"And ... what about Cameron?"

"He's great Mom. I know that it's a big step. I mean, Cam is great, but we haven't spent a lot of time together yet. It's always been a weekend here, a week there.

However, although we are quite different, we get along extremely well."

"If it's any consolation, your dad and I were complete opposites."

"Well, as you know, I like to go all the time. Going to school, nightlife in D.C. or Georgetown, concerts, that kind of stuff. Cam likes to spend his downtime relaxing on a beach. His idea of a night out is dinner dockside somewhere overlooking the gulf. He likes to go fishing. I hate fishing."

"Again Chloe, take that as a good thing. You can open his eyes to your world and he can show you his. You can have all the nightlife you want here. There is plenty to do."

"I know Mom. And I really like him. He's on the list."

"List? You have a list?" she laughed.

"Not really Mom. Let's just say if there is a list, Cam's name is the only one on it." Chloe gave her mom the details about the upcoming weeks. Chloe told her that Cam was flying up to help her move. This relieved her mom and was sure to take worry off of her dad's shoulders.

"Please call me after you speak with Colonial Bank and let me know how it goes."

"I will Mom. It's going to be today or tomorrow. Wish me luck."

"Good luck honey. Dad and I are so proud of you and can't wait to have you near. Love you dear."

"Love you too Mom. Kiss Dad for me."

"Will do. Bye now."

"Bye Mom."

CHAPTER 49
JUNE 14, SATURDAY 10:00 A.M. PUNTA GORDA

"Hey Jim. It's Cameron."

"Good morning Cam. What's up?"

"Well, I want to come see the house again today and I'd love to go out on your boat for a sea trial. Do you have the time? Is Sara available?"

"Sure, I've got the time. Sara is running errands and won't be home till around 3:00. Why don't you get here around 1:30. We'll take the boat out and I'll give you a rundown on her. We'll get back in time to meet Sara and she can show you the house again. Sound like a plan?"

"That's perfect, Jim. Thanks. I'll see you in a few hours." I rang off and spent the next hour cleaning the condo and doing laundry.

Later that day

With the Alfa loaded up to spend a few hours at the beach, I drive north on Tamiami toward Englewood Beach on Manasota Key. I'm quite early, so I take the backroads to the key once I pass Port Charlotte. Shortly before 1:00, I pull into Jim's driveway. He's inside, but hears me, since all his windows are open.

"Go inside the garage and grab us both a beer, then come on in," Jim yells through the open kitchen window.

I did just that. The garage fridge is full of all types of beer. I grab a Corona for me and an Amstel Light for Jim. Inside the house, I find him installing a fan over the stove.

"Hand me that Phillips-head right there. Thanks."

"Weekend project, huh?" I asked.

"Not really. If you buy out here and get the boat, you'll realize there is no such thing as a weekend project. It's all the time. Don't get me wrong. To me, it's a lot of fun. Tinkering with the boat, improving something in the house. I'm just lucky that Sara loves the yardwork. I cut the grass and run the weed eater, but she does the rest."

"About the boat, how much maintenance do you do?"

"It's all about keeping it running. The worst thing you can do to a boat is let it sit. You have to keep up with the fluids, oil, gas, hydraulic, and such. And keep everything clean. That's probably the most work, keeping it clean."

Jim finished tightening a few screws and hit a switch. The fan hummed to life. He flicked another switch and the light came on. Successful, he looked at me and said, "Let's go to the marina."

We took the golf cart to the marina and made our way to his slip and the Wellcraft. Jim took me below deck, giving me details on the galley, head, stateroom, aft bed, air-conditioning, and heat, not that I'd need it. Back above deck, he pulled up the floorboard and showed me the engines, batteries, and generator.

Jim started the twin engines and I untied us and jumped in. We cruise out into Lemon Bay, where he had her on plane in no time. We switched positions and he walked me through the trim tabs and throttles. I circled us back and gave up the controls once in sight of the marina.

Jim pulled us even with his slip, put the starboard prop in reverse, the port prop in forward, and expertly backed into his slip. Securely tied down, he did a quick spray down, removing the salt spray. Jim called Sara, who reported she would meet us at the house with the key in a few minutes. Jim and I had another beer and sipped as he took me through a systems check for shutdown procedures.

We met Sara, who already had the front door open.

"Hello? Sara?"

"Back here Cam," she called from the master bedroom.

'Thanks for letting me see it again," I said.

"This must mean you're interested," Sara smiled.

"I am. Do you think $405,000 is a fair offering price?"

"I do. The market is a little depressed right now and I also know that she is eager to sell. I think the reason it hasn't had many offers is its size. Most people who want a beach house want four or more bedrooms and capable of sleeping twelve or so people. A vacation house. This house is more the size of someone's pool house. A bungalow, cottage. A lover's retreat," Sara smiled, as she said this last remark.

"It feels right," I said. "I like the size. It's less than a half-mile to the marina and the sound. Once in the sound, you're less than ten minutes to the open waters of the gulf. It's not too pricey. Sara, will you call Ms. Stutts and grease the wheels a little? Set up a time that I can speak with her by phone and let me know."

"I'd be happy to Cam. Should I give her your cell number?" Sara asked.

"Yes. And tell her I can be reached at any time that suits her."

"Oh, I'm so excited Cam. Jim, are you excited?"

"Hell yeah! I'm going to sell my boat and buy a bigger one. And if our investments go down, I'll know exactly where to find you," Jim added, with a wink.

"And if the boat is a lemon," I said, "I'll know where to find you!"

Jim and I carted back to his house, where Sara tried to talk me into staying for a steak dinner. It took a lot of willpower to decline her invite and I jumped into the Alfa and headed back to Punta Gorda.

At home, I talked to Chloe about our future. We both seem to be on the same wavelength about the next few months. I have planned out so many things we are going to do and I couldn't be more excited. Too bad that the course of my life is about to be completely altered.

CHAPTER 50
JUNE 18, PUNTA GORDA

I have an appointment with Larry Rudisill of Hancock and Rudisill, a private mortgage company. In less than an hour with Larry, he had me approved for a $400,000 note. I want to put $50K down, mortgage $350, pay $50K for the boat, and get a low interest rate on the home loan.

Satisfied that I've got the financing available, I go to bank number two's deposit box and take out $60K, leaving almost $100K. I've got to deposit less than $10K in order to comply with banking regulations. In the next few days, I have to make several deposits in four different accounts at four different banks. This would be a problem if I did it often, but a few times shouldn't be a big deal.

At my office, my cell phone rings and I don't recognize the number. I answer in full name.

"Cameron Steele. Can I help you?"

"Mr. Steele, this is Linda Stutts. How are you today?"

I sit up in my chair and put on a less formal voice. "I'm great Ms. Stutts. Thanks for calling me."

"Please, call me Linda. And can I call you Cameron?"

"Yes, please."

"Excellent. I hear you may have an interest in my home on Manasota Key?"

"I do Linda. It's a quaint little cottage."

"Very well, Cameron. Is there anything I can tell you about the house? Any questions you might have?"

We discussed the house in detail. The age of the roof, exterminators, siding, air-conditioning and heat, the new appliances and warranties, the plumbing, and even the sprinkler system. Everything seemed to be in good order. We briefly discussed her price and I asked if I could call her on Monday and I'd give her an offer or pass. After agreeing to a 10:00 a.m. Monday morning phone call, I rang off.

Finishing work at 5:30 (yes, I occasionally have to work a full day), I close up my office and head to the Slip-Knot for dinner with a client. After a delicious blackened salmon platter and side salad, I make it an early evening and am home by 8:00. I'm asleep on the couch by 9:00 and crawl into bed around midnight.

CHAPTER 51
JUNE 20, PUNTA GORDA

I'm finishing up at the office shortly past noon when Chloe calls me. "Hi baby."

"Hey Cam. How's your day going?"

"No complaints. Trying to finish up here and get to Manasota Key as soon as possible. What about you?" I asked.

"Just now getting my lunch break. I've got to stop by the drug store, then I guess I'm going to pick up a salad from Wendy's. When I get to Florida, will I be able to take off work early and meet you at the beach?"

"Absolutely. Every day I hope."

"I don't know how you make a living," she remarked.

"I work hard from 6:00 a.m. till 1:00 almost every day, no breaks. That's almost seven hours straight. I just like to hit the beach afterwards."

"Well, let me go, but keep your phone on. I might try you in an hour or so, depending on how busy we get. You can send me another picture of the beach and remind me why I'm moving there."

"No problem. Consider it done. Bye dear."

"Later babe," Chloe said.

I gathered up my belongings, told my assistant to have a good weekend, and that I'd see her Monday. Having no clients to see today, I dressed casually in a pair of chinos and a green solid Tommy Bahama shirt. I'm in and out of the men's restroom, changing into my bathing suit like Superman and off to Manasota Key, all before 1:30.

I drop the top on the Alfa, remove the cooler from the small trunk, and place it behind the passenger seat. I retrieve the leather boot and cover the retracted top. It conceals the cooler and I turn north on Tamiami for the short drive to Manasota Key. I turn left at the crossroads that will take me by the Gasparilla Island turnoff to avoid the traffic. It's another great day in sunny south Florida and it screams to ride with the top down, sipping a cold one.

By 2:30, I'm sitting in my beach chair, toes in the sand at Englewood Beach on Manasota Key, less than one thousand yards from what may soon be my new home.

A few yards away from me, a nice-looking couple with their young son, probably around six, build a sandcastle. The father is showing his son how a little water will help firm up the sand and keep it in place. They are having the best time, while Mom is watching from her beach chair.

CHAPTER 52
JUNE 21 PUNTA GORDA

After my morning run and a quick shower, I boot up my laptop and google Tallahassee State Bank. Chloe pleasantly interrupts me with a phone call.

"What's up Chlo? I was just thinking of you."

"Aren't you sweet," she said. "I've been thinking about you since last night after 9:00."

"After nine," I said. "What happened at nine?"

"Well, let's see. I went to the bathroom."

"I like where this is going," I said.

"Hold on Cam. It's not what you think."

"Oh, okay. Go on."

"I went into the bathroom and I....took an early pregnancy test."

"Oh....wow." We both were silent for a few seconds. "And?"

"It was positive." Silence on both ends. "Cam, are you there?"

"Yeah. I'm here. Uh, are you sure it's positive?"

"It is. I went back to the pharmacy and bought another one. Same result. I slept on it, or rather didn't sleep, determining whether to tell you over the phone or wait until next week and tell you in person. I couldn't wait until next week."

"Are you okay? You feel alright?"

"Yeah, I'm fine. And ... how are you upon hearing this news?" Chloe asked.

"I'm, well, I guess surprised. And, honestly, I'm happy. I mean, we could have planned it better but ... "

"What should we do Cam? What do you want to do?"

"Well, I've never had this discussion before with anyone. I'm against the alternative, but I'll also respect your decision."

"I don't know what I think Cam. I've always wanted children, but I always thought I'd be married first. I'm so confused."

"Well, do you want my opinion?"

"Yes Cam. Please."

"I can't wait to be the father of our baby."

"Oh Cameron. You always know just what to say. Do you really think we can do this?"

"Why not. We're both adults. You're moving here. You're starting a new job and I'm sure we can work around it. We'd be great parents. You'll be an amazing mother."

"I'm so relieved that's what you want. It's what I want, as well. Oh my God Cam, we're going to be parents!"

"I know. Wow, this day surely changed directions quickly, in a good way."

"I can't wait till the 26th and you get here so I can wrap my arms around your neck. I need a big hug and reassuring words that everything is going to work out just fine. Oh my gosh. What am I going to tell my parents?"

"I'd say nothing yet. Let's get you down here and situated and figure everything out together," I said.

"Okay. I won't worry about that right now."

"Please don't. Like I said, we'll figure it out together."

"Together," said Chloe. "I like the sound of that."

Fifteen minutes later

"Hi. Is this Linda?"

"It is. Who's calling?"

"It's Cam Steele, from Punta Gorda."

"Yes Cameron. How are you doing today? Well, I hope."

"I am, thanks. I'd like to make you an offer on your house."

"That's great. I'm glad you decided to move forward. I wasn't expecting your call till Monday. What upped your schedule?" Linda asked.

"Just a little good news, that's all. I hope I haven't called at a bad time?"

"Not at all. Let's deal!"

"Okay. I'm willing to offer $410,000 on the condition we close Tuesday the 24th. I'll throw in an additional $3,000 cash for your moving expenses, if you can have it empty by Wednesday at noon. I noticed there were not a lot of belongings in the house, but I'm willing to pay, due to my wanting to move in by that afternoon.

"Wow, that's quick. Tell you what, make it $415,000 on the house and don't worry about the moving expense. And if we close Tuesday morning, I'll have everything out by the end of that day. Deal?"

"That's a deal Linda."

We made the necessary details about closing on Tuesday and exchanged numbers for our attorneys. We agreed to speak Monday at noon for any last details or changes.

"Thank you Linda."

"Thank you Cameron. Speak with you Monday."

I called Larry, my mortgage broker, and give him the details. It'll be a squeeze, but he said he could make it work.

I then call Jim and let him know the good news about the house, but not about Chloe's pregnancy. We hammer out a deal on the boat and plan to meet tomorrow at his house. I spend the rest of the day in a fog. I'm going to be a dad! I just bought a house and a boat! And tomorrow, I might have to make another purchase.

After an early dinner at Harpoon Harry's and an energy drink from the fridge, I settle in for research on the Tallahassee job. Per my personal calendar, I schedule the job for July 8th, the Tuesday after the 4th. This very well could be my last job. Probably not, but maybe.

CHAPTER 53
SUNDAY JUNE 22 MANASOTA KEY

Jim and I go over the details of the boat. We discuss the price, his personal warranty concerning the engine, and what accessories he wants to keep to put on his new boat. Sara met us a few minutes after I arrived, with chips and salsa and a bottle of Dom Perignon Champagne to celebrate my purchase, their sale.

Not being able to hold back my emotions, I spill the details about my plans to have Chloe move in, but still hold back about the baby. Sara asks all kinds of questions, some of which I answer and others I dodge or hedge. I explain that Chloe's parents live in Sarasota and that she accepted a position with Colonial Bank in Port Charlotte.

We all go to my new house (well, it's almost mine) and Linda opens up the door. I do a final walkthrough, this time spending extra time studying the spare bedroom. Sara notices and asks if I plan to make Chloe sleep here.

"I hope not. I just want to know how much furniture it will hold. Something like a small bedroom suite," I offer.

"How small?" Sara asks and smiles.

I try to dodge the question the best I can. "I don't know, just a queen bed and dresser. Maybe a chest of drawers or a desk."

"Or a crib?" Sara said.

"Sara! Stop bugging the man," Jim interrupted.

"It's okay Jim ... she's right."

"What?!" both exclaimed.

"She's right. I'm going to be a father."

"Oh my gosh Cam. That's awesome! Are you guys excited?" asked Sara.

"Well, it's been quite a shock, but yeah. I'm very excited. And I really think Chloe is the one. She's kind, funny, spontaneous, pretty, and from a good family. I think I'm going to ask her to marry me. Holy shit. That's the first time I've said that out loud. I never thought those words would ever come out of my mouth. And it actually felt good, comforting. I want to marry Chloe."

"Oh Cam, I'm going to cry."

"Me too," said Jim. "Me too."

"Shut up Jim." Sara punched him in the arm. "It's sweet."

"I'm just kidding Cam. It is sweet. Do you think she's going to say yes?" asked Jim.

"I guess we'll find out soon. Sara, I need another favor."

"Name it, Cam."

"Give me the name of a trusted jeweler."

CHAPTER 54
JUNE 23RD MONDAY CHARLESTON, SC

"Anything from last week, Knabb?" Rickard asked.

"I inputted the search criteria to include Florida, Georgia, Mississippi, and Alabama. I finished it about thirty minutes ago. Should have results any minute now. I'm not expecting anything, however. No Florida headlines jumped out to me this morning while I was checking the internet."

"Well," Rickard started, "He's going to strike. I can feel it. I don't know what it is, I just feel it. What say you Knabb?"

"Don't know sir. I just don't know. Don't know if he's smart enough. It's a two-sided question: Is he smart enough to do a job in Florida to prove that he doesn't live there or is he smart enough not to hit Florida, knowing that that's what the profilers expect him to do? Either way, it's smart."

"So," Rickard responded, "what you are saying is it doesn't matter. Either way, we still think he lives in Florida."

"Unless he pulls a job, say, on the west coast or up north in a state he hasn't hit yet. What if he does that sir?"

"He won't. And if he does, we take a back seat on the whole Florida Bandit thing. That, I promised the Director. Not to worry Knabb, he'll hit. He can't help himself."

Just then, Knabb's desk phone rang. The search report was complete. No matches.

"Not yet sir."

CHAPTER 55
TUESDAY JUNE 24 PUNTA GORDA

I wake up just before 6:30 and hop out of bed to take my morning run, but I can hardly move. I spent all day yesterday loading my furniture in a U-Haul out of the condo. I grabbed a couple of the landscapers from the high-rise next door and offered them $100 each for two hours of work. They helped me from noon till 2:00 during their lunch break and moved most of the heavy, bulky items. I still made two dozen trips up and down the stairs, loading things I could carry. I made arrangements for the same two guys to meet me at the Manasota Key house later that evening. The hell with a run. I shit, shower, and shave and I'm off to see Linda to close on the house.

At 2:30, I'm at Harpoon Harry's, enjoying a bacon double cheeseburger, fries, and a cold Corona Light. I'm sitting in my booth, our booth, looking out over the harbor. I look left and see my condo and smile, remembering the good times I made there. Then, I smile even wider, thinking of all the good memories Chloe and I are going to create in Manasota Key. On the table sits the new house key. I fondly caress it and feel, complete.

The sun has set on Manasota Key and my help and I have finished unloading the U-Haul. I lock up the house and return the truck to Punta Gorda and pick up the Alfa. An hour later, I'm in my new house, sitting on the back deck enjoying a cold beer, exhausted. I text Chloe.

"I'm so excited about our future."

She reponds, "Can't wait for US to be in your arms again."

I'm so tired, I don't notice her text till the morning when I wake. The next few days are a complete blur. Sara called her jeweler and I met with him Wednesday morning, purchasing a 1.4 karat, princess cut diamond ring set in platinum. I stopped by bank number two and pulled out $25,000. The ring was $12,000. Then, I go by bank number one to get my credit cards and fake driver's licenses. I spend several hours at the office, making calls and attending to some paperwork that needs my signature. My assistant has made most of my clients' trades under $20,000. The others, above that amount, need my password to execute. I fill several large trades, so June will be a good month for commissions.

In Maryland, we pack Chloe's belongings in the rented Penske truck with the help of a next door neighbor couple, John and Eric. The next morning, before the sun peaked over the horizon, Chloe and I are driving to Sarasota. Unbeknownst to her, we're actually headed to Manasota Key.

A few hours shy of Sarasota, I phone Chloe, who is a few hundred yards ahead of me, and let her know the truck needed fuel. We take the next exit and gas up. I inform Chloe that I'll lead the way and I've got to make a very important stop at a client's house. Chloe calls her parents and tells them we will arrive a little later than previously scheduled.

About a half-hour from Manasota Key, I phone Chloe. "You getting excited?"

"I'm excited, but also extremely tired Cam. Couldn't this have waited till tomorrow?"

"I'm sorry Chloe. My client called me a few hours ago and told me his mother was very sick. He asked me to stop and notarize some important documents in the event she doesn't make it through the night."

"Oh, I'm sorry Cam. Why didn't you mention that earlier when we stopped for gas?"

"It's no big deal. He's just one of my better clients. It shouldn't take me but a few minutes and we've made good time. We'll be at your parents in little over an hour or so."

"Where are we going?" she asked.

"A little island called Manasota Key. It's very quaint and has a small beach town feel. You'll like it." I kept Chloe on the phone the remainder of the drive. I got her talking about baby names and she wouldn't stop.

As I pulled up into the little driveway, I said, "We're here. Come on in." Then, I hung up.

I got out of the truck, stretched, and waited for Chloe. She grabbed my hand and asked who my client was.

"Come on. I'll show you." We walked up to the front door. "That's strange. No lights are on."

"Surely they're home, Cam. Please don't tell me we went forty minutes out of the way and your clients aren't even home!"

I walk up to the front door and ring the doorbell. I then reach into my pocket, pull out the key, insert it, and open the door.

"Hello? Anybody home?"

"Cam, what are you doing?"

"It's okay. Come on. Jim? Sara? Anyone here?" I ask. No answer. I turn on a light and we both look around. My flat screen TV, couch and matching chair, plus the ottoman sit in the small den.

"Cam, this stuff looks like yours."

"What? No. Really?"

"Cameron, is this your house?" she asks as she takes a few steps, looking around at the place.

"I was hoping it could be our house," I say.

Chloe turns around and I'm down on one knee, jewelry box open in my left hand. "Chloe, will you do me the honor, the pleasure, the pure joy of taking my hand in marriage? Will you marry me?"

Tears running down her cheek, she stood there, not saying a word. She has one hand over her mouth and the other reaching for the ring.

"Chloe, will you marry me please?"

"Yes Cameron. Yes."

We went straight to bed.

CHAPTER 56
SUNDAY JUNE 29 MANASOTA KEY

After breakfast, we get started unloading the truck. We are both so happy. Jim and Sara stopped by with a housewarming gift and Jim helped me get a few bigger items in the house. Chloe and Sara worked on organizing the kitchen.

After lunch, we went to Chloe's parents' house, where she told them about my proposal and her accepting. She held back the pregnancy. They both were excited and Chloe and her mom started planning a sunset wedding on Siesta Key Beach. Her mom wanted it planned for next year in March. Chloe told her we decided not to wait and are shooting for October. The 15th fell on a Saturday in October and that day just felt right to both of us.

We left Sarasota and returned to Manasota Key. I told Jim and Sara that we would meet them at the marina an hour before sunset for a nice, relaxing cruise to top off the day. At their boat, Sara and Chloe quickly started to have their own conversation about the wedding plans. I earlier told Jim to mention to Sara to not let Chloe know the boat was ours. I'd do that later.

Jim, out of earshot of the ladies, who were below deck, walked me through a small checklist before shoving off. He let me helm the controls. Barely out of sight of the marina, Chloe popped her head up from below and offered Jim and me a beer. Seeing me at the controls prompted her to say I looked good behind the wheel. She also commented about the cute galley below. She asked when we were going to get one.

"Slow down pumpkin," I said with a smile. "We've got some pretty big purchases still to come."

We hit the gulf and head south toward Gasparilla Island. I give the controls over to Jim and look out over the beautiful, calm gulf. Chloe nudged up behind me and slipped her arms around my waist.

"What are you thinking about Cam?"

"Just how happy I am. Then, I think of the little one you're carrying and think, wow, I'm going to get even happier." I look at Chloe and hold her face with both my hands. "Duchess, I'm the luckiest man on earth."

"And I'm the luckiest woman."

We kiss gently. We cruise around Gasparilla Island, dock at the local marina, and head on foot to the raw oyster bar a short stroll away.

After a bucket full of oysters and beer, Chloe has a chef's salad and bottled water. We take the scenic long way back to the marina. Boarding the boat, Chloe whispers to me if we could get a boat someday? "Possibly" was my reply.

On the ride back to Manasota Key, Jim pointed out several points of interest. There were a few other boats on the water and we waved at each passerby. Jim explained the channel markers and landmarks to help inform me of the safest route. There are many sandbars throughout the gulf beaches and one constantly has to be aware of your depth monitor to avoid running aground. We watched as the sun dropped into the ocean, experiencing the unique green flash so often missed by most. No one said a word for several minutes, then Chloe turned to me and said, "I want to experience this with you daily."

"I'll see what I can do." I smile and she kissed me on the forehead.

We arrive at our marina, back in, and tie down. I help Jim wipe down the boat, while Sara and Chloe disappear below deck to clean the galley. When the girls returned on deck, Jim and I were discussing last-minute details.

"What do you think Chloe? You like it?" I ask.

"Like what, the boat? The house? The lifestyle? Yes, yes, and yes," she responded.

"Well then Jim, you've got a deal. We'll take it!" I stick my hand out and Jim takes it.

"Awesome Cam. I'll get the paperwork ready. As far as I'm concerned, it's yours now. Legally, it'll be yours Wednesday, Thursday at the latest."

"That'll be fine. Chloe, what should we name her?"

"Name what....the boat?"

"Yeah. Name our boat?"

"I don't know Cam. What do you think?"

"I kind of like 'Licensed to Steele'."

"Steele, like your last name?" asks Chloe.

"Yep. Do you like it?"

"It has a nice ring to it."

Sara had disappeared below deck, brought up three Coronas and a bottled water, and proposed a toast.

"To new friends. A new family, new house, and to sunshine."

"Yes, to sunshine," I reiterated, winking at Chloe.

"To sunshine," Chloe agreed.

The next couple of weeks came and went. Chloe and I shopped for whatever we were missing for the house and the boat. We furnished the nursery with furniture purchased at a boutique baby shop on St. Armands Circle at Lido Beach. Chloe started her new job at Colonial Bank in Port Charlotte. I made final plans on the Tallahassee job for July 8th. We spent every other evening on the boat out in the gulf just exploring. Jim and Sara tagged along a couple of times. They were a few weeks out from finalizing their new purchase and Sara was trying to keep Jim from spending more than $150,000.

One night, Chloe and I were shopping for groceries at the local Publix grocery store. She sent me to get some bread while she kept to her list, picking out fresh vegetables. I was wandering around aimlessly and found myself browsing the potato chips section. Searching the endless options for the best deal, I reach for the Lay's Hot & Spicy Barbecue, grab two bags, and turn around to see Chloe with her right hand over her heart and her left cupping her mouth. I look at her confused.

"Chloe. Are you ok? You look like you've seen a ghost. Chloe? Can you hear me?"

"Yes," she whispered.

"What is it honey?"

"It's nothing. I'm okay."

"No you're not. You're shaking. Are you hurt? Is it the baby?"

"No. It's nothing. Really Cam, it's nothing."

"Bullshit Chloe. Don't block me out. Tell me, so I can help."

"No, you'll get mad," she said, wiping back a tear.

"Mad? Why would I get mad, dear? Chloe, you're not making any sense. Tell me what it is. I promise I won't get mad."

"It was him."

"Him who?"

"Him. You. You know, him."

"Chloe, I still don't know what you're talking about."

"Just now, when I saw you down the aisle, you look exactly like the bank robber."

"Honey, we've been through this. It's okay. Calm down. You know it wasn't him. You know I'm not him. It's just a mild resemblance. Based on what you told me, we are about the same height and build. But, didn't you say he had blue eyes?"

"Yes. But at certain angles, you look just like him. I don't know. It's just some stupid trick my mind is playing on me. Things are going so great with you and me that my brain just has to sabotage it. Nothing can be this good. Something bad has to happen."

"No Chloe, it doesn't." I take her by the waist and look deep into her eyes. "This is going to be great. We, and I do mean we, have a beautiful little beach cottage, my career is going strong, we've got a baby on the way, and a sunset beach wedding to plan. Chloe, look at me. I love you. I'm not going to let anything happen to you. To us. I promise."

"You better promise Cam. I can't do this by myself. It's just, nothing like this has ever happened to me before."

"Hell, I hope not," I chuckle.

"Cam, you know what I mean. It's just, things are going too good and my brain is trying to prepare me for a bombshell. Trying to warn me of something. I don't know. I'm being paranoid. It must be the hormones."

"Chloe, this is your new normal. I'm going to make you the happiest woman which, in turn, is going to make me the happiest man. Then, we will become the perfect family once our child is born. I'm going to do everything to make this new life of yours not a fantasy, but reality."

"Cam, look at me and promise this is real. That we are real. Don't you back down on me. No surprises."

"None Chloe. You can trust me. This is me. Laid-back, financial adviser, beachgoing, beer drinking Cameron Steele. I am what you see. I love you Chloe. You love me. We love our child to be. We're going to live the dream."

"Okay Cam. You're right. And I do love you and can't wait to have your baby. Everything seems to be happening so quickly."

"Because God wants it to."

"God wants it to, huh? You're right. Can we go home now? I don't feel like staying here."

"Let's go."

We leave the cart in the center of the aisle. At home, thirty minutes later, I lead Chloe to the bedroom and convince her to lay down for a nap. Once she's asleep, I slip down to the marina to work on the boat. I'm back an hour later and she's still sleeping. I grab a few steaks from the freezer, thaw them in warm water, and wait for my duchess to awaken.

CHAPTER 57
FRIDAY, JULY 4TH MANASOTA KEY

I wake without disturbing Chloe and sneak out of the bedroom. A few minutes later, I'm jogging the beach. This is the life I want. At my halfway point, I turn around and head south toward home. I stop and look out over the gulf. It's so peaceful. There are a few people walking about getting a little exercise before the heat blankets the beach. The gulf water is at a literal standstill. A couple of private fishing boats a few hundred yards offshore are lazily crossing the horizon.

I almost start to cry. I've got so much now. That also means I have a lot to lose. Having a strong inner battle about the Tallahassee job, I start to run again. My mind is in overdrive and the only thing that makes any sense is to pound the sand until my thighs burn. Do I need this next job, the money? Not really. I've got enough saved to last me ten years, so why am I planning my next heist? I pick up the pace. My lungs beg for more oxygen. Is it the rush, the thrill of getting away with it? The feeling of being alive? Doesn't Chloe give me all those feelings and then some? Absolutely.

I rationalize that I have to do the Tallahassee job to throw investigators off my track, to prove I don't live in Florida. A deluge of sweat is pouring out of my body. Am I lying to myself? If I'm caught, I'll lose everything, including Chloe, the love of my life, my soulmate. I'm dizzy. Shit, what do I do? As I ask, I already know the answer.

I look up and I'm at the end of the island. I'm at least a mile past my cutoff toward home. I'm out of breath and about to collapse. What the fuck am I running from? Back home, I strip down and rinse off under the back porch outdoor shower. The water is cold and I feel like I'm emitting steam. I shake my head like a dog and wrap a towel around my waist. I enter the kitchen from the deck and find Chloe cutting up cantaloupe and watermelon for breakfast.

"It looks like a gorgeous day to be on the boat Chlo. The gulf is perfectly calm. I say we hit Gasparilla till about 4:00, then go south to Harpoon Harry's. We can grab dinner and do a little shopping, then anchor in the harbor to watch the fireworks. We'll be back home by midnight. Sound like a plan?

"Sounds like a long day, but I think I can keep up. Did you run it by Jim and Sara?"

"Yep. Both are gung-ho. Jim wants to really open her up today and see how she runs. He wants to give me a few lessons on working the trim tabs and motor angle for the smoothest ride."

"Okay. I'll run to the store and get us some lunch supplies while you get the boat ready."

"Perfect. Meet us at the marina at noon. Love you," I say as she walks out the door.

"You too," as the door closes behind her.

It was a perfect fourth of July. The boat performed perfectly and the weather was straight out of a dream. Jim brought snorkels and fins for everyone and we used them anchored near Boca Grande. It was the first time Jim and Sara had dined at Harpoon Harry's. I pointed out my condo from our usual table. It appeared that my neighbors were having a cookout in the backyard overlooking the harbor. About twenty or so people were enjoying themselves, eating, drinking, and playing with a dog.

Dinner and cocktails, except for Chloe, were enjoyed by all. Afterwards, we strolled through the shops of Fisherman's Village, buying a T-shirt and a "beach house" decorative sign to put up in the new house. The fireworks viewed from the harbor, with Chloe by my side, were magical.

The evening was capped off by an incredible moonlit cruise home. Jim and I were at the controls and Sara was below deck taking a nap. Chloe was spread out on the lounge behind us, looking radiant and softly sleeping.

At the marina, we tied her down and said goodnight to Jim and Sara. Chloe and I were going to stay for a bit, she down below cleaning and myself up top wiping down. Sara wanted to help, but Chloe insisted they go home.

I go below deck and take Chloe in my arms, kissing her bottom lip softly. I make my way slowly to her neck, up to her ear, and return to her lips. Reaching around her back, I undo her bikini top, then pull her shorts and bikini bottoms down. She kicks out of them and pulls my shorts off as well. She kisses my chest and moves downward to my waist. She takes me in her mouth and works me into an immediate erection. She keeps me happy for several minutes till I tell her it's her turn.

I back her toward the state room and push her gently down with her legs hanging off the end. Now, it's my turn to taste her. I bury my face in the warm, wet folds of her sex, as her hands grasp my hair. I'm harder and thicker than ever and I try to stay calm for the final act.

"Now baby," breathed Chloe.

I laid atop her, then rolled her over, so she was on me. She picked herself completely off me, then lowered herself and guided me into her. Her warmth nearly takes me over the edge. Chloe rocked her hips toward me and back, slowly lifting, then dropping, to feel the full length of me. Just before losing myself, Chloe stops and tightens and shakes her head.

She rolls me over, with me on top, and pulls my buttocks toward her over and over, both of us gasping with each thrust. She digs her nails in my back and I grab the back of her hair. She motions for faster movement and I keep pace as long as possible, until I explode inside her. Seconds later she gets hers and cums, as well. We lay still with me on top of her, breathing quickly.

CHAPTER 58
JULY 6, SUNDAY MANASOTA KEY

I've got the Tallahassee details finalized. I told Chloe last week about my three-day business trip to Jacksonville. I'll leave tomorrow morning around 5:00 for a 10:30 meeting, I explain to her. I chose Jacksonville as my lie because it's close to the same distance away as Tallahassee. If everything goes as planned and I'm not sitting in the local jail, I should return home late Wednesday evening. She's got training with the bank till the eighteenth of this month at several different branch locations.

We spend the afternoon working around the house. Around 2:00, we pack a small cooler and walk to the beach. After some sun, a good swim, some innocent necking, and a little heavy petting, we make our way back home. Out back, under the outdoor shower, we take the heavy petting to the next level. A good ten minutes later, we dry each other off and journey to the kitchen for an early dinner.

That evening, I pack for my trip. I have to pack two suits and accessories for appearance sake, including ties and dress shoes. I double check the internet for directions and triple check my IDs and credit cards. With the exception of a few minor things I keep on hand, I'll pick up a few disguises and a rental car on the way.

Before retiring for the night, Chloe apologizes for the scene at the grocery store from a few days ago. I assure her everything is fine and she blames it on her hormones. As a heavy rain comes down, I spoon Chloe as she gently falls asleep. Before I follow suit, I whisper, "I love you Chloe. And I love you too little one," as I rub her belly.

CHAPTER 59
JULY 7TH

On the way to Tallahassee, I go through Tampa. My internet research has pointed me to Ray's Costume and Military Clothier just outside downtown. After spending about an hour and $130 cash, I'm out the door and off to my second stop at the Tampa Airport for a rental car. Shortly before noon, I'm driving an impressive Ford Taurus toward my final destination. By nightfall, I've checked into my hotel room. I'm going over my checklist when Chloe calls.

"Hi Chloe," I answer.

"Hey handsome. How were your meetings?"

"Easy breezy. I've already had dinner and I'm chilling in my room watching TV. What're you up to?"

We small talk about our day. I'm lying and she's telling the truth. She makes me promise to call her when I return from my morning run. I ring off and get back to my details, walking through the steps one more time. Satisfied with my preparations, I crawl into bed, set the timer on the TV, and dose off to the local news.

CHAPTER 60
JULY 8TH CHARLESTON, SC 9:00 A.M.

"Do you feel that Knabb?"

"Feel what Captain?"

"That feeling ... like something important is about to happen."

"Can't say that I ... "

At that moment, a ladder with a 275-pound HVAC repairman atop it falls directly onto Knabb, the extra large man cushioning his fall with Knabb's body. Knabb falls backward, striking the back of his head on the corner of a desk, then falling, face forward, with his forehead breaking the fall with a sick, wet slapping sound.

Rickard rolled him over on his back. "Holy shit Knabb! Are you okay?" asked Rickard. The repairman was holding his knee beside Knabb's lifeless body, but appeared to be fine. Knabb, on the other hand, wasn't moving. "Knabb!" Rickard checked his neck for a pulse and found one. A little blood trickled on the floor beneath his head. Rickard slapped him at midstrength in the face. "Knabb!"

Knabb opened his eyes, blinking several times.

"Can you hear me Knabb?!" Rickard yells.

"Fuck yeah. Stop shouting," he answered.

"Good, good. Now, can you tell me how many fingers I'm holding up?" Rickard displayed two fingers in the classic peace sign two feet from his face.

"Yeah, Thursday Coach," he replied.

"What?"

"Thursday Coach. Now put me back in the game. It's the fourth quarter."

Rickard recalled a story Knabb told him about his high school football days. Knabb was small, but quick and not afraid of anyone. A backup safety, he was called off the bench when the starter, Mick Foltz, injured his right knee in the first half. Knabb was the last man to beat when Red Denton, a 190 pound solid rock of a tight end, was racing toward him full throttle. Knabb lowered his shoulder and Red leveled him, knocking him back five yards. Knabb gets up like a drunken fraternity boy and walks over to the visitors' bench and takes a seat. The other team's doctor asks him if he knew where he was. "Thursday Coach" was his only answer.

Rickard chuckled from the memory. "Just sit tight Knabb. Jennifer, get me the first aid kit from the breakroom."

"It's 4th quarter coach!"

"I know dammit, relax. I took a timeout."

Jennifer brings the kit and Rickard gets out the smelling salts, opens the package, and places it directly under Knabb's prominent nose. He pulls his head violently back and to the side.

"What the hell was that?" he asked.

"Smelling salts Knabb. You were out cold."

"Damn, it smelled like your mom's douchebag."

The few agents that had gathered around the commotion tried not to laugh, but were unsuccessful.

"I'm going to let you get away with that one. Just once though," Rickard replied.

"Everyone, get back to work," he said to the others, still suppressing their laughter.

Same day 1:00 p.m. Tallahassee

I go through the motions once more before I get dressed. The props needed to pull this off are displayed on the bed. Earpiece, hat, laminated ID badge, walkie-talkie, and the remaining minor pieces to complete my disguise. I apply a fake tattoo of a spider on my neck, exposing the top half of its body above my shirt collar. I draw a dark mole on my upper lip, a la Elle Macpherson. I tear up bits of toilet paper and place them between my cheek and gums Marlon Brando Godfather style, then spray my hair silver gray. The last step before getting fully dressed are the light blue contacts. I suddenly remember my fingerprints. I can't use gloves on this job, so I've purchased some super glue. After coating each finger and letting it dry, I dress and leave the room precisely at 2:30, one hour before contact.

2:30 Charleston

Knabb is holding a cold pack to the back of his head. The first thought was a concussion, but since he didn't throw up it was probably just a disorienting blow. Eight hundred milligrams of Advil a few hours ago have kicked in and he's feeling better.

"How long was I out?" he asked.

"About ten minutes. No big deal."

"Ten minutes! Just laying there?"

"Yeah," Rickard replied.

"Why was my belt undone?" he asked.

"How the hell should I know?" Jennifer thought it would be funny to undo his belt and make him wonder why and how. It worked.

"Whatever. So, what was that feeling you got? You know, right before tiny fell on me."

"You really want to know?"

"Not really. But you're going to tell me anyway."

"I just had this feeling that he was about to strike. Sit down Knabb, before you fall over. Good. He always strikes on Tuesday, Wednesday, or Thursday. I don't believe he'd try the week of the fourth. It kind of makes me think sometime this week. He wants to do it." Rickard stands and runs his fingers through his thinning hair. "I bet he's practically going through withdrawals."

"Calm down sir. We'll get him."

3:15 Tallahassee

I feel like I'm having withdrawals. I couldn't stop shaking earlier, but now I'm in the zone, dopamine tickling my brain. I park the rental on the side of the bank directly in front of the branch manager's office window and enter the front door.

"Hi everyone," I say. "Is Mrs. Thornton here?"

"Um, no sir. She's in an all-day conference and won't return until tomorrow. Is there something I can do for you?"

"You can, Ms ... "

"Call me Tina," the nearly six foot brunette beauty responded.

"Okay Tina. I'm Bud Fox with the Tallahassee Fire Department. I'm here for your annual checkup. I need to inspect your fire extinguishers, exits, and fire alarms." Scanning the room I say, "All your faces look new, except for you Tina."

"You are correct. I was here last year when you stopped by. I'm now the senior teller," she beamed.

"Excellent. Then you know the routine."

"Sure do," she replies. "Help yourself. You know where the breakroom is in the back. There's an extinguisher back there, along with our exit map on the wall by the back door."

"Thanks Tina. I'll only be a sec." I walked to the back, find the extinguisher, and make a motion to inspect it in the event someone was watching the camera monitor. Walking back out to the lobby, I press the "talk" button on the walkie-talkie. It makes the "shhs-cka" feedback sound and I can barely make out the distinct sounds of a police conversation. "I also need to check behind the line for obstructions."

"Come on back Bud," Tina said, opening the half door for me.

"Thanks dear. Just for you, I have a small, personal micro-extinguisher. It's great for your car or the kitchen." I remove the extinguisher from my belt. It's coated in rubber, so that plus the superglue should make it harder to detect my prints. It looks like a double-sized personal mace container. "Just twist the top, aim, and pull the trigger, aiming for the base of the fire," I say, handing it to her.

"Thanks Bud. That's kind of you."

"While I'm here, I need to cash a check. Can you do that?"

"Sure thing," Tina responded.

I handed her the note and a bag: This is no joke. Open your first and second drawers. Give me all the bills. No bait money. No dye packs. Then, open your bottom vault. Give me all the bills. Do not trigger the alarm. The fire extinguisher I just gave you is a bomb and I can set it off with my cell phone. My radio is a police scanner and I'll know if you press the silent alarm. Stay calm and hurry.

The other tellers are helping customers. Tina reads the note, looks up at me with half a smile, and looks back at the piece of paper and says, "Really?"

"Really. And hurry. Do as the note says and you will not be hurt."

Tina looks at me again, then opens her top drawer. She cleans it out and moves to the next one. She looks at me and tells me she needs to kneel down to get to her vault.

"Go ahead. No alarms, okay?"

"Okay."

She's back up in less than fifteen seconds. She hands me the bag and I remind her the extinguisher bomb is right behind her. After asking her for the note back, she complies and I put my index finger over my puckered lips, wink at her, turn, and walk out.

A policeman pulls in as I'm walking out the front door. He makes eye contact with me and we share a nod. I tighten up my sphincter in order to not shit my pants and stroll toward the rental. In the car, I calmly start her up, reverse out of the space, and leave the parking lot before the officer leaves his cruiser. In my rearview mirror, I spot the officer casually enter the bank.

I proceed to the Super 8 Hotel just minutes away. In my room, I discard my disguise, including the contacts, and dump everything in a grocery store plastic bag, tying the handles into a knot. I put on a suit, tie, and dress shoes and slick my hair back, resembling a young Gordon Gekko, putting the money bag in my briefcase. Just thirteen minutes after leaving the bank, I exit the hotel's back door.

Soon after, I'm driving east on I-10, doing exactly the speed limit. I bet the police don't know what the fuck is going on! Greed is good.

4:08 p.m. Charleston, SC

"Knabb, what the fuck is going on?" yelled Rickard.

"I'm not sure sir, but I just got word of a 3:30 robbery in Tallahassee."

"How?"

"How what?" Knabb asked.

"How did you hear about it forty minutes after it happened?"

"Three weeks ago, I sent an email to the fifteen top precincts in upper Florida, asking them to call me if something comes up matching our perp's M.O. I told them to be especially alert at 3:30. A Tallahassee patrolman was entering the Tallahassee State Bank when a perp walked out disguised as a fire marshal. According to a bank employee, that same person was there for their annual inspection when he robbed them."

"And!"

"And he walked out, nodded to the officer, and escaped undetected with over $30,000."

"Fuckin' A," Rickard sighed.

"Yeah. Fuckin' A."

"Shut the fuck up Knabb."

Same day, North of Tampa

The AM news station had a brief report about the robbery, but no details. I decided to drive to downtown Tampa and get a room. I told Chloe that I'd be home tomorrow around sunset, so I've got time to kill. I splurge a little and book a room at the Hilton Tampa, using the fake ID and paying cash. Minutes later, I'm sitting on the bed counting my money, $31,660. Not bad. Paid for the ring. I spend the rest of the evening wandering on foot through downtown Tampa, checking out the sights. I enjoyed a Delmonico steak, rare, with a side of crispy shiitake mushrooms brian and a bottle of 1986 Livio Felluga Merlot at Bern's Steak House. Damn, I could get used to this level of dining.

On my stroll back to the Hilton, Chloe calls and I lie about my day. I tell her the meeting was boring and that I hope to be home tomorrow around 7:00. Maybe we can take the boat out for a little sunset cruising. She likes the idea and we make plans to talk in the morning. In my room, I grab a Heineken from the mini fridge. I turn on the TV and find an episode of Law & Order. Kicked back on top of the covers, I drift off before the Order started.

Same day 8:00 p.m. Charleston

"Do you think this could be him, sir?" asked Knabb.

"You bet your ass I do."

"Could this be his last?"

"Not on your life Knabb. It's in his blood. It's who he is. He doesn't want to admit it, but he can't stop. If I had to guess, I bet he's financing a bad habit."

"Drugs?"

"Not hardly. He would have screwed up by now. He's too levelheaded and precise to be strung out. My guess is women or gambling, maybe both."

"To me, that would put him down in Miami. Plenty of women and plenty of gambling, both legit and underground," added Knabb.

"My thoughts as well Knabbster. But that doesn't give us shit. Did those numbnuts in Tallahassee get anything? A latent print, half a license plate number, any fucking thing?"

"Nothing that I know of. I'll check with my contact in the morning."

"Do that Knabb, because we have no idea when or where he'll strike next. But I tell you this much, he will."

CHAPTER 61
SATURDAY, OCTOBER 15TH SIESTA KEY BEACH

It's an unforgettable day in southwest Florida. The temperature is in the mid-seventies, not a cloud in the sky, and there's a soft breeze coming off the gulf. It's 6:45, sixteen minutes till sunset. Last night's rehearsal dinner was perfect. Chloe's parents had suggested Michael's on East. After a test dinner a few months ago, they reserved the back room for the occasion.

For the dinner, I donned an off the rack charcoal gray, pinstriped Brioni suit, classic white Brooks Brothers French cuff dress shirt, accompanied by a Hermes coral print silk tie, and cushioned by a sleek pair of black Mezlan Italian Bilbao shoes with matching leather belt.

Chloe was ultraelegant in a black Givenchy asymmetric ruffle, little black dress complimented by a Bianca Pratt black diamond choker that I gave her earlier that day. Her bohemian waves hairstyle fell just below her shoulders and she pulled it all off in three-inch black Manolo Blahnik heels. The cut of the dress accentuated every curve of her delicate figure and her refined legs showed off the pumps. She looked sensational. A duchess. My duchess. She has never looked more radiant. Until now.

She's walking across the sand down the aisle escorted by her father. We decided that the rehearsal party was our formal night. The beach wedding would be considerably more casual. Chloe is wearing a short vintage white wedding dress in tulle and chiffon. It had a scalloped edge along the V-neckline with long lace sheer sleeves. I decided on Tommy Bahama khakis with matching vest over a white linen shirt. We are both barefoot.

After our vows, we kiss and go back to Michael's on East for the reception. The next ten days we spend traveling throughout Italy and return to Manasota Key. With a few days to spare before we both return to work, we spend the weekend opening wedding gifts and writing thank you notes.

CHAPTER 62
NOVEMBER 25TH SARASOTA, FLORIDA

Chloe and I are waiting in the doctor's office for our six-month checkup of our soon to be born son, tentatively named Cash. All reports have Cash and Mom healthy and developing on schedule. His arrival date is February 22, conceived May 25th of last year.

Mom is doing well and still working at the bank. Our plan is for her to work till the end of January, then stay at home till delivery. We've worked the past three months getting the nursery ready, including painting, purchasing a crib and matching changing table and of course, a diaper genie.

Chloe has had two more episodes where she saw me and thought I was her robber. Both times, it took a few seconds for her to calm down and regain her composure. They were nothing like the episode in the grocery store months ago.

My work is going great. My clients are excited about our new edition and with the market moving upward, a lot of transactions with hefty commissions pour in daily. I'm on a better routine these days, clocking eight to four at the office. I usually get home before Chloe and prepare dinner. We work together afterwards on the house or spend time relaxing on the boat or simply walking the beach. Nothing has alerted me that my true identity might be revealed.

CHAPTER 63
DECEMBER IOTH, CHARLESTON, SC

"Knabb, for the past five months, we haven't gathered any new information on our Florida Bandit," said Rickard.

"I know sir. I guess he's taking some time off. Maybe waiting for spring."

"I wonder why? Why stop now? Is he smart enough to know what we were all predicting, that he lives in Florida? Is he laying low thinking the authorities were honing in on his location? Something must have changed in his life. Maybe he was arrested."

"I think," interrupted Knabb, "he is either locked up or taking time off to let the dust settle."

"For some reason, I don't think he was arrested. He's too meticulous, careful. He's taking time off. For all we know, he's married with a kid on the way."

Same time that day, Manasota Key

"Chloe, I can't believe we are married with a son on the way. This time next year, we'll be shopping for Christmas presents for little Cash." I hugged her from behind as she stirred spaghetti sauce on the stove. She turned her head and kissed me on the cheek.

"I don't know if I want to return to work after Cash is born," she said.

"Maybe you won't have to. I bet that you'll want to, however."

"Why do you say that?"

"I'm sure you're going to love being a mother, but you love your work also. After six weeks, you're going to be begging to go back to work."

"What about breastfeeding?"

"You can pump at work Chlo. Just close the blinds and lock your door. Pump and refrigerate. We'll get a nanny to care for him during the week and you can pump nights for him to have during the day."

"How do you know all this stuff?" she asked.

"Duchess, that's only the tip of my knowledge concerning your breasts."

"They're getting huge."

"No shit."

CHAPTER 64
JANUARY 18TH, PORT CHARLOTTE

"Stephanie," Chloe called, "can you come in here?"

"On my way Chloe," she answered via intercom. Stephanie held her breath as she gathered her notepad in preparation for Chloe's instructions. Chloe has been a little edgy lately. Having some trouble with her pregnancy, she's scheduled to stay home starting next week; however, the entire branch prays daily she won't return.

"Stephanie, I'm not feeling well. I'm going to close my door and lay down for an hour or so. Will you wake me at 2:00? I've got a 2:30 appointment with a new client."

"Not a problem. If you'd like, why don't you go home. I'm sure Janet can handle the new client for you."

"Thanks, but I'm okay. Just need a quick nap."

Stephanie closed Chloe's door on the way out. Chloe only got a few minutes of rest before Peter Baker, regional manager, showed up at the branch wanting a few minutes of her time. He asked Stephanie if Chloe was alone, but before she could answer him or inform Chloe, he opened Chloe's door and entered.

Chloe was half-asleep when she heard Peter's voice calling her. Mr. Baker was over the southwest footprint of the bank, from Naples to Tampa. He was personally responsible for forty-eight branches and wore the concern on his forehead. Although a star wide receiver for Florida State thirty years ago, he never turned pro and his once six foot three, 190 pound frame is now pushing 250 pounds.

Peter was very demanding of his branch managers and rewarded those that excelled. He also had a slight reputation of flirting with them. Thrice divorced and currently single and on the prowl, Chloe had been warned of his demeanor and habits.

"Chloe, are you feeling okay?" he inquired.

Half-asleep, she answered slowly. "Yes Mr. Baker. I'm all right. I apologize. I just needed a little rest."

Chloe started to stand up, but her extra weight pulled her back down to the low sitting couch. Peter immediately went to her aid and placed his hand on her waist, the other on her back, helping her up. When she was standing, he let his hand linger a little too long on her stomach and when he did pull it back, he let it brush open-handed across her left breast.

Not sure if it was accidental or on purpose, Chloe tried not to react. In the back of her mind, she recalled Stephanie's warning of Mr. Baker and assumed he meant to. Putting it aside, she asked "What can I do for you Mr. Baker?"

"Please, it's Peter. Please call me Peter or Pete."

"Okay. Pete, what brings you to Port Charlotte?"

"Nothing really, Chloe. I only wanted to stop in and officially meet you. We met briefly at the regional meeting in Cape Coral, but I had a plane to catch and couldn't stay. I feel bad it's taken me nearly six months to sit down with you."

"It's okay, Peter. You cover the entire southwest for the bank and I'm sure that keeps you busy," she said.

"Yes it does. However, I always try to see my hot new talent ASAP. I hear your employees enjoy working with you and your numbers are already impressive. Keep up the good work. And speaking of work, when are you due?"

"February 23rd."

"And you plan on taking six weeks off for maternity leave, right?"

"That's the plan."

"Good. Good. Of course, please take all the time you need, but at the same time, I need you here. The first and second quarters are the best for our business. Lots of commercial loans and mortgages. We do almost 70 percent of our business during that time."

"Lord willing, I'll be back the first of April, the fifteenth at the latest."

"Excellent. You hungry? Had lunch yet?" Before she could answer, he said "Come on, let me take you to lunch, you being my new star employee and all."

"I've got an appointment in forty-five minutes."

"That gives us half an hour. I'll have you back in no time. Come on, you're eating for two."

They dine at Sunset Grill on the Harbor for lunch. Pete made a few off-color comments, but for the most part kept it clean. Chloe assured him that she wanted to return to work after the delivery and promised to work extra hard in the meantime to build up her numbers. Peter accepts this, takes her back to the branch, and wishes her a healthy baby and childbirth before leaving for Fort Myers.

Chloe met her client in the lobby when she entered the branch and proceeded to open a checking account and certificate of deposit. After filling out paperwork for a home equity line, it was close to closing time. She packed her belongings and left to meet Cam at the house.

CHAPTER 65
FEBRUARY 21, MANASOTA KEY

"Cameron," Chloe called from the bathroom.

"In the kitchen Chlo. What do you need?"

"I need your help."

"Dammit Chloe, I've told you to check for toilet paper before you sit down!" I go to the spare bathroom and get a roll from under the sink. Walking to the master bathroom, I find her standing over the bowl.

"I think my water just broke."

"Okay. Keep calm. We're packed. Let me get your bag in the car. You get your pillow and I'll be back for you pronto."

I do just as I say. A minute later, I'm helping her into her BMW. The Alfa is too low to the ground. Pulling out of our street, I pray we make it to the hospital in time.

We pull into the emergency drop-off of the Bayfront Health Center of North Port, where an orderly meets us with a wheelchair. He wheels her in, I park the car, and by the time I return, Chloe is in a private delivery room.

Everything happened so fast, I didn't know what was going on. All the information and advice you get still will not prepare you for the actual moment your child arrives. A couple of RNs, an anesthesiologist, and what appeared to be a janitor getting a free show are milling about while Chloe is spread eagle on a table. Finally, the doctor makes an appearance. Our doctor, Dr. Sink, is on vacation, so Dr. Dorsett is standing in for him.

Chloe was the perfect patient and communicating with all in the room. I was holding her hand, asking her what she needed. She, they, needed me out of the way.

After what seemed to me like minutes, but closer to two hours (just ask Chloe), she delivered a healthy and beautiful baby boy, six pounds, eight ounces, and twenty-one inches long. He was a little skinny, but with a healthy set of lungs.

"I love you so much Chlo. You're my hero," I say, kissing her lightly on the lips as she held Cash Parker Steele.

CHAPTER 66
FEBRUARY 26TH, MANASOTA KEY

The Steele clan is home. Mom is taking a nap with son in her arms. Dad is doing laundry. I spend the afternoon making phone calls to family and friends, relaying the good news. Young Cash wakes and Chloe quickly gives him his life supply. All is great in the Steele household.

The doorbell rings and I answer to a florist handing me a huge vase of mixed flowers. The card is to Chloe. I take them into the bedroom where Cash is still nursing and hold them up to show her.

"They're gorgeous Cam. Who are they from?"

"Don't know, didn't read the card. Here, it's for you," handing her the envelope.

Chloe reads the card aloud. "'A beautiful arrangement for a beautiful new mom and baby. All my best to you - Pete Baker'. Hmm. That's nice."

"You don't seem thrilled babe."

"It's okay. Just … "

"Who is Pete Baker?"

"I guess, technically, my boss. He's over the southwest footprint and came to see me a month ago at my branch. He kind of gives me the creeps."

"Huh. In what way?"

"Well, I'm not sure if it was on purpose or not, but he felt my boob."

"Do what?"

"Felt my boob."

"How?"

"Calm down Cam." She explained what happened and how it was no big deal.

"So it was no big deal, you say."

"Don' sweat it hon. I'm sure it was an accident. Can we just drop it? I don't want to upset Cash."

"Of course, we can drop it. Please just tell me if something like that happens again."

"I will Cam. I promise."

CHAPTER 67
MARCH 8TH, CHARLESTON, SC

"Knabb!"

"Sir," he answered.

"Get your ass in here!"

"Yes sir. Whatcha need?" he inquired.

"A box of tampons."

"Sir?" asked Knabb.

"What the fuck do you think I need? I need information on the Florida Bandit. The Director gave us an additional twelve months to work it, starting from the date of his last known job. The Tallahassee hit was last July, so we don't have much time left."

"Well, I've ran a new search every Monday and little has shown up so far using our search criteria. And what has popped up, I've quickly ruled out," Knabb countered.

"Well, I need something dammit. I want you to give me your best ten matches that you've previously ruled out. In thirty days, if we don't have something legit, I'll massage something out of what you do have."

"Sir, I'm starting to think it's a lost cause. That we'll never catch him. I'm really starting to think he's retired."

"Knabb."

"Yes sir."

"Shut the fuck up."

"Yes sir."

CHAPTER 68
APRIL 4TH, PORT CHARLOTTE

"Welcome back Chloe!" exclaimed Stephanie. "How are you and that handsome boy of yours?"

"Great Steph. Thanks. How's everything here at work?"

"We're good. A few of the other branch managers from North Port, Venice, and Englewood covered us on Tuesdays and Wednesdays, so our branch numbers look good. They took the personal credit for the accounts, but coded them all to us. They also booked the loans to our branch. We're only slightly below goal."

"That's great. And our staff?" Chloe asked.

"Everyone is still here. We are real excited to have you back. But enough about that, let's see some pictures!"

Chloe spent the next couple of hours showing everyone pics of Cash and Cameron. A steady stream of regular customers stopped by her office to offer congratulations and ooh and aah over the pictures on her desk.

Just past 2:00, Chloe received a phone call from Pete Baker, welcoming her back to work. His tone was friendly and sincere, but she still picked up a flirtatious edge to his voice. She didn't expect him to ask if the little one was taking to nursing. Then, asking if she was going to pump while at work. Of course, she was planning to pump, but didn't feel it was any of his business. All things considered, she blew it off to him just being insensitive.

About an hour before closing, she called home and spoke to her mom. Cash was doing great and Grandma had put him down for another nap. Chloe inquired about Cam and her mom informed her that he was at the marina working on the boat. Chloe told her mom she'd be home in an hour and rang off.

CHAPTER 69
APRIL 8TH, CHARLESTON, SC

"Director, here are three cases that we believe our perp is responsible for since October of last year. As you can see ..."

"Rickard, hold it a minute," Director Munley interrupted. "Are you telling me you're not sure about these three?"

"Well sir, they are very similar to our perp's MO. The physical description matches. They used disguises. The first took place in Chattanooga, one in Cincinnati, and the other in Sacramento. All fit, but they do have a particular flaw."

"What, is the perp black?"

"No sir. It's the time of day the crimes were committed. See, our guy's MO is to strike almost exactly at 3:30. I'm not sure of the significance of the time, but it seems to be his schedule. All the crimes in my report happened before noon."

"Senior Special Agent Rickard, how long have you been in law enforcement?"

"Twenty-six years last November," Rickard answered with pride.

"And in all your years of service, you don't know the significance of using 3:30 as a go time?"

"Uh, no sir."

"Tell me something Rickard. In all your time working as a police officer, what time did the afternoon shift start?"

"I think at 3:00, sir."

"That's right. And the shift they replace, they get off at … "

"4:00 p.m. sir."

"Again, you are correct. Now, the afternoon shift is briefed at 3:00 every day till about 3:30. The morning shift is relieved at 4:00 and usually return to the station around 3:30. Any of this shit connecting for you yet?"

"It's the best time to break the law," Rickard mumbled, half to himself.

"And it's pretty standard police procedure in any major city. It gets the day shift off the street before rush hour. I'm giving you another ninety days Rickard, then it's closed. Between now and," Director Munley consulted a desk calendar, "July 8th, please don't waste my time."

Fifteen minutes later

"Knabb! Why are you wasting my time?"

"Sir?"

"Don't sir me. How long have you been in law enforcement?"

"Well, I did six years with the Greenville, North Carolina Police Department before you recruited me. I've been here for five years. So, almost twelve."

"And you don't know why the perp uses 3:30 as a go time?"

"Uh, no sir."

"Well, go figure it out and don't show me your face until you do."

"Yes sir." Knabb walked out of Rickard's office and rubbed the back of his head, tracing the scar from last year's fall.

Later that night, Manasota Key

"How was your first day back Chlo?" I asked.

"It was good. I missed Cash soooo much. I want to work, but I don't know if I'm ready. I can't stand to be away from him, not even for a few hours."

"I know. I feel the same way. Why don't we see if we can get your mom to help us till Christmas, for nine months or so. That will give us time to save up a little extra money and maybe you can stay home full-time. What do you think?"

"Oh Cam, that would be great."

"And easy. Look, let's take your check every month and put in a special savings account. I've always planned to use my pay for the mortgage and other monthly bills and expenses. I bet you could save almost $25,000 by the end of the year, don't you?"

"I can sure as hell try. I'd love it. It will be a goal. Work hard knowing my reward will be to stay home with Cash."

"That's right. And I'll try to log a few more hours at the office. If I try, I can probably make a few extra grand, as long as the market cooperates." I take Chloe in my arms and look deep into her eyes. "We can do it."

"We will do it," she said, full of hope.

Over the next few months, Chloe worked at the bank without complaint. She had an Anne Geddes calendar in the kitchen, where she crossed out each day completed. She placed a big, highlighted star on December 31st.

I worked my business harder than ever. I also used my paycheck for investing. I paid my mortgage by bank draft from my checking account, but all the other bills by cash, spending nearly a full day mid-month to drive to each location. Every month, I was putting almost five grand in a trading account and playing the market aggressively, at times making a few grand, but bleeding it away on the next trade.

Another concern was Chloe thinking I was her robber from over two years ago. She had another "sighting" one afternoon as I was returning to the house from the mailbox. She was on the front porch holding Cash and tried to hide her feelings, but I could see it in her eyes. I knew immediately what was going through her mind. Again, I calmed her down, but she still had a touch of apprehension for the next few days.

Chloe was finishing up her day when Stephanie bounced into her office.

"I'm leaving. Everyone else is already gone," she said. "Oh, I see Mr. Baker pulling in. Do you want me to stay?"

"No. That's okay. Thanks though. You get out of here and I'll see you in the morning."

"I'll unlock the door and let him in. I'll also hang out for a few minutes before I go."

"Thanks Stephanie," and they gave each other a knowing nod.

Pete Baker entered Chloe's office decked out in a Hugo Boss navy blue pinstriped suit, Robert Talbott silk tie, and Gucci loafers. He greeted Chloe with a hug and asked about the baby.

"He's good. Growing fast. My mom is somewhat local, so she looks after him during the day, but I rush home as soon as I finish up," hoping he'd get the hint.

"It must be tough, he being less than a year old and such. You're missing some of the best bonding moments."

"It is tough. Sometimes, I wish I could bring him with me to work."

"I bet. Maybe there is something we can work out." Pete looked up and to the left, as if to ponder the situation. "What could we work out?"

Chloe didn't like the sound of his voice, but countered, "Work what out?"

"I don't know. What if you came in to work around 7:30, instead of 8:15, don't take a lunch, and stay till 1:00? You get your numbers and I don't think anyone will have a problem with it.

"Really!? Do you think I can do that?"

"I don't see why not. I mean, I am the boss. Again, as long as you keep your numbers up, I can't see where anyone can complain. And I'm sure you can figure out a way to repay me."

Chloe got a chill down her spine. Something about his eyes when he said, "repay me." Hesitantly, she responded "It would be nice to be home everyday by 1:30."

"See, and everyone will be happy," Peter said as he patted her on the knee and left his hand on it.

"Mr. Baker, I'm not sure exactly what you may be implying, but I'm a happily married woman."

"I'm sure you are. And I'm also sure you'd like to be home earlier each day. That being said, I feel certain we can work out an agreement to make us both happy."

"I'm not so sure Mr. Baker."

"Pete, Chloe. I told you to call me Pete."

"Pete, I value my job and I appreciate your offer; however, I value my marriage above everything."

"No one would have to know Chloe. Just you and I."

"I can't Pete. If the first part of the offer is contingent on the second, then don't bother offering it again."

"Think about it Chloe. Go home, see your son, and think about it. I'll call you soon and we'll discuss it further." With that, he turned and walked out of the office and left the branch.

Chloe cleaned up her desk, set the alarm, got into her BMW, and drove home to her husband and son.

Later that evening, she told Cam about her conversation with Peter and how she was sure she had interpreted his intentions correctly. It was definitely a pass, a proposal. Cam wanted her to report him to his boss.

"Turn his ass in!"

"For what? It'll be his word against mine."

"So. You can still tell someone. What if he's got a pattern of doing this to other employees? Maybe one more complaint and he's gone."

"I'll think about it Cam. But don't worry, I can handle him."

"Well, do your best not to be alone with him."

Drawing him into her arms, Chloe said, "I love it when you're protective babe."

"Do you now?" I push her down on the bed and lay on top of her. I kiss her neck and she purrs. Cash cries a little from his crib, but I hold fast. Next thing I know, milk is bleeding from her chest.

"That's it boy! You're really starting to crimp my style. Enjoy them while you can, because I'm claiming those puppies back .... and soon."

CHAPTER 71
MAY 30TH, SATURDAY NORTH PORT

"Did you bring the list?" I ask.

"Of course I did. You get Cash out of the car and I'll get us a cart."

Outside Publix, I place Cash, still in his car seat carrier, in the shopping cart. I push the cart and make car sounds as I turn left and right like a NASCAR driver warming up his tires. Upon entering, Chloe heads straight to the fresh vegetable and fruit section, while Cash and I stay in constant motion.

"Go pick up your beer and chips and meet me over by the dairy," she said.

"Okay Mom," I said, like a child responding to, "Make your bed." "We'll go get some beer." To Cash, I said, "Man, she can be so bossy. Go get your beer. Go get your chips. What are we going to do with her, little buddy? I know. We'll keep her." Cash just cooed and looked at the overhead lights as we made our way down the aisle.

"Beer, check. Doritos, check. Pretzels, check. Okay buddy, back to Mommy."

Approaching the milk section, we spot Chloe with her arms full of small plastic bags with all kinds of green leafy healthy stuff. She drops her stash in the cart and proceeds to add milk, shredded cheese, yogurt, and half-n-half. Cash and I follow her down the next aisle, while she continued to add to the cart.

At checkout, we get behind a lady whose teenage son was sent back to get an item they forgot, holding up the line. I'm entertaining Cash as Chloe is looking at the covers of tabloid rags. "Oops, Britney Did It Again," "Lilo Arrested," and "Fire Marshal Robs Bank." Chloe picks up the "Fire Marshal Robs Bank" and turns to the two-page spread in the center. There, in black and white, grainy but somewhat clear, is a picture of the Fire Marshall Bandit.

The son has returned to the line with the forgotten item and it's finally our turn to check out. The clerk starts the process of weighing the leafy stuff and looks up at me.

"How are you doing today sir?" she asks.

"Oh, probably better than I deserve," I reply.

"I'm sorry sir. What did you say?"

"Yeah Cam, what did you just say?" asked Chloe.

"I said, probably better than I deserve. Why? It's just a saying."

"I'm not sure I've ever heard that one before," the cashier responded.

"I've heard it before, once" Chloe said.

Chloe puts the tabloid magazine back and I pull out my wallet to pay. She picks up Cash in his carrier and heads for the door.

"Good idea hon," I say, tossing her the keys. "Pull the car up."

I pay and put the bags in the cart and push it outside. I scan the parking lot and see Chloe leaving in the BMW, turning north toward Manasota Key. What the hell? I reach for my cell phone.

"Uh, hello Chloe. Forgetting something?"

"Nope, got Cash right here," she said very matter-of-factly.

"Okay, but the groceries and I are back here."

"I know where you are. Stay away from me, from us."

"Chlo, what is going on?"

"Go check out the National Enquirer in the checkout lane we were in. Oh, and better than I deserve, where have I heard that before?" Chloe hung up.

What the hell. I walk back in, leaving the cart of groceries curbside, return to our lane, and scan the papers. Nothing. What's the big deal? And that's when I saw it. That's when I saw, ME!

Holy shit, that's me. I hand a fiver to the cashier and don't wait for the change. I grabbed my cell phone and called Chloe again. No answer. I try again. Straight to voicemail. Right then, I spot Sara driving her SUV through the parking lot, heading straight for me. I jump out in front of her, making her slam on the brakes to avoid hitting me.

"Cam, my god, I didn't see you."

"It's okay Sara. Look, I need your help. Can you give me a ride home?" I ask.

"Sure Cam. Just let me pick up a few things first ..."

"Now Sara. It can't wait. It's an emergency."

"Well sure, Cam. Being it's an emergency and all. Is Cash okay? Chloe?"

"Yeah," I said, trying to regain my composure. "We just had a little spat. I said something I shouldn't have and she left me here."

Sara giggled. "Cam, you know she's still very hormonal. You've got to be careful around her."

"I know, I know. I'm stupid sometimes. I'll get home and beg for forgiveness."

"I'm sure it will be all right. Jim and I argue like that at least once a week. It's even healthy. It clears the air."

"I hope so."

We drive the rest of the way in relative silence. Sara makes a few comments, but I don't even hear her words. I just mumble. I rack my brain for some kind of explanation to give to Chloe.

"Here we are. Now be sweet and sensitive, young man," she says, patting me on the shoulder.

"I'll try. Thanks Sara."

"No problem. Good luck."

I approach the house and I have no idea what I'm going to say. I walk in the front door, surprised that it's unlocked. The BMW is in the driveway beside my Alfa. I hear Cash softly crying in the master bedroom. He's sleepy and Chloe is trying to get him to take a nap. What am I going to say? To do? Oh well, got to try something.

"Chlo?"

"What?"

"We need to talk."

"I'd say so Cam. But not right now. Let me get Cash down. I'll be out in a minute. Leave the room please."

I turn and leave the bedroom for the kitchen. Grabbing a Corona Light and a lime, I walk out on the back deck to get my head straight. Just tell the truth Cam! Everything. Well, maybe not everything. Admit to about 25%. No, come clean! I can't, she'll leave. You've got a son to think of. I don't care, spill it all. No, she doesn't deserve that pressure. Protect her. Protect Cash. Protect yourself.

"Cam," Chloe started. "I don't know what you can possibly say to me."

"How about the truth? You deserve the truth."

"That would be a great start."

I start at the beginning, explaining about the first job I did in Myrtle Beach and end with the latest one in Tallahassee. Of course, I admit to the Maryland heist and tell her of a few others, but hold out on half the truth. Her only reactions bounce back and forth between nodding and shaking her head. Sometimes, she throws in a "I can't believe it" or "Oh my god." I bend down on one knee and place both my hands on her thighs. She doesn't offer her hands.

"Say something hon."

"What the hell do you want me to say Cam?"

"What are you thinking?"

"I have no fucking idea what to think. You're a thief."

"Right."

"Cam, you met me when you robbed me!"

"I know, I know. I fell in love with you the moment I saw you. Please know that I'd never hurt you. I've never hurt anyone doing a job."

"You've never hurt anyone physically. You've hurt plenty of people in other ways. Hell, I still have nightmares. And today, I find out I'm sleeping next to it. You're the father of our son Cam. I share my bed with my worst fear. Our child is the product of your criminal acts."

"Chloe, that's not fair."

"Don't talk to me about what's fair asshole. Look, I want you out. I don't care where you go, but you have to leave. For how long, I don't know. Leave! We'll talk tomorrow."

I go into the master bedroom and carefully kiss Cash on the cheek while he's sleeping in the middle of our bed. I grab my dopp kit, a pair of shorts, and a tee shirt and leave.

I drive to a convenience store, grab a bag of ice and a twelve pack of Bud Light and head for the marina. I take the boat out for a cruise and try to clear my head. Before I know it, I'm at Boca Grande and I turn in to Gasparilla Sound. I admire the large beachfront houses and the beautiful aqua marine clear water. All the while, I'm worried about my marriage and the fact that my picture, although unrecognizable, is in the National Enquirer.

Dropping anchor in a private little bay, I take my shirt off, grab a beer, settle in the captain's chair, and pull out the paper to read the article.

Last year on July 8th in Tallahassee, a brazen man robbed the Tallahassee State Bank dressed as a fire marshal … The article gave a vague description of me, height, weight, and so on. Nothing that could lead directly to me. That was good. But, the article contained the picture. Who else that knows me has seen this picture?

I think I'm okay. I wonder how much the police have. After a quick dip in the gulf, I weigh anchor and turn toward home.

All the way back to the marina, I try to decide what to do next. What can I say? Am I days from being caught? I never meant to drag anyone into this. I never really knew true love till I met Chloe. And now, I've jeopardized everything I love. Chloe, Cash, not to mention freedom. I return to the dock, back into my slip, and kill the engines. As I tie her down, I look up and see Chloe holding Cash a few feet from our slip.

"Cash wanted his daddy," she said with tears streaming down both cheeks. "He wants his daddy to come home."

"His daddy wants to come home too."

9:30, at home

Cash is down for the count, we hope. Chloe and I decide

to convene on the back deck, me with a Bud Light, her with a Diet Cherry Dr Pepper.

"So, how many banks have you robbed?"

"Let's just say seven."

"So, there is more than that?"

"Chloe, let's just say seven, in seven different states."

"And how much have you got stashed away?" she asked.

"Right about $400,000."

"$400,000! Where?"

"It's in a safe place. Not to worry."

"And was that you in the picture? It said Tallahassee back last July."

"Yeah, it was me."

"You told me you were on some kind of business trip. In Jacksonville, I think."

"Yeah. That was it. I didn't plan to do any job once you moved in with me, but I had to."

"Had to? You just said you had $400,000. Why did you have to?"

"It's complicated duchess," I say, going to the kitchen to retrieve another beer. "I don't want to tell you too much. I mean, you do have spousal rights, which means you can't be forced to ever testify against me, but I'd rather you not know too much."

"Are you done now? Can you quit? You are a stockbroker, aren't you?"

"Yes, yes, and yes. Honey, I had to do the last job to throw the investigators off my tracks. I don't want or plan to do another job, period."

"Well, I'm not saying I'm okay with any of this, but I will give you one ultimatum. Do one more job, whether you get caught or not, and I'm gone. And Cash goes with me.

"I promise dear. No more. Ever."

"Okay. I don't want to talk about it any more tonight. K?"

"Not another word."

"Cam?"

"Yeah."

"You said you've got $400,000 stashed?" she asked.

"It's probably closer to half a million."

"Half a million, huh?"

"Yep."

"Knabb, get in here," Rickard yelled from his office.

"Yes sir."

"You got a pic?"

"A pic of what?" Knabb asked.

"A naked pic of your mom. What do you think?"

"A pic of our bandit perp?"

"Thatta boy Knabb. You know, you're a lot smarter than you look."

"We've got a pic of the Tallahassee job last July. It was pretty shoddy, but I had our lab run it through a bunch of enhancements. It's a lot better," Knabb said, looking at the photo. "It's still not perfect, but pretty strong," he said, handing Rickard the photograph.

Rickard studied the photograph for a few seconds while rubbing his chin. "So this is our guy, huh?" he said, handing it back to Knabb. "We got a name, anything?"

"Well, the 800 hotline with a twenty grand reward is getting over fifty calls a day."

"Can we put a filter on the results and get copied on the Florida calls?"

"You say the word and it will be done," Knabb replied.

"Word. I've got a meeting with the Director at 11:00. I'm hoping, with this evidence, he'll let us hang on a little longer."

"Maybe make a little trip to the sunshine state, huh boss."

"Maybe Knabb. Just maybe."

CHAPTER 73
JUNE 8TH, NORTH PORT

"Chloe, Mr. Baker is on line one," Stephanie yelled from her desk.

"Thanks Steph. Hello Peter, how may I be of help today?"

"Well hello Chloe. I was hoping you were going to ask me that. How about meeting me for lunch? I'd like to discuss our proposal.

"Listen Peter," Chloe started sincerely, "I'm very flattered of your offer, but I'm going to have to decline."

"I'm not sure that's an option Chloe. Look, I'm a nice guy. I'm clean and disease-free and I'm not looking for anything freaky. You get to keep your job, work half a day with full pay, and have afternoons with your son. It's a win-win. All for spending a couple of hours with me every other week or so. It'll all be very discrete. I promise."

"Please Mr. Baker, I'm fine with working full days. I'd like for our relationship to stay professional."

"I could pay you if it would help. Say $500 per visit?"

"Mr. Baker, please. Now this has gone on far enough. Anything more from you and I'll take it up the ladder."

"Chloe, calm down. No need for idle threats."

"As they say Mr. Baker, it's not a threat, it's a promise," and she hung up forcefully.

Stephanie overheard Chloe raise her voice and came in to inquire. "Everything okay?"

"It's just that snake Peter Baker. You know what he just said to me?"

"What?" Stephanie asked.

"Never mind. It was nothing."

Later that night, Manasota Key

"He did it again Cam."

"Who did what again? I asked.

"Peter Baker. This time, he calls me up and says he's even willing to pay me $500 per meeting."

"What the fuck, Chloe! If you don't report him, I'm going down to your Fort Myers headquarters and talking to him myself. And anyone else who wants to listen."

"Stop it Cam. I can handle this myself. I'll figure out a way to report him anonymously or something."

"No, the hell with that. Call the bank president. Get this guy fired! Look, I'll be down at the boat. I need to cool off a little."

I decided to walk to the marina to give myself a chance to think. At the boat, I go below to grab a beer. What's with this guy? Who the fuck does he think he is? I'm not kidding. If Chloe doesn't do something, I am.

I figure the boat needs a good cleaning. I switch the spigot to fresh water, soap up the bucket with "Sally's Professional Boat Wash," and get started, working off aggressive energy. Three beers and an hour later, I've got the outside washed and dried. I use a special solution to clean the isinglass and another to protect and condition the seats. By 9:00, I'm half-drunk and start thinking about Chloe and her job. I know one way to get that bastard back.

Back at home, thirty minutes later

"Cam?"

"Yeah dear."

"Can you come here?"

I walk into Cash's room where Chloe is folding his onesies and putting them away.

"I was thinking ... I know one way we can get Peter Baker back."

"Chloe!"

"You can't be serious Chlo? Are you?"

"I don't know. You're the one who has done it, seven times." She does the two-finger air quote. "Can you get away with another one?"

"Chloe, we don't need the money. My business is going well. You can quit the bank anytime you want. Another $25 grand isn't going to take us over the top."

"Yeah, about that. I was thinking more like $200 grand."

"What!? The banks don't carry that much cash. Maybe $100,000, $150,000 tops," I say.

"Besides the day before Thanksgiving and the week of Christmas, there is one day the banks are always flush with cash."

"Right, a day before a holiday. Still, it's only around $100K."

"Not for this year's fourth of July. This year, the fourth is on a Friday. It's also the beginning of the month. Government checks, payroll, and the like. We've already preordered $125,000 to be delivered that Tuesday. Come Wednesday, we should have close to $200,000. Interested?" Chloe asked, smiling.

"You serious about the amount?" I asked.

"Yep. See, the fourth is also a big shopping holiday. Businesses of all types will come in on Thursday the third to stock up on cash. They need change for the extended weekend."

"Getting that much cash would take a lot of time. I'm usually in and out in less than five minutes. It would take at least fifteen minutes to pull off that much cash. There is a plan I've always wanted to try. It might just work."

"That's my man."

CHAPTER 74
JUNE IOTH, CHARLESTON, SC

"Looks like we have permission to go south for a week," Rickard said to Knabb.

"The Director signed off on it?"

"Yep. That's the good news. Bad news is he wants us to go the week of the fourth. We'll drive down Monday and return Thursday night, the third."

"Well," Knabb asked, "what's the plan when we get there?"

"Tallahassee first to talk with TPD. I called Florida DMV this morning. They're working together with TPD to run a face recognition software to match the black and white pic of our perp. By the time we get there, they should have several real leads for us to track down."

"Probably a shitload sir. More than we'll have time to work."

"I'm aware of that Knabb. They promised me a list a week before we leave. That will give us time to eliminate 90 percent and we can concentrate, hopefully, on a handful of suspects," Rickard stated.

"Florida is a big state boss. It's going to take a lot of legwork, or should I say luck, for us to make any headway."

"I agree Knabb; however, it's what the Director has granted us. Get a lot of rest between now and the twenty-third, 'cause I'm going to work your ass off afterward."

"I'm with you sir."

CHAPTER 75

JUNE 18TH, MANASOTA KEY FOURTEEN DAYS TO GO

"Do you think it will work Cam?"
"I think it should. If the disguise is believable, I don't see how it won't work. How many employees should be there at that time?"

"Let's see. Me, Stephanie, Janet, the three tellers, plus one in the drive-thru. Do you want me to set it up so Mr. Baker is there, or is that pushing it?"

"Hell yeah, he's a big part of the plan. You, on the other hand, I wish not."

"I thought we already went over that. It's going to look very suspicious if I'm not there. I think it's a better cover for you."

"I know. You're right. But, I'm still trying to figure out a way for you to be conveniently away from the branch."

"It won't work Cam. You need me there to keep everyone calm and to tell them to do as you say."

"Okay. You go take care of Cash. Your boobs are leaking and I need to spend time on my ID badge."

Looking down at her chest, Chloe says, "Damn, you're right. That boy cries and I start lactating. I can't wait for this to end."

"You aren't the only one," I said.

CHAPTER 76
JUNE 23RD CHARLESTON, SC

"Here's the report sir," Knabb said, handing Rickard a fifty-page file. I've marked through the obvious ones, eliminating them based on weight and height. I couldn't reject based on eye or hair color, since they can be easily changed."

"So how many does that leave us with?" asked Rickard.

"Uh, ballpark, about half the original. Maybe 120."

"One hundred twenty! Shit Knabb, we don't have the time to check out twenty-five while we're in Florida. What else can you do to lower that number?"

"We'll, DLs issued in the past three years should cut out a few more. Then, also geographically," Knabb responded.

"We can also eyeball the pics ourselves. I think this guy has multiple IDs, all within a two hundred mile radius."

"Good idea sir. I'll start the process now and update you before 5:00."

"I'll call the Director and give him an update. One more thing Knabb."

"Yeah sir?"

"Get that list down to forty and check for matching addresses. He might have been lazy."

"That's two things sir."

"What?"

"You said one more thing sir and that was two things."

"Knabb?"

"What?"
"Shut the fuck up."
"Yes sir."

CHAPTER 77
JUNE 24TH NORTH PORT EIGHT DAYS LEFT.

"Hey Pete. It's Chloe here."

"Well hello Chloe, to what do I owe the pleasure?" responded Pete.

"Well, I've been thinking about your proposal and how I reacted last time we spoke. I don't want you to think I'm not happy with my job."

"Thanks Chloe. That means a lot."

"I also need to go over a few things work-related and was wondering if you'd have time to meet with me next week."

"Give me a second." Baker fished out his calendar from his Armani jacket. "The week of the fourth? I've only got Tuesday and Wednesday open."

"And I've only got Wednesday and Thursday available. Can you do Wednesday at 3:00? Shouldn't take more than two hours max?" Chloe asked, keeping her fingers crossed.

"That, uh, yeah. I can make that work. Just have to rearrange my 3:00 to an earlier time. Not a problem. Anything for you Chloe. Can I take you to dinner afterward?" he asked.

"I think that would be okay," Chloe lied. "I just need to be home by 7:00 or so."

"That'll be great. I look forward to it. Do me a small favor and email Janice, my assistant, so she can put it on my calendar."

"I'm doing that as we speak."

"You're the best Chloe. Till next week."

"Till then. Goodbye Pete."

"Bye Chloe."

Later that evening, Manasota Key

"So, it's all set up?"

"Yep. He was putty in my hands," Chloe answered.

"Is that what you're feeding Cash? Putty? This shit is toxic," I say, while changing his diaper.

"Oh stop it. It's no worse than usual."

"It smells like burnt hair. How long does the doctor say he should breast feed?"

"I haven't asked. How long were you breastfed?"

"Till my freshman year in high school. Must be why I don't mind drinking milk past the expiration date."

"Oh shut up Cam," she laughed. "That's nasty."

"Anyway, back to Baker. So he's good for the second?"

"Yep. He asked me out to dinner afterward."

"Did you say 'yes'?"

"Of course I did," she responded, smiling.

"So you're going out to eat with him afterward, huh?"

"Think about that Cam."

"What, oh, oh yeah. I guess that was a stupid question."

"There are no stupid questions, just stupid people that ask them."

"Very funny Chlo. Dammit, Cash took another dump. You got this one," and I ran to the kitchen and grabbed a cold Corona Light.

"Lightweight," she yelled from the other room.

"You damn right," I said more to myself than her.

Knabb was looking at his completed report, going over each detail before presenting it to Rickard. He narrowed it down to thirty-two suspects. Out of those, he was confident he could cut that in half, possibly down to twelve. He nervously picked up the eight-page report and walked toward his boss' office.

"Got a sec, sir?"

"Come on in Knabb," Rickard responded. "Have a seat, but hold your tongue. Let me finish this report." He was typing on his laptop, which was always a task and a treat to watch. Rickard's heavy, thick fingers always depressed the keys too long, which caused his words to have repeating letters where none are needed. It's always fun to watch him go back and delete half his report.

"This damn keyboard is too sensitive. Why can't they make these things for people with heavy hands like me?"

"I don't know."

"Shut up Knabb. Rhetorical question. Okay, what have you got?"

"It's not a lot, but I think it's significant. Our FBI and DMV reports gave us too many hits. I narrowed it down to twenty-four based on certain criteria, then to thirteen using the Knabbster method."

"What the fuck is the Knabbster method?"

"I guessed."

"Okay. Let's see it."

"There are three each in Tampa, Miami, and Port Charlotte, two in Sarasota, one in Jupiter, and another in Punta Gorda. With the exception of the Jupiter ID, the other ones look similar to each other."

"Meaning what Knabb?"

"Meaning all the Miami driver's licenses could be the same person. The same goes for Tampa and Port Charlotte. There's is a slight difference in all of them, but similar features. I'm starting to think the same guy has several fake, but legit, Florida driver's licenses." "Fake, but real? Simplify it Knabb."

"I think he used counterfeit paperwork to walk into several different DMV offices to obtain real IDs from different cities. The ones I've highlighted could be the same person with a slightly different haircut, eye color, or body stats, such as height and weight."

"That's good work Knabb. But why the single one in Jupiter?"

"He's just creepy. That one looks the most like the fire marshal job in Tallahassee. But, there isn't another resemblance ID in a thirty-mile radius. Honestly sir, all these IDs could be the same person."

"Okay," Rickard interrupted. "Let me look at this over the weekend. I'll call you Sunday night. We leave Monday morning, 5:00 a.m. sharp."

CHAPTER 79
JUNE 28TH, MANASOTA KEY FOUR DAYS LEFT

"Let's go Chloe."

"I'm coming dear. What's the big hurry?"

"I want to get some sun. It's a half-hour ride to Boca Grande and I want to be there by noon. Have you got everything we need for Cash?"

"That's what I'm doing now. Get his bathing suit off the back deck please. I put clean towels on the boat yesterday."

Chloe comes around the corner carrying Cash and hands him off to me. She's already got her pre-pregnancy figure back so shortly after giving birth. She's wearing a cute pair of khaki shorts over her bikini bottom and a white tank over her strapless top.

"We'll be outside waiting when you're ready. Come on Cash, you wanna go on a boat ride? Sure you do, you motorboatin' little booger."

I set Cash on my lap behind the wheel of the Alfa for the short ride to the marina. Chloe comes out and jumps in the passenger seat, promptly grabbing Cash away from me.

"You know I don't like him not riding in a car seat."

"Chlo, it's less than five hundred yards. He'll be fine. It'll be no different when we get a golf cart. Tell me we're not putting a car seat in the golf cart?"

"I guess not Cam. I just don't like it."

"Point taken."

We hop on the boat and immediately start our routine.

We've done this enough times now that we both know our respective jobs. Chloe takes Cash down below and puts him in his pack 'n play. She checks the fridge and grabs two beers, a Bud Light for me and a Killian's Red for herself. She puts three feedings of breastmilk in the refrigerator and has three more back at the house. She pumped all last night and some this morning so she could have a few beers and still let Cash have the good stuff.

I check the gas and batteries and turn on the stereo, adjusting the CD magazine to play Chairmen of the Board for a little beach music. Opening the beer and draining nearly half in a few sips, I start the engine and untie us. After checking with Chloe about any last-minute details, we shove off and minutes later hit the open gulf.

Gasparilla Island is perfect. We anchor a short swim from the main bridge onto the island. The water is such a teal blue it looks as if dyed. We're in about fifteen feet of water and you can see straight to the bottom. I dive in and swim completely around the boat, giving her a once-over.

Once I'm back on board, Chloe gets on her float that's tied to the swim platform and asks me to hand her another beer.

"Are you nervous about next week Cam?"

"I'm always a little nervous hon," checking on Cash below. The air- conditioner is keeping the galley a comfortable seventy-four degrees and the boy is sound asleep. "Being nervous keeps me sharp. Makes me check my details over and over."

"Have you done that, check the details over?"

"Not enough. That's what the next few days are for Chlo. I also need something from you."

"Yeah? What's that?"

"I need for you to get me the name of the IT guy in your region, as well as the one in Miami. Full names and spelled correctly."

"What's an IT guy, Cam?"

"Information technology guy. Your computer geek," I replied.

"Gotcha. How's Monday morning by 10:00?"

I grab another Bud Light and answer, "No later than noon. I've got work to do afterward."

Chloe splashes herself to cool off. She's so beautiful. So perfect. It makes me think again about calling the whole thing off.

"Should we call the whole thing off Cam?"

"No. It's perfect. It'll give you a perfect reason to quit the bank. You know, being all shook up about the robbery, having a newborn at home. And, it's a big enough haul, added to the rest, can carry us for many years. Maybe twenty if invested correctly and we don't blow it." I've purposely held back on Chloe the actual amount I have stashed. Consider it a rainy day fund.

"Won't it look suspicious that I've been in two robberies in three years?"

"I've thought about that a lot and the answer is no. You told me you haven't mentioned to anyone here about the robbery in Maryland."

"That's right. Not a soul," she said.

"So unless the cops ask you about it, and I see no reason why they should, nobody is going to make the connection." I jump in the water and swim up to Chloe's float, resting my arms on the edge, holding her hand.

"So, all in all, you feel good about this."

"And scaring the shit out of Mr. Peter Baker is just a bonus!"

"I love you Cam," Chloe smiled.

"Get used to the lifestyle babe, because I love you and all this," I say, spinning in the water, pointing all around.

We board the boat from the swim platform and Chloe goes below to check on Cash. She pops her head up and calls me to the steps. "I need some help," she says. I look down and she's completely nude.

"Help with what?" I ask, smiling ear to ear.

"Come help me with my sunshine, captain."

"I'm just the man for the job."

"And I'm a woman looking to give one."

"Cash, my boy, close your eyes. It's naked time."

CHAPTER 80

JUNE 29TH SUNDAY, MANASOTA KEY THREE DAYS LEFT

"I'm off Chloe. See you in a few hours."

In the Alfa, I make my way to I-75 and head south toward Naples. I plan to shop for supplies there, so as not to purchase within forty-five miles of North Port. Items in need of buying include red hair spray, lamination plastic, thick black frame nerd glasses, and a pocket protector.

It takes me less than an hour to get it all and I'm back on 75 heading home. On one of the Fort Myers exits, I can see the Colonial Bank South Florida headquarters building. Such a beautiful building. Stately and expansive, the sunlight bounces off the exterior glass, giving the complex a water-like image, almost as if it's an apparition. Like a desert oasis, you can see it, but it's not really there.

Smiling, I think of the years ahead with Chloe and Cash. All the time we are going to spend on the water, teaching him how to fish and to respect the ocean. I can't wait till he is strong enough to swing a golf club. All the things he and I are to explore. For the first time, I wonder if Chloe would like to add a little sister or brother to our little clan.

Thinking of the wonderful life we have to look forward to carries me all the way to Englewood. I stop at Publix and buy a bouquet of Gerbera daisies for Chloe. On the card, I write "To an awesome mommy, love Cash (and daddy)." At home, I enter to find mom and son sleeping together on the couch.

CHAPTER 81

"Last night, I mapped out our trip. First things first," said Rickard. "Tallahassee Police Department. We've got a meeting at 10:30 with Chief Patterson and Detective Rittenmyer. He's the dick who caught the case. Afterward, I want to go to First Tallahassee State Bank and talk with the employees."

"Sounds like a plan."

"Shut up Knabb. Then on Tuesday, I hope we can get to the three IDs in Tampa in the morning and the two in Sarasota after lunch."

"Then down to Port Charlotte on Wednesday?"

"Yep, then Miami Thursday morning and Jupiter. We should be on our way home hopefully by 2:00, hitting the South Carolina line by 9:00, speeding all the way, of course."

"Of course," Knabb replied. "Who do you like the best?"

"Hard to say. I'm hoping TPD or the bank can shed some light on our IDs. We're going to have the employees look at all of them. Maybe we'll get lucky."

Three hours later North Port

"Cam, I got the information you needed."

"Great hon."

"You want me to text it to you?" she asked.

"No. Absolutely not. Don't text a thing. Read off the names."

Chloe relayed the information I needed.

"When's the delivery coming in?" I asked.

"Should be tomorrow morning."

"Cool. Now I need you to go to the third office, the one nobody uses, and unplug the phone line connected to the back of the computer. Got it?"

"Yeah. You want me to do it now or later?"

"When you hang up is fine. Have you confirmed Mr. Baker yet?"

"No. I'm going to call his assistant in the morning and make sure I'm on his calendar."

"Excellent. Just be cool. Act like everything's normal. I'll be at the office until about 3:00. I'll go home afterward and relieve your mother. I'll see you when ... around 6:00?"

"About then. Have a good day Cam."

"You too Chlo."

11:30 a.m. Tallahassee Police Department

Detective Rittenmyer was a short, stocky man, built like a fire hydrant. He greeted Senior Special Agent Rickard and Agent Knabb with a smile and firm handshake, offered them coffee, then led them to the Chief's office.

After formal introductions were made all around, Chief Patterson asked how they could help.

Agent Rickard explained his theory of their perp, giving both a history lesson, starting with the Myrtle Beach robbery, details of the Los Angeles and Manhattan, Kansas jobs, and concluding with the Tallahassee heist. Rickard relayed the similarities of over twenty different bank jobs and why he and Knabb think they are related.

Rickard listed the disguises, the amount of money, the notes the perp used, and the general description of the unsub, and why he believes he lives in Florida.

"Now gentlemen." Rickard paused to clear his throat and emphasize the importance of his next few words. "Our perp, we believe, has completed twenty-seven robberies in twenty-one different states. All crimes were committed within a half-hour of 3:30 p.m. local time."

"Right at shift change, smart," Rittenmyer remarked.

Rickard shot a glare at Knabb, then continued, "Looks that way. And as I previously stated, we believe he lives in Florida."

"How so?" the Chief finally spoke.

Agent Knabb, with an approving nod from Rickard, explained their theory, including the thoughts of several professional profilers why the unsub may have Florida as a permanent address.

Patterson and Rittenmyer exchanged glances and didn't disagree.

"What else you got?" the Chief asked.

Rickard told Knabb to get out the report of the IDs. The four of them went over each suspect and offered their thoughts. Not having that "ah-ha" moment, Rickard asked the Chief if he could spare Rittenmyer and escort them to First Tallahassee State Bank. He didn't object and Rickard and Knabb followed the detective to the bank.

1:00 First Tallahassee State Bank

"Hello Mrs. Thornton. I'm Detective Rittenmyer."

"Hi Detective. What can I do for you and please, call me Sandra."

"Thank you Sandra. These are FBI Agents Rickard and Knabb from South Carolina. I was assigned to investigate the robbery in July of last year. I, we, were hoping to ask a few questions with some of your staff." He paused to look at his notes. "Do you still employ Tina Rice and Janet Bonner?"

"Yes. Tina and Janet are both here. Who would you like to speak with first?" Sandra replied.

"If it's okay with you, we'd like to ask you a few questions first."

"Sure. Please, let's go to my office." Sandra led them to the branch manager's office, nicely appointed with a round table set with leather chairs to accommodate clients.

"Let's go back to last year, July 8th. What do you remember of the events that transpired that day?" Rittenmyer probed.

Sandra quickly explained that she was in an all day long conference when the robbery happened. She verified the events of the robbery as were explained to her, while Knabb and Rittenmyer took notes. She left everyone in her office to retrieve Janet, allowing the interviews to take place in her office. She returned with a petite lady, five foot two, sixtyish, with a grandmotherly warmth about her. She wasn't the actual teller robbed but, according to Rittenmyer's notes, she recalled the perp.

After introductions were made, Agent Rickard placed pictures of the IDs in front of her, asking if she recognized any. She took several minutes, flipping the pages back and forth, studying each photo.

"They all look similar," she said. "Each one could be him."

Knabb spoke up. "Can you eliminate any?"

"Not really. I mean, this one seems most likely to be him and this one the least."

"Do you remember anything odd about him?" Knabb asked. "Something that to this day stands out to you?"

"No. Not that I can think of."

"How about tattoos or a birthmark?"

"No."

"Do you think it might be possible you ever met him before that day last July?"

Janet shook her head.

"Ever see a likeness of him after that day?"

Again, she shook her head no.

Agent Knabb retrieved a business card from his inside jacket pocket and handed it to her, telling her to call if she remembered anything, however insignificant she thinks it might be. They all thanked her for her time and asked if she could send in Tina Rice.

Tina Rice, late twenties, nearly six feet tall with shoulder-length jet-black hair, was bubbly from the moment she entered the room.

"Hi guys. What can I do for you?"

Introductions were made by Detective Rittenmyer and he explained the purpose of their visit. Knabb showed her the same pictures he had given Janet. Like Janet, Tina flipped the pages, turning back often, and making slight approval noises like she was humming.

"Any particular picture stand out to you Ms. Rice?" Rickard spoke.

"Please, call me Tina. And is this some kind of test? Are you guys trying to trick me?"

"No ma'am. Why do you say that?" Knabb asked.

"Because the same guy is in half the pictures."

"Come again?" Rittenmyer asked.

"Please explain," Rickard continued.

"Look here. The two from Sarasota, this one from Tampa, this one from Miami, and these from Port Charlotte are the same guy. Possibly, this other one from Punta Gorda, as well."

In disbelief, Knabb asked, "And how do you know that? All these photos were run through an extensive facial recognition software program by the FBI."

"Well, your computer program is a little misguided at best. Look, I was a hairstylist before I became a teller. And believe me, after that day at the bank, I was questioning my choice of leaving hair. But, what I can tell you is each hairstyle and variation will change a person's appearance." She paused to readjust her gum.

"Go on." Knabb scooted to the edge of his seat.

"See, longer hair will make you look thinner and younger. Short hair makes you look chubby and older. Long bangs make your forehead smaller. Medium length should capture your true age, for a man that is.

"See, look here. In this photo, his cheekbones look higher and his neck and chin seem thinner because of his long hair. In these other two pictures his face looks fuller because of his shorter hair. My guess, it was cut with a number one or two guard. On that one, he's wearing wire-rimmed glasses and it makes him look older. The pic with tortoise shell glasses is more stylish, makes him look ten years younger.

"Then, the normal length hair is a nice merger of the two. If you put something over everything but his mouth and eyes," (Tina used her thumb and index fingers to illustrate) "you can spot the similarities. See, you can't change the eyes or mouth much without surgery."

"I'll be damned." Knabb tried it. "She's right. Look sir, try it yourself."

"Why didn't the FBI face recognition software pick this up?" asked Rickard.

"Not sure, but probably ran it at 80 percent match," Knabb answered.

"So Tina, is this the guy who robbed you?" Detective Rittenmyer asked.

"I don't know."

"For crying out loud," Rickard meant to say to himself, but didn't.

CHAPTER 82
JULY 1ST NORTH PORT THE DAY BEFORE

"Is this Ms. Post?"

"It is. And you are?"

"This is Chloe Steele, branch manager in Port Charotte."

"Yes Chloe. How are you?"

"I'm great, thanks. Mr. Baker and I have a meeting set for tomorrow and I want to make sure he's got it on his calendar."

"It is. I put it there myself. Let me double check the computer though. Things have a way of disappearing. Mr. Baker moves things around from time to time." As keys were tapped in the background, Chloe spotted the Brink's truck pull into the bank's parking lot. "Here it is. Yes, he's got 3:00 to 6:00 blocked. Location is Port Charlotte branch."

"Perfect. Thank you Ms. Post."

"My pleasure Chloe. Have a nice day."

Same day, same time Tampa

"The damn address doesn't exist Knabb!" said Rickard.

"What the fuck! Doesn't the DMV have some kind of program in place to verify addresses?"

"You'd think so. I'm starting to think Tina is right. What's the address of the other ID from Tampa she thought may be our guy?"

Knabb fished out the report and entered the information on the Garmin GPS attached to the dash. Seconds later and after an illegal U-turn, lights flashing, they were racing toward the west end of Tampa.

Fifteen minutes later, Port Charlotte

"Chloe," Vanessa, the senior teller, called over the intercom.

"Yes."

"I need your signature. Can you come to the vault and verify the Brink's shipment?" she asked.

"Be right out."

Any shipment over $200,000 has to be signed by both the senior teller and the branch manager. In the event the manager is unavailable, the assistant branch manager plus an extra teller can sign in her place.

Entering the vault, Chloe asks, "What's the total?"

"With our change order, we've got $244,000."

"That much! Why?"

"It's the fourth on Friday, three-day weekend plus the beginning of the month. Believe me Chloe, we'll go through it."

"If you say so Vanessa. Where do I sign?"

Twelve minutes later, Tampa

"What the hell is this?"

"It sure isn't Disney World. I wish it was. I love Space Mountain."

"Knabb, shut the fuck up. I mean, what the hell is this place, a condemned apartment complex?"

"Looks more like a warehouse to me."

Rickard and Knabb get out of the car and look around. In front of them stands a five-story brick building near its death. Constructed probably in the 1950s, the building had a burned down, but still erect, feel to it. There weren't any parked cars out front and a sign on the front door read "Condemned by the City of Tampa. Do not enter." In small print was a phone number for the Tampa Housing Department.

"Knabb, call that number and see what this place was, is, and what happened to it and when."

"Sir, I think … "

"Knabb, don't do that. Every time you do that a kitten dies. Now call the damn number."

"Yes sir."

Rickard tried the door, but it was visibly chained. It looked like an old school, New York City-style, he thought. Peering through the windows didn't shed any light on the building's identity.

"Sir, city records indicate it was a housing project. Six years ago, when tax revenues dropped drastically, they had to close it. For several years, it was a squatters' paradise. The city locked it up for good last year. It's owned by the county, but there are no plans to reopen it. The address on the ID matches the location, but no records of an Ira Robert Banks on file."

"Just our luck. Ira Robert Banks, huh?" Rickard repeated a few times. "Knabb!"

"What?"

"It's him."

"It's who, sir?"

"Ira Robert Banks."

"That's the name on the ID. You want me to run it for all of Florida?"

"No dipshit. It's a fake name Knabb!"

"Fake name? I don't understand. Oh, because Ira is a made-up name?"

"You're a genius Knabb, but wrong. What's short for Robert?"

"Um, Bobby?"

"Fuckin' A Knabb. It's Rob. His name is Ira Rob Banks. Do you get it now?"

"Oh, I see now."

"No you don't. Get in the fucking car Knabb."

Same day, an hour later North Port

"Hey. It's me. Everything a go?"

"I think so," Chloe replied. "How about on your side?"

"Finished laminating the ID a few minutes ago. I took care of everything else this morning."

"Good. Can you think of anything else I need to do?" Chloe asked.

"Did you verify the meeting?"

"Yep, it's on his calendar. Including dinner afterward."

"Bad girl."

"You like it when I'm bad."

"You damn right I do."

"Cam?"

"Yes dear."

"Where are you? What do I hear in the background?"

"You mean this?" I hold up a Bud Light and open it into the phone's mic.

"Yeah, that. And I hear seagulls."

"You got me. I'm trolling tarpon and snook a few miles out."

"Cam, do you ever work?"

"I try not to."

"See you at home after work. Be safe babe."

"Okay."

"And don't drink too much."

"No worries Chlo."

Same day, 3:00 Sarasota

"Is this right?"

"It says Evergreen Street, lot fourteen sir."

"Well, there's nothing here."

"Doesn't look like there has been a trailer here for quite awhile."

"I agree. Let's ask some neighbors. Knabb, go to that one," pointing to the right. "I'll get this one."

Rickard and Knabb met back at the car with nothing new to report. There was no answer on the trailer Rickard knocked on and Knabb spoke with the owner of the other, but he didn't know the perp. He said that there hasn't been a trailer there since he's been here and that's been over three years.

"Did he recognize the name?" Rickard asked.

"He said he never heard of," Knabb checked the report, "Richard Franklin Sutton."

"Come with me Knabb. Let's ask the lady across the street. I just saw her peeking through her blinds."

After several minutes of wasting their time chatting with a grandmother who showed them pictures of all her grandchildren, twelve total, and where each lived, they were back to square one. She never heard of Richard Sutton.

"What kind of pompous name is that anyway? Sounds like he should have been a Senator. Richard Franklin Sutton, Jr.," Rickard said with a terrible British accent. "Shit!"

"What sir?"

"Richard Sutton, aka Willie Sutton. The notorious bank robber in the middle 1900s. He always used a disguise."

"How do you get Willie Sutton out of Richard Sutton?"

"What's another name for Richard, Knabb? Dick. And what's slang for Dick? Willie. Willie fucking Sutton. Got it?"

"Not really sir." Knabb looked at Rickard a little confused. "I should shut the fuck up and get in the car, huh."

"Yep. But first, get me the other IDs."

Knabb fumbled in the back and came up with the report and read the names to Rickard.

"I got William Theodore Childress and Howard Myers Richard Tate."

Rickard said the names over and over.

"Got it. William Theodore Childress is actually Billy the Kid. That one was easy. But Howard Myers Richard Tate? What the fuck is that?"

"It doesn't even sound like a name to me."

"That's right Knabb. It's not a name. You're a fucking genius."

"Cool. But what does it mean?"

"How's my dick tate?"

"Excuse me sir?"

"It's an old joke Knabb. Google it."

"Okay."

CHAPTER 83
JULY 2ND MANASOTA KEY DAY OF

I sneak out of bed and slip on my running shoes. A few minutes later, I'm pounding the sand, running toward the north end of the island. I hit my two miles and turn toward home. Less than a half-hour later I'm washing the sweat off, using the outdoor shower on the back porch. In the kitchen, I grab a bottled water from the fridge.

"Good run?" Chloe asks, sipping coffee gowned in her robe.

"Not bad. Clears the cobwebs," I answer.

"You ready?"

"Yeah. I feel good. It's more complicated than my past jobs, but I'm ready. And yourself?"

"Not going to lie, I'm a little nervous. I don't want anything to happen to you. To us."

"I know. And it won't. Now, just in case something does go wrong, here's a letter that explains everything. Where certain things are stored. My lawyer's phone number and what to say to him. Certain things to get rid of and how to go about it. This letter," holding up the envelope, "will be in the top drawer of my dresser. If everything goes well and after six months, we'll open this letter together. Right now though, it's information that shouldn't burden you. Got it?"

"Got it. There's no big surprises in there, right?"

"What kind of surprises do you mean?"

"That you've killed someone or something."

"No Chlo, nothing like that. Think of it as a treasure map with instructions."

"I like treasure maps. Is there a pot of gold?" She walks up to me and grabs my crotch. "Does X mark the spot?"

"You just found the treasure, babe."

Two hours later Punta Gorda

I enter my office and check with my assistant, Crystal, about any messages I might have. Around twenty, she tells me. I spend the next two hours buried in my office with the door closed, making calls.

My next call is to a client, Kim Drum, a successful real estate agent I've done business with in the past. I let her know that I want to list my Punta Gorda condominium and we agree to meet there in half an hour.

I finish up a few trades and a couple more phone calls to confirm to my clients their strike price, then put away their files. I call Jim and Sara, speaking with Jim, and invite them to a sunset dinner on our boat this evening. Sara is out and Jim will let me know later.

Pulling up to the condo, Kim is already out of her car looking at the exterior. She knows the place well, selling it to my late uncle some ten years ago.

Kim is striking, as usual. She stands only five foot two, but with the confidence and charm of a six footer. She has long blonde hair, a perfect tan, and a smattering of freckles across her cheekbones and chest. She has a perfect little body built for speed and agility. Today, she's wearing a white knee-high sundress, exposing just enough cleavage to make me glance.

Kim and I discuss life for a few minutes, then get down to business. Letting her into the condo, I give her my idea of an asking price and ask how long it might take to sell. She feels $220,000 is a few thousand below fair value and should make it move fast, maybe less than a month. There is never a shortage of snowbirds looking to buy in southwest Florida and they generally bring cash to the table.

Same time, Port Charlotte

"Where to Knabb?"

"Well, the three in Port Charlotte are pretty spread out. The first one actually has a Punta Gorda address, just a mile over the bridge on West Marion Avenue."

"How far?"

Knabb enters the information in the GPS and reports, "Eight miles, twelve minutes. Keep heading south on Tamiami."

"What's the guy's name?"

"Um," Knabb flipping pages, "Cameron Grey Steele."

"Cameron Grey Steele, you say. Let's think. Cam Steele. C. Grey Steele. I got nothing. You?"

"Nope. So probably not our guy."

"Let's go check him out and cross him off our list."

Same Time, Punta Gorda

Kim agrees to take the listing and wants to run several comps before settling on a listing price. On the back lanai, we see Harpoon Harry's extending off Fisherman's Village into Charlotte Harbor. A few private fishing boats dot our view, most heading out for deeper waters.

"My uncle really loved this place," I said.

"Yes, he did."

"Every time I talked to him, he'd tell me how a hot woman was jogging by or walking her dog." I smiled while replaying our conversations. "I hate to sell it, but the thought of renting it out seems disrespectful some way. He wanted me to have it and I've loved it also. I just needed more."

"Your uncle was a good man Cameron. He'd be happy for you buying your beach house. Now, just leave everything to me."

Kim gave me a hug and we kissed one another on the cheek. In the parking lot, what looked like an unmarked police cruiser with two occupants and a South Carolina plate passed the condo entrance. The passenger had an arm out the window pointing toward us. Kim didn't see it, but I did and my heart began to race. I tell Kim I have a meeting and I'll call her later. Getting into the Alfa, I notice the cruiser turning around a block past my place. I pull out and Kim is right behind me. Pulling away slowly, I spot the cruiser turn into my condo via the rearview mirror. In third, I downshift to second and head toward the bridge leading to Port Charlotte.

Five Minutes Ago

"Have we passed it?" Rickard asks.

"Not according to the GPS."

"What's the address?"

"1434 West Marion Avenue."

"Knabb, you dumbass. You've got 2434 in the GPS."

"1434 you say. We're passing it now," Knabb indicates, pointing out the window to what appears to be a large house divided into four condominiums.

They pass the condo's turn-in and go to the next stop light located in front of the Punta Gorda Yacht Club. Obeying the traffic laws, Rickard turns around in the yacht club's parking lot and waits for the light to let him turn left onto Marion.

Rickard, but not Knabb, noticed the green Alfa Romeo Spider Veloce with its top down leaving the small parking lot serving the condos. Walking the property, they knock on all four condo doors, but no one answered. They peek through the window of unit four, Cameron Steele's place, and find it empty. A check of his mailbox only reveals junk mail and grocery store circulars.

"Knabb, find out what kind of car is registered to Cameron Steele."

A few minutes later

Oh shit. What was that? Did that officer point at me or someone else? Was it even a cop? I drive home to grab lunch and to prepare for the afternoon. Cash is at his grandmother's in Sarasota until this evening. Chloe is to pick him up after work.

I calm down and fix a roast beef and pepper jack cheese sandwich on an onion roll with mayo and spicy mustard. I reach for a Bud Light, change my mind, and grab one of Chloe's Diet Cherry Dr Peppers and twist the top.

After lunch, it's preparation time. It's 1:30 and I need to be at the bank by 4:15. I apply red-tinted hairspray, basically paint, to the desired color I'm aiming for. I put on navy blue straight leg pants from Old Navy and a short sleeve white button down with a front pocket I purchased from Sears a few weeks ago.

I insert my pocket protector and attach my fake Colonial Bank employee laminated identification card. Adding a few pens, a small Phillips/flat head screwdriver combo, and a pen flashlight, the pocket protector is in full effect. Rounding out the disguise, I put in fake bottom teeth, which gives me a slight underbite, a rather large birthmark on my left cheek, and a pair of black, thick framed glasses with clear lenses. Once complete, looking in the mirror, I barely recognize myself.

The day before, I rented a car from a local non-chain rental lot advertised as "We Rent Wrecks." I chose a 2009 White Ford F-150 pickup truck.

I check the clock again. It's 3:00 and it's a thirty-minute ride to Colonial Bank in Port Charlotte. Before I leave, I pull up YouTube on my business phone and search Jimmy Buffett's Pencil Thin Mustache. I hit play and leave the phone on my dresser.

Same time, Colonial Bank, Port Charlotte

"Pete, so good to see you. And right on time," Chloe said pleasantly.

"It's good to see you also Chloe. How's everything since the last time we met?"

"Business is good."

Pete followed Chloe into her office. She noticed he closed the door behind him before she could even get comfortable in her chair. They spent the next hour going over reports, comparing Chloe's branch to nine others in her direct region. Pete seemed to pay more attention to her than the numbers.

Same time, Port Charlotte

"The DMV says that Cameron Grey Steele owns a 1991 Alfa Romeo Spider Veloce, registered to him about four years ago. As of today, they still have him at the condo's address on Marion Avenue."

"That was him. He pulled out of the condo's parking lot when we passed it earlier. Check the county property records for Charlotte and surrounding counties. Maybe he has purchased something new."

"Yes sir. Where to meanwhile?"

"The next address on the list."

"Okay. 1601 Waterford Plantation in Port Charlotte. GPS says it's nine miles away, be there in fourteen minutes.

"What's his name?" asked Rickard.

4:00 Colonial Bank, Port Charlotte

"Hi, I'm Jerry Paxton," I say, introducing myself and showing my ID badge to Charity. "I'm the IT guy for the Miami area. Michael Evans, your IT guy, is on vacation, so I'm covering for him this week."

"Nice to meet you Jerry. I'm Charity. What brings you out here today?"

"We got an alert on the mainframe in HQ yesterday that computer number nine is down. Do you know which one that is?"

"The five behind the line are numbered one through five. I'm guessing Stephanie's is six, Chloe, our branch manager, is seven, Kelly is eight, and I think number nine is the spare office on the left. Let's go take a look, shall we."

Charity takes me to the spare office, stopping at Chloe's office to introduce me and let her know what I was doing. Chloe looks me up and down and I seriously think it takes her a moment to recognize me. She smiles and resumes her conversation with Pete. After showing me into the spare office, Charity returns to her window behind the teller line.

I close the door and open my computer tote bag full of tools. I spend the next thirty minutes either under the desk or tapping keys and referencing a computer manual. I've put super glue on all my fingertips, so I don't have to worry about fingerprints or gloves. I've got everything I need for the job and at 4:45, I'm a few minutes ahead of schedule. I look for the men's room.

5:00 Colonial Bank, Port Charlotte

"Have a nice evening Bailey," Charity waves as Stephanie walks the customer to the door, unlocks it, and lets the customer out. She relocks it and returns to her seat. I come out of the spare office and knock on Chloe's door.

"Come in," she says.

"Sorry to bother you," I say, "but I need everyone in the lobby for a minute. I need to explain something about the computers and I'd like to do it only once."

"Um, okay. Come on Pete." Chloe walks with us to the lobby. "Hey everyone, our IT guy, what's your name?"

"Jerry."

"Our IT guy, Jerry, needs your attention for a minute about the computers."

"Thanks." I say. "If I can get everyone to get behind me at Stephanie's computer, I'll show you, instead of tell you."

I need them all in the same place, away from their windows and pushbutton floor alarms. There is a silent alarm just under Stephanie's desk, but with her standing behind me, it's out of reach. Once everyone, including Peter Baker, is standing behind me, I turn around in the chair and get started.

"Good afternoon. I've got C-4 plastic explosives right here." I pull out a ball of Silly Putty the size of an orange, with red and green wire running from it to a battery pack. Everyone takes a step back. "Now, don't be afraid. It's very safe and stable, as long as I don't hit this switch right here. If you all do as I say, no one will be hurt. Now, let's all turn around and walk slowly to the conference room."

The employees all look at Chloe and Peter.

"Don't look at them. I'm the one in charge for the moment. Now let's move."

Charity led the way and everyone followed. Once through the double glass doors, I ask Charity to close the blinds. Walking to the opposite corner, I rip the phone cord from the wall, rendering the phone useless. I then ask everyone for their cell phones. Only two phones were produced. I asked Peter to come toward me, turned him around, and frisked him, finding a phone in his inside coat pocket. Next was Charity. She was clean. Then Stephanie, phone in hip pocket. The other tellers were phoneless. Next was Chloe.

"Turn around, Miss."

"Go to hell. Don't touch me," she warned.

I force her around and push her against the wall. Although she is wearing a skirt suit that comes to just above her knees, I start at her ankles and keep my hands on her all the way up to her thighs.

She turns around and slaps the shit out of me, nearly knocking out my fake teeth. I spin her back toward the wall and press her forcefully, pinning her face-first against the wall.

"Don't do that again. That's the one freebie of the evening. Next time, I press the 'send' button on my cell phone. I'll detonate the C-4."

"Now Charity, you're going to be my helper. You think you can do that?"

"Uh, yes sir Mr. Paxton," she answered.

"Who?" I ask.

She pointed to my ID badge on my chest and nervously said, "Mr. Paxton."

I look at my chest and say, "Oh, yeah. Right. Now first Charity, I want you to get everyone's keys."

Charity walks around the room and collects keys from those that have them.

"Okay, next we're going to put some plastic zip ties around Peter-boy's hands. Charity, think you can figure these out?" I hold up the cuffs and Charity nods. With Peter securely tied, I ask Ms. Chloe if she can behave or do I need to tie her up, as well. Satisfied that she is no longer a threat, I ask Charity to take me to the vault.

With cell phones and keys collected, Charity and I step outside the all-glass conference room, locking the double glass doors at their base. Charity takes me behind the line to the vault.

"You're the senior teller. Open the vault." The vault is a series of small safes, eight in all, one for each teller window located behind the massive door you see behind the teller line. In this branch, only five are used. The senior teller gets the money shipment and will "sell" it to the other tellers as they need it throughout the day. She spins her combination, releases the latch, pulls open the door, and steps back.

"Wow," is all I can get out. Brick straps of ones, fives, tens, twenties, fifties, and hundreds. "How much is that?"

"Should be right at $235,000."

"Great daddy, that's a lot of cash." I hand her my tool bag and tell her to load it. "Let's hit the teller line now."

Back out of the vault and behind the line, I check the drawers and safes. Those that are locked I get Charity to open with the gathered keys. Each window has anywhere from $10K to $30K. We clean out each window being used, making sure Charity doesn't include the dye pack, nor hit the foot alarm on the floor.

Satisfied, I ask Charity to gather everyone's purse. I open each and get the billfold, personal keys, and cell phone and place them in my bag. I take Charity to Chloe's office and get her wallet, keys, and phone, as well.

"Now, let's go back to the conference room."

In the conference room, everyone is looking at Chloe and Peter as if they have the answer. When Charity and I return, I ask her to have a seat and for Peter to stand. I turn him around, check his wrists, and find them secure, then pull out his wallet. I remove his driver's license and return his wallet to his back pocket.

"Now, listen up everyone. I've got everyone's ID, keys, and cell phone. The only landline in this room has been ripped from the wall. Now, because I have your IDs, I know where you and your family live. When I leave, these double glass doors will be locked and I'll place the C-4 at the bottom, touching both doors. If either door loses contact with it, it will detonate. If it fails, I will be notified by my cell phone," I hold up my phone for everyone to see, "and I will enter the 'go' code. Exactly one hour from now," I check my watch, "at precisely 6:20, the C-4 will power down and will not detonate. You all have family and loved ones, so I'm sure the police will be here by 6:15 or so to check on you.

"This brings us to a few rules for later tonight. When the police get here and remove the C-4, they will separate you and interview each of you for details. Before I leave, I will take the videotape that has recorded me since I arrived. Remember, I have your address. When the police want a description, some of you will say he was five foot five or six foot two. He was Hispanic, white, Asian. Dark hair, blue eyes, blond with green eyes, or maybe red hair and brown eyes. He weighed two hundred." I stick out my gut. "No, more like 160." I suck in my gut.

"He had a goatee, no a mustache, clean shaven. He had a southern accent ya'll. No, he was from Boston and wicked funny. Or was he a surfer dude. But one thing you'll all agree on is," I smile real big to show my screwed-up teeth, "his teeth, were perfect. Again, I've got the tape. They'll never know.

"Okay, everyone stand up. This brings us to our conclusion. Peter, if you'd be so kind to join me here on my left. Thank you. Peter, it took me only a few seconds to size you up. When I saw you trying to look down her blouse," I point to Chloe. "And even in here, during this stressful time, you've been checking out her legs," pointing to Stephanie, "and her ass," nodding toward Charity. "What kind of twisted fuck are you? So everyone here gets to take a shot at ole Peter-boy.

"Now, don't come up here and give a little love pat across the cheek, because then I'll have to do it myself, twice, and much harder than you. So, who wants to be first?"

They all look at Peter and then back to me, but no one moves an inch.

"Don't be shy guys. This is going to happen. This pervert deserves what's coming to him. Now again, who's first?" Twenty seconds pass by. "Stephanie, I nominate you. Come on up."

Stephanie sheepishly approaches Peter and myself.

"You want me to just slap him?"

"Slap, hit, knee him in the nuts. Whatever you want. But do it hard or I'll do it for you."

Stephanie looks at Peter and says, "I'm sorry Mr. Baker." Then, she winds up and slaps the shit out of him.

"Boom! Holy shit Stephanie, that was awesome. How did it feel for you?"

"Um, pretty good, I guess."

"Okay, who's next?" I ask.

"I'll go," little Mrs. Stevens, who works the drive-through window, says rather anxiously.

"All right dear, you're next." I act like I have an imaginary microphone in my hand and treat her like we're on The Price Is Right. "Now, Mrs. Stevens, how old are you and where are you from?"

"I'm sixty-two and originally from Staten Island. We moved here four years ago when Stanley, he's my husband, retired and wanted to fish all day." She's actually talking into the make-believe mic.

"Excellent Mrs. Stevens. Now, let's get to it. Get yourself a good angle."

Mrs. Stevens leans back and steps forward, punching Peter hard in the stomach.

"Hot damn, I think we have a new leader!"

Maggie, the other lobby teller, bounced up for her turn.

"Damn, Peter. These girls are ready."

Maggie gives him a purple nurple and steps on his left foot.

"Holy cow! Maggie goes for the titty twister and finishes it off with a toe stomp. Not sure about the pain scale, but I give it a nine point five on originality. You Ms.," I point to Chloe, "how about you?"

Chloe gets up and half-heartedly slaps him.

"No, no. Hit him like you hit me or I'll do it for you."

Chloe looked at her feet.

"Do it," I say.

"Yeah, do it," said Mrs. Stevens. "Knock him on his ass. I never did like that son of a bitch."

"Easy Mrs. Stevens. You've had your turn," I say.

"I'm sorry. It's just so exciting."

"I know. Fun, isn't it?"

Chloe makes a fist, reaches back, and punches him right in the nose, splitting it open with her ring and drawing quite a bit of blood.

"Pa-dow. Mrs. Branch Manager comes through with a right hook to the face. Oh shit Peter-boy, you look fucked up! What do you think Mrs. Stevens? Good enough?"

"Give me another shot and I'll dot that eye."

"All right, all right, we'll see. Now, the best for last." Doing my best Michael Buffer impression, "Please help me welcome, at six feet even and weighing in at, umm, very little. The senior teller from another fellar, the tower of power, the vagabond amazon with a python, Ms. Chariteeee!" The girls actually applaud.

Charity, all of six foot two in heels, eyes Mr. Baker closely. She walks up, whispers something in his ear, then smiles, and brings her right knee up directly in his crotch. As he bends over whaling, she uppercuts him in his chin, sending him to the floor, balled up in the fetal position. I start my count.

"One, two, three." Charity comes up behind me, trying to taunt him.

"Get up bitch!" she screams.

I push her back a few steps and continue my count. "Seven, eight, nine" and wave off the fight. "Ding, ding, ding. Winner by knockout." I grab Charity's right wrist and put it in the air. She raises her left one on her own. "our senior teller, Cha-a-a-a-a-rity! Thanks for playing guys. I got to go."

I leave Peter on the floor. The girls are laughing and hugging one another. I grab my bag and go out the double glass doors, locking it behind me. I place the Silly Putty at the bottom, pressing it so it touches both doors. I look up and make eye contact with Chloe, giving her a little wink. I think Charity saw me.

On my way out of the bank, I stop and put all the purses and cell phones and all but one set of keys in the men's restroom. I go to the communications closet beside the teller line and get the security tapes. I grab all my belongings, use the set of keys I kept to lock the front doors after me, then toss them in the bushes. In the F-150 pickup, I drive to a Walmart Supercenter parking lot, park, then get into the Alfa to head home.

Same day, same time Port Charlotte

Rickard and Knabb are at Hooters eating an early dinner. In the table next to them are three Port Charlotte police officers with their radios on. Just after muffin-top dropped off a burger for Knabb and an order of wings for Rickard, the radios come to life.

"All units, we have a possible 211 at Colonial Bank at 19720 Cochran Boulevard, Port Charlotte. The suspect left on foot. More details to follow."

Rickard looked over to the officers, flashed his FBI badge, and asked, "Was that a robbery at Colonial Bank?"

"Yes sir."

"Here, in Port Charlotte?"

"Yes sir."

"How far is that?" Rickard asks.

"Not six miles north, one block east of Tamiami. I'm sure it will be lit up. Can't miss it. It'll be on your right."

"Come on Knabb!" Rickard barked, throwing money on the table and heading for the door.

Same time

It's a little past six. I've got to get home, store the money, toss the evidence, go back to Walmart, return the truck, then jog the two miles back to Walmart and get the Alfa. Five minutes from home, my phone rings.

"Hello."

"Cam. Hey, it's Sara. Got your message."

"Great. Chloe and I would love to have you guys out tonight."

"Wish we could Cam. Jim went to Miami yesterday with some old army buddies, but he'll be back Friday around noon. How about this weekend?"

"That would be great."

"Okay. I'll call you Thursday. Got to go. Give my love to Chloe and Cash. Bye."

"Bye Sara."

That was easy, and a strong alibi. At home, I grab a waterproof gym bag I got and tested from DICK'S Sporting Goods. I move all the cash to the bag. I then take off all my clothes, the ID, the pocket protector, everything, and put them in a trash bag. I put on swim trunks and a T-shirt and drive to the marina.

Once parked, I grab the money bag and the trash bag and walk calmly to our boat. A quick look around satisfies me no one is watching. Money bag in hand, I jump into the water, make my way under the dock, and secure the bag on a nail a few inches above the water.

Back on the dock, I untie "Licensed To Steele" and start her up. A quick ten-minute sprint and I'm in the gulf. I throw the pants, shirt, pocket protector, and pens individually in the water. I take out a lighter and burn the ID until it's unrecognizable, then with scissors, cut it up, letting the pieces fall harmlessly into the gulf. Removing the security tape, I slide back the tape lid and pull the film out with several quick yanks, draping the film on the deck. Grabbing up the film, I place it in a steel bucket and douse it with lighter fluid. A flick from a lighter and the evidence is destroyed. A quick sprint back and I'm docked and back in the Alfa by 6:40.

Twenty minutes earlier, Port Charlotte

"FBI, South Carolina." Rickard showed his badge. "Who's in charge here?"

"That would be Owens, sir."

"Where is he?"

"Who?"

"Owens!"

"Owens is a she."

"Okay dammit. Where is she?"

"I'm Sergeant Owens," a five foot five, 180 pound, thick-boned woman behind Rickard said. "Can I help you?"

"Yes ma'am. I'm Senior Special Agent Rickard with the FBI, South Carolina office and this is Agent Knabb. Can you get me up to speed on the robbery?"

"Why are you here, Senior Special Agent Rickard of the FBI, South Carolina office?"

"We came to Florida to track down and interview suspects of a serial bank robber. Our research points to Florida as a possible home base. We just happened to be in Port Charlotte when we heard about this call. So … "

"So you decided to see if we could help you grab a career criminal and let your office take all the glory," she said.

"No ma'am. Just the opposite. I don't give a rat's ass who gets the credit. I just want him stopped."

"Yeah, yeah. Heard it all before. Who knows you're down here investigating?"

"We cleared it through your Governor," Rickard lied.

"We did?" Knabb asked.

"Yes we did, Knabb! Now Mrs. Owens … "

"Sergeant Owens!"

"Yes, my apologies. Sergeant Owens, I would just like to ask a few questions. Maybe get a copy of the report before any ink dries."

"I don't have time for this right now. You can stay and listen, but don't let me catch you talking to any witnesses. Got it?"

"Yes ma'am. Got it."

Rickard and Knabb walked around outside the branch, picking up as much information as possible. So far, all they heard was a white male, five foot six to six foot one, 140 to 200 pounds, from the south, but with a northern accent with black or blonde hair, and walked with a slight limp. The employees were being interviewed individually inside the branch. All Rickard and Knabb could do was to wait for the detectives to conclude the questioning and come out with some answers.

7:10 Port Charlotte, Walmart parking lot

I park the Alfa and jump in the truck. A few minutes later, I park the F-150 in the designated "car return" space and place the keys in the night drop box. I re-tie my running shoes a little tighter and hit the pavement for the short jog back to Walmart. In less than fifteen minutes, I'm in the Alfa and driving in the direction of the bank. I figure a dozen police cars are clogging up the parking lot about now.

7:15 Colonial Bank, Port Charlotte

As the "inside" detectives start to file out of the branch, Sergeant Owens rounds them up in the drive-through lane, away from curious pedestrians lined up outside the yellow crime scene tape. Rickard becomes part of the "officer" crowd and listens as the Sergeant gets an update.

Knabb tries to work the crowd and keeps an eye on the ever-increasing number of spectators. It's quite common for serial criminals to return to the scene as a concerned citizen or even a reporter. To Knabb, no one looks suspicious or familiar.

The crossroads the branch sits on become jammed with curious drive-byers. Knabb notices a green convertible sports car, but can't recall the significance of it, if any. Rickard said something earlier, but Knabb can't quite put a finger on it.

Rickard gets the details of the crime, including a preliminary count on the amount taken. Nothing adds up to suspect their guy. He waits until Sergeant Owens dismisses everyone, then decides to find Knabb.

"Let's go Knabb. Doesn't look like our guy."

"Yes sir."

CHAPTER 84

"Happy birthday dear Cash, happy birthday to you!" Chloe and I and Jim and Sara sing to little Cash on his first birthday. Cash is in his portable high chair on the deck of Licensed To Steele and he's got cake all over his face and hands.

"Okay boy. It's naked time," I say. Chloe takes off his outfit, including his diaper, and hands him over to me.

With Cash in my arms, I lazily fall backward into the warm gulf water, making sure to keep his face above the water. Cash squeals in delight and immediately starts to kick and giggle. I wash him down and we float, father and son, in the beautiful tropical water of the gulf. In less than ten minutes, he's asleep on my chest as I float on my back. This is my life. Want it?

EPILOGUE

Rickard and Knabb showed up at our house four days after the Colonial Bank robbery. They traced the Alfa back to me in Manasota Key and also made the connection that Chloe not only worked at the bank, but married me the previous year.

They interviewed us for several hours about my whereabouts the day in question. Since they didn't take me in after the first hour, I realized they didn't have enough information, nor the authority or evidence, to arrest me.

"Question Mr. Steele." Rickard recited a phone number. "Is that your phone number?"

"Yes, it is."

"And do you have another phone? One for business?" he asked.

"No. Since I more or less work for myself, I use my cell phone for business and personal."

Rickard tossed out several robberies that I'm guilty of, including the original Myrtle Beach, Winston-Salem, Los Angeles, and about ten other jobs he "thought" I was responsible for. His big problem, he admitted, was there was "no dead ringer." No solid ID by a witness. The videos were not clear and no DNA or fingerprints were recovered to positively ID the perp.

"I will get you sooner or later. Mark my word, Cameron Grey Steele. I'll bring you down. You can't stop. It's a drug to you. You can't quit. And when you get that itch again, I'll be there. I'll scoop you up."

I walked Rickard and Knabb to their car, leaving Chloe and Cash on the front porch watching us.

As Knabb leaned against the passenger side door, I asked Rickard to join me for a quick, private conversation. He agreed and we walked toward the marina. I offered him a cigar, a Dunhill. He accepted.

We walked in silence to the marina and approached my slip. Rickard had no idea that he was standing directly over a quarter million dollars. Pointing at my boat, I said, "She's a beauty, huh?"

"Catchy name, Mr. Steele."

"I think it has a nice ring to it."

"What do you want to tell me, Mr. Steele?"

"Agent Rickard," I began, "you've got good instincts. I have no doubt that you've received numerous commendations and awards and I'm sure you have catapulted past your peers all through school, work, and life. But let me tell you something. You're not going to pin this on me. Ever."

"You know that because you're innocent or just cocky?" Rickard asked.

"Why can't I be both?" I replied and gave him a wink.

"You know, I cleared you on this last job because we tracked your phone. It didn't leave the house between three and seven the day of the robbery. You better hope it doesn't show up at any of the random states where bank robberies have occurred. You know I'm going to check."

"Good. That should clear up any thoughts you have about my involvement."

Turning around, walking back to the car, Rickard asked, "Why banks?"

"Sutton's Law," I answered with a cigar held between my perfectly straight teeth. I flashed him a $1,347,000 smile, winked again, and turned and walked back to Chloe and Cash.

"Sutton's Law?"
"Google it."

Later that day ...

"What should we do now?" asked Chloe.

"Well, you need to quit the bank, with the reason being that you're a new mother and you're not comfortable with the risk working around so much money."

"I can do that, but what's next?"

"I still have my job as an investment advisor. We can live comfortably with me working a half schedule. I continue to go to the office, you stay home with Cash, and nobody's the wiser."

"I really like that idea Cam; however, do you think we might be able to do better?"

"Better?" I asked.

"Yeah. You've spoiled me. I'm getting used to the finer things in life."

"Sweetheart, I'm hanging up my wild ways. Can you live with the boring, Jimmy Buffett lifestyle that we've come to love?"

"Only if we travel a bit."

"It just so happens that I have a client near the Keys, Paulie Iannuzio, on Islamorada. He called me yesterday, invited us all to his beach house for a long weekend."

"Oh Cam, that sounds terrific. How long of a drive is it?"

"Not sure, but it's only about eight hours by boat."

"We're going by boat?"

"Yes. He insisted."

PRAISE FOR LICENSED TO STEELE

"Incredibly detailed, well thought out fun read. A real guilty pleasure. Can't wait for the movie!" **Lisa B.**

"Fast paced, brilliantly written page turner! A world that truly comes to life. You won't put this down!" **Molly N.**

"Grips your attention from the start. Grab a seat as you are in for a ride!" **Kevin R.**

"A fresh new storyteller has arrived and his name is Noland Mattocks."
Jonathan H.

"Pure adrenaline rush! Makes you wonder what would you do?"
Katherine R.

CPSIA information can be obtained
at www.ICGtesting.com
Printed in the USA
FFOW03n1552190817
39038FF